# A Matter of Iodine

# A Matter of Iodine

DAVID KEITH

COACHWHIP PUBLICATIONS

GREENVILLE, OHIO

To My Wife

*A Matter of Iodine*, by David Keith
© 2017 Coachwhip Publications

Title published 1940
David Keith, pseud. Francis Steegmuller (1906-1994)
No claims made on public domain material.
Front cover: Bottle © Marina Mariya

CoachwhipBooks.com

ISBN 1-61646-417-8
ISBN-13 978-1-61646-417-2

# ABOUT THE AUTHOR

Francis Steegmuller (1906-1994) was an award-winning author (including two National Book Awards) who specialized in biographies and translations of French classics (particularly Flaubert). He contributed to the *New Yorker*, as well as writing a few books on his travels. His life-long interest in Europe led to early travels after attending Columbia University in the 1920s, exploring England, France, and Italy, until the World War, when he went into the military. Returning to France, he worked in military intelligence and became a recipient of the French Legion of Honor. His first wife, artist Beatrice Stein, who suffered from polio, died in 1961; he married writer Shirley Hazzard in 1963.

Aside from his literary interests, he also appreciated well-written detective novels. Once asked to name the 10 best mystery novels, he countered with "a dozen which I enjoyed very much." These included Graham Greene's *This Gun for Hire*, *Ministry of Fear*, and *Brighton Rock*; Frances Noyes Hart's *The Bellamy Trial*; Ethel Lina White's *The Wheel Spins*; Francis Iles' *Before the Fact*; Eric Ambler's *Journey into Fear* and *A Coffin for Demetrios*; and Dashiell Hammett's *The Thin Man*, *The Maltese Falcon*, and *The Glass Key*. He also included David Keith's *Blue Harpsichord*, which was certainly very well-received, and in fact his own title. Steegmuller wrote three mystery novels under that pseudonym, starting with *A Matter of Iodine*, and *A Matter of Accent*. Unsurprisingly, *A Matter of Iodine* is no simple murder mystery, rather a strange adventure involving sub-par shipments of iodine from France that must be investigated, leading to a labyrinth of mysterious characters and deadly threats.

FRANCIS STEEGMULLER

A MATTER OF IODINE

# CHAPTER 1

Rain was falling in torrents the morning after my arrival in Paris. I breakfasted in bed, as I always do; and then, still in bed, I set about getting in touch with Monsieur Binbonnet.

Monsieur Binbonnet had been notified in advance that I should be arriving. He had certainly received Pearce Brothers' letter long before this. All I had to do was to telephone him and ask him to drop around to see me.

That is what I thought.

But to my annoyance the operator informed me that there was no telephone listed for Achille Binbonnet, commodities broker, of 404 Rue Saint-Martin. That seemed to me incredible. Monsieur Binbonnet was, after all, a broker with a large business. From us alone he had been clearing an important sum of money every year for some time. But when I told the operator some of this she could only express her regrets. "I am sorry, but Monsieur Achille Binbonnet has no telephone, Monsieur," she patiently repeated.

I remember that when I was finally convinced that this was so, and had hung up, defeated, I had a fit of temper, lying in bed there by myself in the hotel. A fit of temper against Al and Jim for forcing me to come to France in the first place. Quite unjustifiably, against the entire French nation for being backward, inefficient, perverse and annoying. Particularly strongly, against Monsieur Binbonnet for forcing me to travel to the Rue Saint-Martin, wherever that might be, to get in touch with him.

For I was unwilling to send him a note, to risk a delay in his reply. I wanted to make him see me right away. The *Normandie*, on which I had just arrived, was leaving again in two days, and I wanted her to take a letter from me to Al and Jim with something about Monsieur Binbonnet in it. I wanted to impress them, at once, with the speed and efficiency I was displaying on their behalf. It was important to me that I do this.

I'd go and see Monsieur Binbonnet tomorrow. Today was too rainy, and I was too tired.

My very fit of temper was due largely to fatigue, I suppose—fatigue after the rough crossing, after the swaying train-ride from Havre. I'm not my best on boats or trains or other things that sway and move. Shortly after my defeat on the telephone I fell asleep again, and felt better when I awoke. I had lunch, a delicious one, brought to me on a tray by a very correct waiter. Correct and something more than that. For in the course of a bit of rearranging I had had her do during the morning the chambermaid had removed my braces and crutches from their accustomed place beside my bed and had forgotten to bring them back; and now the waiter, after he had cleared away lunch, quietly restored them to their proper position without being asked. He had realized that I was helpless without them. That was more than correct service. It was an imaginative and intelligent sort of kindness that is rare indeed. I thanked him warmly. He assured me it was nothing.

It was by mere chance that I had come to the Clarence—an attractive publicity folder about the hotel that I had found one day in my cabin on the boat. A lucky chance, I felt, if this man was typical of its staff.

After lunch I went to sleep once more. That was evidence of pretty considerable fatigue, even for me; or, looking at it another way, it was better sleeping than I'd been doing for some time. When I woke up again it was midafternoon, the rain had stopped, and from my bed I could look out through the long windows and see bright blue sky and a low sun pouring yellow light onto the Tuileries Gardens. I decided to make a day of it—to do something I hadn't done for quite a while: spend the entire day without putting on my braces, without using my crutches. That was a restful thing to do, if I didn't do it too often, and for the past few weeks it hadn't been possible. On the boat

I had wanted to spend as little time in my stuffy cabin as possible, and in New York before leaving I'd been busy every day.

So I stayed in bed with the braces and crutches standing up against the wall beside me, and took up an absorbing novel that remained unread from the boat, and read until it grew dark. I knew no one in Paris except a few picture dealers whom I hadn't seen for ten years and whom I didn't intend to see now.

And then, when I looked out the windows again and realized that the day had ended, I had a visitation of real panic.

In the morning, I should have to do my errand—and morning, since the daylight was gone, was almost here! I suddenly felt weak through and through, as I hadn't felt since I was a boy of 17 getting up to deliver my valedictory address at High School graduation. Bad enough to have had to come to France at all and to talk over these matters with Monsieur Binbonnet and Monsieur Gerard, people whom I'd never met; bad enough to have Monsieur Binbonnet come to my room for a discussion, perhaps a dispute; but for me to have to go to see him, assume the entire effort of the thing myself—I could scarcely believe that I was going to do it. I discovered, as I looked fearfully into myself, that I was trying actually to skip, in my mind, the entire period that my mission in France would take, and trying already to live in the future beyond it—that calm-looking, serene-seeming time after the work was done. And this panic, I knew, was not due to fatigue, but to something deeper than that, which I recognized quite well but could do nothing about.

And, it occurred to me, once my work in France was done—what then? Would life be calm and serene, as I was now pretending? Or would it be more accurate to say that it could at best only become again what it had been for the past ten years—empty?

# CHAPTER 2

Not that there was anything romantic or complex or perilous about the errand that I had come to Paris to do. It was the simplest of business affairs.

My two brothers-in-law are the president and the secretary-treasurer and the chief stockholders of their firm of Pearce Brothers, Incorporated, Manufacturing Importers, of New York—formerly known as Matthew Pearce, Inc., during the lifetime of their father, who founded the business. It is a close corporation—that is, the company's stock is never placed on public sale but is entirely held by the members of the firm. When a member dies, his estate is obliged to sell his stock back to the firm, unless he has left it to an heir who is in the firm himself. In addition to Al and Jim there are only two other officers, the first and the second vice-presidents, two good men who have grown up with the firm and each of whom now owns a medium-sized block of stock. There is only one member of the firm apart from the officers.

That person is now myself, T. S. Weaver. Formerly, however, it was someone else. Shortly before Matthew Pearce's death it was written into the firm's constitution that Matthew Pearce's daughter, Lucille Pearce, whether or not she take an active part in the firm's business, be considered, from the moment of Matthew Pearce's death and for the rest of her natural life, a member of the firm, and as such entitled to hold stock, and that she be further entitled to bequeath her stock to her heirs as she might see fit. And on his death, Matthew Pearce left his daughter a large block of stock.

As it happened, Lucille Pearce, although she would have been an excellent businesswoman, never did take an active part in the business of Pearce Brothers, Inc.

Lucille Pearce was my wife. I met her in 1921, the year after I came back from service in an American military hospital in France, when she was in her early twenties and studying painting and drawing at the Pennsylvania Academy of Fine Arts. I had been studying there before I went to the war, and had resumed my studies on my return. Rather quickly, however, I came to feel that it was futile for me to continue and that I should henceforth be happier living with art in some capacity other than that of fumbling, clumsy, would-be creator. Lucille was the first person I told about my plans. I decided to take some of the capital I had been left by my family and with it establish a picture gallery in New York. I had picked up a few pictures in Paris myself after the Armistice, enough to start with. If I had luck, and made a sale or two, I knew I could find a lot more over there, at prices which would be sure later to rise. For one thing the big Degas sale had just taken place in Paris under wartime conditions, and the market was flooded with Degas pictures at prices which seemed low even then and are now incredible. Shortly after I met Lucille I fell in love with her and we were married and went to live in New York. At first most of my income went into the gallery, and Lucille's income from her Pearce Brothers stock took care of our living expenses. Soon our daughter Caroline was born. I shall say nothing about our married life, except that it was perfect.

Financially, we prospered. The times were with us—as they were with almost everyone else. The gallery did well. Pictures sold themselves, in those days, particularly pictures as good as mine. Lucille was often in the gallery, helping with her tact and taste. Every summer we went to Europe and bought new pictures in Paris. Pearce Brothers, Inc., thrived likewise, and on a far greater scale. Matthew Pearce had made it into a solid, money-making house; under Al and Jim it expanded. Lucille's stock was split several times; she was well-to-do in her own right.

In the spring of 1929, when Caro was almost seven, we took her with us on a short motor trip through the West. A week or so before we were to take the train at Los Angeles for New York (whence

Lucille and I were shortly to leave for Paris as usual), we were driving one afternoon down the high coast road below Santa Barbara. We were driving fast. We had no chauffeur; I was at the wheel. During the past several days, for the first time in my life, I had been feeling strangely unwell. Now, suddenly, as the car was speeding along the top of the cliffs, I began to feel much worse. It swept into my mind that I shouldn't be driving, that I should stop, see a doctor immediately. Then my eyes and brain seemed to be blurred over, and all of my body felt queerly the same; certainly the first thing to do was to slow down; I jammed on the brake, hard—or at least as hard as I could, for strangely I couldn't seem to do it very well. Everything was much more blurred now; I heard a cry of wonder from Lucille beside me, a childish question from behind . . . the last sounds I was ever to hear from my wife and my child. . . . There was a sickening motion, a crash. The blur became completely black.

I was in the hospital a long time before I learned what had happened. The first weeks I was unconscious. Then I came to sufficiently to hear—couldn't see or speak, because the muscles didn't work. Then those muscles slowly came back. It was at that point that I asked my first question. Nobody wanted to answer it—so of course I knew what the answer was. After I knew it, somebody told it to me.

The answer took away my will to live. But other muscles stubbornly persisted in coming back. Several weeks later, I asked my second question—about myself, this one. The answer was, "Poliomyelitis and fractures."

I was in the Santa Barbara hospital the better part of a year. The muscles in my neck and arms and hands and chest and stomach gradually came back. The rest didn't. There was a question of my going to Warm Springs, but the doctors thought I could do as well where I was, so I took a bungalow in Santa Barbara and stayed there another year. By the end of that time I had learned to walk with support, and there was no use staying any longer.

Al and Jim came out separately to see me several times, and once together. Mildred and Eunice would have come too, had I let them. But I couldn't bear to see them. Not that I don't like them—far from it. But wives—living wives, with living children! I was close to insanity on such subjects as that.

I had Al and Jim give up the gallery and the apartment and store everything. There weren't many pictures left anyway—I'd had a good season and was pretty well cleaned out.

When I went back to New York I took a small furnished place on Murray Hill and lived there with a series of unsatisfactory manservants. Life went on, as life can, for eight years. I don't enjoy thinking of those years now. I didn't enjoy living them then.

To get back to the business end of things, Lucille and I had made wills in which each of us left everything to Caroline. Not to each other—neither of us seemed to need more than he already had. Thus by the terms of Lucille's will Caroline was the inheritor of the Pearce Brothers stock. But since what had happened had happened, it was I who got it.

By the time the matter was adjudicated by the probate courts, the Pearce Brothers stock was the only capital I did have, apart from a dozen or so pictures. My old personal capital had gone the way so much went during those years, and—like the muscles in my legs— it never came back. Pearce Brothers weathered the depression well. It suffered, of course, but less than many. I wasn't rich, but I was comfortable. Nowhere else, during the depression or after, could I have got so good a return on the amount of capital represented in the investment, and there was every reason for me to hold on to that stock.

I well remember the day when Al and Jim came to lunch and told me they'd have to call the stock in.

I've always liked my brothers-in-law. We've got on well from the day we first met, and what I should have done without their friendship and backing during those months in California I don't know. During the eight dreary years following my return to New York I'd been in the habit of having them to lunch every once in a while. There were sometimes things I wanted to talk over, and anyway I enjoyed their company. Al lives in Montclair beside his tennis court, Jim in Great Neck near his golf course, and since I never got out into the suburbs they were always willing to see me in my place—I'd chosen an apartment near their office partly to make it easy for them to come often. I think they always understood, too, how I felt about their homes and children. I didn't see my nieces and nephews at all. For a long time it remained hard for me to see even Mildred and Eunice. But they're tactful women, and gradually I lost my feeling, and they began to come in too. It wasn't always I who did the inviting. Occasionally Al or Jim or one of the girls would telephone and ask to come to lunch that day, and sometimes they dressed and dined at my place before going to the theater. So I wasn't surprised, that day early last October, when Al phoned and said that he and Jim would like to come.

But I confess I was surprised—aghast, in fact—at their news.

"Ted, every close corporation's got to crack down on stock not owned by members of the firm. Orders from Washington—a new law. We'd like to make an exception of your case, but . . ."

I quickly held up my hand. The news was bad, but why should they make an exception of my case? I didn't want pity or favors. "Don't apologize," I ordered. "Above all, don't apologize."

"Apologize?" They looked at each other. "You're going a little fast, Ted. What makes you think we're apologizing to you?"

Well, they had said they'd like to make an exception of my case *but*, hadn't they? "What was your *but* going to introduce, if not an apology?" I asked.

"We were going to say 'but we don't know whether you'd care for the only conditions on which an exception could be made.' It depends on your taking certain steps, which would be to our advantage. We don't know whether you'd want to take those steps or not, whether you'd think them worth while, in order to hold on to the stock."

They had me there, all right. Steps to be taken—action, activity: the boys' delicate manner of speaking made me wonder whether they knew what terror such words as those struck into me. I didn't want them to know. I wasn't proud that it should be so, and yet it was. I hadn't undertaken an action in ten years, and the last thing I wanted to do was to start now. I had come to dread activity, seeing people, doing things. I wanted to be left alone, quiet. I wasn't happy, in my quiet, but I wanted to be left in it. One of my most constant fears was lest I be disturbed, forced out of my stagnant existence.

And yet, on the other hand, I quickly calculated that the loss of my Pearce Brothers stock, with subsequent reinvestment of the principal, investment counsel, and so forth, would mean the cutting down of my income by almost half—at least a third; and that, for me, would be a serious inconvenience. It would mean loss of my ease. I should have to move, radically reduce my comfort—be forced into some form of activity in any case! "Tell me the whole story," I said, uneasily. "What new law calls in the stock? I've had it for ten years and Lucille had it for ten years before that. What's come up?"

They told me. It was a question of taxation—I forget, now, the exact details. In some way, the fact that I held stock without being a bona fide member of the firm was threatening to cost the firm five figures a year. I had to be cracked down on.

That was quite clear. "Obviously you have to crack down on me," I said. "Why should you try to avoid doing it, particularly, under the circumstances?"

"Purely for our own advantage." They looked at me steadily as they said that—the two men said it almost in unison—and I looked back at them, hunting for pity in their eyes.

"Do you mean I can actually be of service to you?"

"You can."

I looked at them a moment longer; then suddenly I felt silly and truculent. "Shoot," I said. "Tell me the story."

"That's what we've been wanting to do, Ted," Al said, a bit wearily. Then we all grinned. I knew, and they knew, that the difficulty that always came up when I felt that somebody was pitying me was finally surmounted. When I think, now, that I had been as difficult as that for ten years!

After that, the talk continued more easily.

Unexpectedly enough, it was a matter of iodine.

I don't know, though, why I say "unexpectedly." I've come to expect to find almost anything among the products of my brothers-in-law. I remember my mirth when I first heard them referred to, quite seriously, as the "burlap kings of New York," and since that day I've grown used to hearing them called the "tapioca kings" and the "oakum kings" as well. So I was not too surprised, that day at lunch, to learn that in addition to their other accomplishments they were the manufacturers of an iodized breakfast food which enjoyed a brisk sale in the Middle Western and Rocky Mountain states—those areas where goiter is an ever-present danger, combatted by constant imbibings of iodine in any one of a hundred forms. Iodized salt is of course the most familiar of these goiter-preventing foods, but by skillful salesmanship, including medical testimonials and radio publicity, Pearce Brothers had brought their iodized breakfast food—called Idena—to a very wide popularity indeed, particularly among children, to whom the radio programs were chiefly addressed. In fact Idena had become one of their "best-selling numbers," as Al put it, and they intended to do everything in their power to keep it so.

Their difficulty was with the iodine. The slogan "Keep Idena Pure" had, I learned, long been semi-comically circulating about the office and the factory, such had been the difficulty in sufficiently refining the iodine for edible purposes; and an equal difficulty had been in obtaining crude iodine of sufficient potency to make shipping economical. They had tried crude iodine from several of our own states, from Chile, from Japan, Norway, and Scotland; but it was only after they had been put in touch, by the American consul in Paris, with a Parisian broker, that they had obtained an iodine which was in its crude state sufficiently powerful to keep shipping charges from being excessive, and which was capable of being easily refined to fit Middle Western alimentary standards.

For the past year or more they had been happily buying large quantities of this French iodine ash—the exact source, it seemed, was the coast of Brittany, where it was obtained by burning particular varieties of seaweed—and during this time the profits from the already popularized Idena had shown a great increase. It was desirable, therefore, that Pearce Brothers maintain cordial and unchanged relations with the French broker and the French supplier.

This, however, was exactly what Pearce Brothers had of late, despite their best efforts, been unable to do. About three months before the date of our lunch, a shipment had been received which was of a quality wretchedly inferior to the usual, and a letter had been sent to the broker in Paris saying that a mistake was suspected.

They had come to consider him a treasure, this broker, Monsieur Achille Binbonnet. In addition to having found them their precious source of iodine in the first place, he had invariably, in his communications and his other efforts on their behalf, been exact and prompt, and the flowery courtesy of his letters they had come to take for granted. What was therefore their astonishment to receive from him in reply to their complaint a letter which was chiefly remarkable for rudeness, almost abuse, and which informed them that the change of quality which they noted was no more than the usual seasonal change inherent in iodine seaweed, and that they should be prepared for even greater deterioration of quality in the future. This was not only shocking and bewildering, but absurd and unjust. Seasonal changes were inherent in iodine seaweed, as in every other natural product, and Pearce Brothers knew it quite well, and provision for them had been made in the contract signed with the French producer: it had been stipulated that no crude iodine was to be shipped which had been adversely affected by these natural changes beyond a certain degree. And this new shipment was far below the minimum quality called for.

Another letter was accordingly written. Not to Monsieur Binbonnet, but to Gerard et Compagnie, the producers, of Brest in Brittany, with whom a less voluminous but equally cordial correspondence had also been maintained. But the reply from Gerard et Compagnie to this latest letter was as disappointing as the answer from Monsieur Binbonnet had been; it was cold, evasive, completely unsatisfactory.

The three-cornered correspondence which thenceforth took place was no more helpful. Binbonnet was asked to furnish iodine from some other source, since Gerard could no longer meet requirements. He replied only to express his complete loyalty to Gerard et Compagnie and his inability to understand why Pearce Brothers should suddenly begin a campaign of complaint. It was hinted to Binbonnet that Pearce Brothers would be willing to increase their price a trifle, if dissatisfaction with the existing price was what was being indirectly expressed. He replied that this suggestion caused him nothing but astonishment. Gerard et Compagnie were carefully sounded out, to see whether they might prefer to deal directly with Pearce Brothers, or through some other broker of their own choosing; they replied expressing complete loyalty to Monsieur Binbonnet. None of the French letters troubled to be polite. And meanwhile shipments of blatantly low quality continued to arrive.

Pearce Brothers, naturally, were greatly troubled. They considered returning to their previous source of supply. Idena had after all been profitably manufactured from the earlier, inferior, non-French iodines, though much less profitably than lately. The other alternative was to manufacture Idena, as best they could, from the wretchedly inferior product now being shipped from France. This was possible, at a loss (due to the weakness and impurity which would have to be expensively overcome); and there was always the chance that the French iodine might suddenly return to its original excellence as mysteriously as it had left it. It was this latter alternative which Pearce Brothers had adopted. During the past months Idena had been manufactured and sold at a loss. But the hoped-for return to normal had not taken place. In some shipments the quality was worse than ever, and shipments now began to come short—as much as several tons less than the quantity ordered. It was impossible to continue.

That was where I came in.

Iodine excepted, all of Pearce Brothers' imports have always come from the East—from Asia, Africa, Australia and the archipelagoes. In many cities in the Orient they have offices or agents; and they have forwarding agents, too, in San Francisco and other West Coast ports. In Europe they have never had representatives; have never had reason to have them. Thus there was no one in Europe who could help them out in this iodine matter, consult with Binbonnet and Gerard, try to unravel the mystery and bring things back to normal—or, failing that, find a new source of equally fine iodine. And yet it was highly advisable that someone do just that; large profits were at stake. Al and Jim had thought that one or the other of them, or one of the vice-presidents, might go over; but not one of them could conveniently leave the office at the present moment, and the thing should be done at once. Furthermore, none of them spoke French, and the Frenchmen concerned seemed to know no English; letters to and from Binbonnet and Gerard were translated by the office translator, a clerk linguistically endowed but incapable of undertaking a mission. They were puzzled as to what to do, when suddenly the issue of my continuing to hold Pearce Brothers stock came opportunely to the fore and they thought of me.

God knows I'm not a businessman. Selling pictures during boom days to wealthy customers who competed with each other to take them off my hands at a handsome profit was the extent of my commercial experience, and Al and Jim knew as well as I did that that had done little to equip me for participation in their world of big business. But, as Jim said, "You speak the lingo, Ted, and you're used to being with Frenchmen." And the chief point they made was, that if I'd undertake the mission they could perfectly justifiably make me a bona fide member of the firm and I could hold on to my stock.

That was the step to be taken, the activity, which they had come to lunch to put up to me. I could help them out. And by doing so I should be helping myself.

Or should I?

I sat there thinking about it when they'd said what they had to say. Could I perhaps set about reducing my scale of living with less discomfort, less mental anguish, than would be entailed by taking on their job? And yet, living meanly would go on and on, uncomfortably, forever, in addition to the first painful effort; whereas, once the French job was done, I could be as quiet as I pleased, and continue to be well off. The success or failure of my attempt abroad would not affect my status, Al and Jim assured me. I might well fail, they said; this iodine impasse was too mysterious, too outrageous, to be simple. Just by undertaking it, irrespective of the outcome, I'd retain my stock.

And yet, in the last analysis, I think it wasn't that consideration— or even a desire to do the boys a good turn—that made me decide to do the job. Wretched neurotic that I was in those days, I think it was the confidence shown by Al and Jim in offering me the job at all, their implied esteem for my intelligence, that made up my mind. That and the desire to show them that I was good for something.

But I was silent a long time. It was hell itself for me to make up my mind to do a thing like that. I was silent so long that even Al and Jim were finally impatient. They squirmed in their chairs. I could feel them looking at each other. Finally they couldn't stand it. "Will you go to France, Ted?" Al asked.

There it was. I was cornered.

"Yes, I'll be your iodine king," I answered in a voice that I didn't recognize. And immediately I was seized with such a feeling of fright that I can't remember what happened just after. We all shook hands, I think. I do remember thinking that my panic must be apparent on my face, and wondering that Al and Jim should look at me quite naturally, and talk to me as though I were myself. Then quite suddenly the panic subsided. I drank a glass of water, and in a natural voice said, "Of course I'll go," a remark which did make them look at me a trifle oddly, since quite naturally to them it seemed a kind of belated redundance. No longer did I feel fear, merely a sensation of being loaded with a distasteful burden which I was eager to throw off.

And from that moment I had no other onrush of panic until I looked out the window of my Paris hotel, the evening after my arrival, and knew that the next morning actual work would begin.

There was a lot to do, of course, before I left.

What a change in my life it was just to go to Pearce Brothers' office! I spent a good many hours there, going over the French iodine files and having copies made of correspondence, contracts and invoices. How different and how exhausting this new activity was! My braces and crutches weren't any more used to such a strain than I was, and I remember I used to wonder whether either they or I would stand up under it. We did.

I was greatly struck by the efficiency evidenced by the earlier correspondence of the French parties to the deal. There had been a straightforwardness about Monsieur Binbonnet and Gerard et Compagnie which differed agreeably from what even my experience had taught me about business as it can be conducted by firms and brokers abroad, a straightforwardness which made their more recent correspondence all the more striking by contrast. How suddenly and completely the tone of their letters had changed! The quality of their product, too. Al and Jim had the Idena foreman from the factory in Astoria come over to the office with samples of various grades of iodine ash, and I fingered and smelled and dissolved the powdery stuff until I became a kind of novice iodine-connoisseur. It was easy to perceive the greater blackness and the greater fineness of the best Gerard product. Quite clearly, Gerard had perfected a technique of burning seaweed unknown to his competitors, and it was that secret—plus, perhaps, a particularly good grade of seaweed to begin with—that explained its superiority. But the samples from the recent shipments were pale and coarse—not the same stuff at all. Something had happened either to the burning or to the quality of the weed; perhaps to both. That was what I had to find out.

It was amusing to read in a trade journal—some organ published for American importers of Oriental products—that "Mr. T. S. Weaver has joined the firm of Pearce Brothers, Inc.," and to put in my wallet a few of the newly printed cards—"T. S. Weaver. Pearce Brothers, Inc., New York."

A week or two after my lunch with Al and Jim I had all the iodine papers and information I needed, my shopping was done, I'd got my letter of credit and taken passage on the *Normandie* sailing October tenth. My instructions were: 1) I was to straighten out the Binbonnet-Gerard situation; and 2) if that situation proved incapable of settlement, then I was to seek another French iodine source. I was to remain abroad, if possible, until two successive, satisfactory monthly shipments of iodine had been received by Pearce Brothers.

Shipments had always been made, and were still being made (such as they were) by Gerard on the first of each month. The October shipment had not yet been received, but would undoubtedly be bad. I could scarcely hope to be so rapidly effective as to secure a good shipment on November first. Therefore, I should probably have to wait in France until the December first and January first shipments were received and approved by Pearce Brothers. In other words, until after the middle of January at the earliest.

It was quite a party, my sailing. Al and Jim and Eunice and Mildred were all there. They brought champagne and toasted me, and when it came time to go ashore the warmth of their affection surprised me, even though I knew full well that they were all affectionate people. They seemed to be expressing something beyond mere affection, something special of which they were all conscious. What it might be I couldn't imagine, unless perhaps they were a little worried by my sailing unaccompanied—without a servant, that is. Against everybody's advice I had let my man go, wanting to see how well I could manage by myself. Maybe that was what was troubling them.

As I have said, I like Al and Jim. And I like Eunice and Mildred. But despite all that, and despite the particularly significant-seeming warmth of the affection to which they treated me at parting, they hadn't been gone two minutes before I felt as I usually did, servant or no servant: alone in the world.

There was something that I wondered about occasionally on the ship, during that dull crossing. Why, since the desire of Al and Jim had been that I join the firm and do their business, had they begun their conversation with me as they had? Why hadn't they said, "Ted, we want you to join the firm," or "Ted, we want you to help us out," instead of "Ted, every close corporation's got to crack down . . ."? Why had they put it in the most alarming way they could? Why had they tried to scare me, corner me? It wasn't like them. Whenever I thought about this it seemed odd. But by the time of my second panic, in Paris, I'd pretty much forgotten about it. My call on Monsieur Binbonnet was preoccupying me by that time.

# CHAPTER 3

The next morning—the fatal morning—was glorious. I woke to find
golden sunlight flooding in through the long French windows onto
the red carpet of my hotel room, and though Paris October air is seldom as exciting a tonic as October air in New York, that morning's
air was the next best thing to it I've ever breathed. My coffee and
rolls were brought in by the same waiter who had served my lunch
and brought over my braces and crutches unasked the day before.
He bade me good morning with correct formality and respect and
uttered the correct number of "Voilà, Monsieur's" while arranging
the table. His response to my mention of the beauty of the day, however, was so enthusiastic as to contrast a trifle oddly with his precise
performance of his duties. Then the source of his enthusiasm became quickly apparent—civic pride. "Monsieur is experiencing Paris
October air for the first time, perhaps?" he said, eagerly. "There is
nothing like it anywhere else in the world—nothing!"

I didn't have the heart to undeceive him—and besides, the state
of my French, though it sufficed for most purposes, wouldn't have
permitted me to give him an adequate description of American October air. (Who, for that matter, has ever adequately described it in
any language?) I contented myself with asking, "There's nothing like
it even in any other part of France?" and then suppressed a smile
at the seriousness with which he considered that question. After a
long, reflective pause he admitted that the autumn air in Alsace-Lorraine was very fine indeed. I assumed that he had been born in one
of those provinces, but no—he had fought there during the war and
apart from that sojourn had almost never been outside Paris in his

life. At that point his bell rang out in the hall, and he retired, telling me that his name was Pierre and that he was completely at my
service. That this last was true I realized a moment later, when he
returned bearing my shoes, which I had sent out to be shined the
night before. It is not among the duties of a French room-waiter to
carry in a guest's shoes. One who does it is expressing approval of
the guest. I thanked Pierre heartily, making sure he saw that I realized the significance of his gesture. He informed me that he was the
chief waiter for the floor. That made his action even a greater favor.
The day was beginning well.

I didn't hurry to get up. What was the use? No French businessman ever gets to his office before ten, and besides, I wanted particularly to avoid giving Monsieur Binbonnet the impression that I was
eagerly hurrying to see him. I must evince no anxiety, no eagerness
or concern. The call must be utterly normal. Above all, Monsieur
Binbonnet must not know that I had crossed the ocean especially to
see him. I wanted to arrive at his office about eleven—not conspicu-
ously early, and yet early enough to allow a satisfactory conversation
before the sacred French lunch-stop at noon. I knew that I'd be more
nervous if up and dressed and hanging around than lazing in bed,
so I stayed there till late, reading over and over again the meager
newspapers, both French and American, which Paris provides in the
morning. Finally I rose, shaved and dressed. The time had come. I
felt pretty jittery.

The evening before, as my panic had slowly subsided, I had gone
over for the hundredth time the correspondence and other documents that Al and Jim had given me, to refresh my memory as to
figures and details, and in the taxi that morning on my way to Monsieur Binbonnet's I avoided going over them yet again in my mind.
I wanted my forthcoming conversation to be as fresh and unstud-
ied-sounding as possible. I well knew, from my previous French con-
tacts, to what extent trite but opinionated conversation is expected
and appreciated by the French, how rude it is considered if even
a businessman gets to the point too quickly. Therefore, as the taxi
sped along I thought of various topics of conversation—the glory of
the weather, my delight at being back in Paris again, my hope that

France would be able successfully to outwit some of the blustering neighbors who were threatening her security, and several others. By the time I had arrived, I knew that I should have no difficulty in supplying polite topics of conversation to Monsieur Binbonnet for at least twenty minutes, even were he to reply in monosyllables, which was most unlikely.

This was absurd, of course, an exaggeration on my part and symptomatic of the jittery state I was in. And as it turned out, such precautions were quite useless—for when I arrived Monsieur Binbonnet was out.

His street, the Rue Saint-Martin, I discovered to be a long, noisy, commercial thoroughfare, choked with trucks and lined on both sides with dirty old buildings housing shops on the ground floor and offices and lofts above. From the pillows and bedclothes bulging from some of the windows, it appeared that there were living-quarters up there as well; I knew that thrifty French businessmen often combined their homes and places of business, and clearly they were not the most ostentatious merchants of Paris, those of the Rue Saint-Martin. Monsieur Binbonnet's house, No. 404, was exactly like the others: dirty gray paint peeling off the front, on the ground floor a dreary-looking shop selling tapes and braids wholesale, and beside the street-door leading to the upper floors a cluster of small commercial signs and nameplates, among which I detected, from my taxi, that of "A. Binbonnet."

I wasn't surprised by the shabbiness of the neighborhood or the house: even in New York, brokers in raw materials are often located in the less imposing parts of town, and in France lack of ostentation is widespread among the commercial. What did surprise me, however, was another detail about the house, which I discovered only when I'd got out of the taxi: I had never had much hope that Monsieur Binbonnet would have an elevator, but what was my dismay to discover that even his concierge lived up a flight of stairs!

The usual place of residence of the concierge—the everpresent demon janitress and watchdog of French buildings—is a tiny suite of rooms just beside the main entrance, where she can command a view of all who come and go, and where she is easily accessible—even too easily accessible!—to visitors. But my heart sank at the view of the long, steep, difficult stairs here at 404 Rue Saint-Martin, up which pointed a hand painted on the wall just inside the entrance door, a hand bearing the word "Concierge."

They were certainly the worst stairs I have ever climbed. Clutching the taxi-driver's arm with one hand, and grasping the stair-rail with the other, I pushed and hoisted myself up from one step to the next. I confess that I came near to repenting, just then, my decision not to bring a personal servant, who might have helped me more expertly. The driver was a strong and willing soul, but I—and he too, I guess—arrived at the top feeling as though we'd been climbing those stairs forever. I was filled with despair because I knew that if the concierge lived up one flight, Monsieur Binbonnet must live up at least one flight more and quite possibly two or three. And I was suddenly filled with anger at myself for having come rather than written—or for not having had at least the wit to send the driver upstairs first. But chiefly I was panting—panting so hard that it was quite impossible for me to answer the questions that were barked at me up there in the hall. As I had approached the top of the stairs I had first seen her through the glass door of her loge—an old crone sitting at a table with a checked tablecloth, peeling potatoes. Then, peering suspiciously, she had caught sight of me, and as I reached the hall she had pushed her work aside and hurried out, rattling the glass door as she came. "Well? What is it? Tell me what you want!"

Parisian concierges are famous for their bad tempers and bad manners, but never had I encountered one as savage as this. Particularly ill-flavored, too, a horrid, filthy-looking old woman. Standing there, trying to catch my breath, I incongruously imagined a cause for her ill nature: probably she was soured by her inability to look out into the street and watch the crowd go by, like her colleagues! After all, a concierge's life isn't a glamorous one, and the ability to sit in her room and watch the street-life outside is one of its few compensations. Deprived of this by her unheard-of location, I pleased myself by imagining, Monsieur Binbonnet's concierge was filled with bitterness! Even the taxi-driver, who was likewise in breathless state, appeared momentarily taken aback by our reception; then he pantingly retorted for me with an unprintable piece of Parisian slang that caused the old woman to glare at him and turn for her answer to me. "Well?" she said, again.

When I finally got out the name "Binbonnet" she replied in one word—"Out"—and started to return to her potatoes.

"Wait a minute, please."

"Well, what is it?" (Arms akimbo.)

"When will he be back?"

A shrug. "This evening."

"Do you mean before dinner or after dinner?"

"After."

"Then will you please tell him that I called and will come back after dinner this evening?" I took out one of my Pearce Brothers cards, scribbled my address on it and handed it to her. "If he wishes me not to call tonight, ask him to communicate with me at my hotel."

She took the card without even nodding and started once again for the potatoes; but once again I called her back and gave her five francs, which I hoped might insure delivery. This she also accepted without acknowledgment.

"Since Monsieur Binbonnet has no telephone," I said angrily— now thoroughly indignant—"it is difficult to make an appointment with him in advance."

To that she made no reply except to stare at me, and then she did go back to her potatoes, banging the glass door behind her, and the driver and I were left alone in the hall, at the top of the stairs we had so laboriously climbed and with nothing to do but descend them.

We looked at each other. "Charming," I murmured.

"She's —," he said vigorously, using again one of the words he had addressed to her. "She's —, triple —."

Then we clumped slowly and noisily downstairs.

Even before I was back in the taxi I was sorry I had made that remark about the telephone. If Monsieur Binbonnet had no phone, then it was undoubtedly normal for French businessmen of his cat-egory to have none, for I was already of the opinion that Binbonnet was a typical smaller French businessman. My angry remark had been an indication of ignorance, and a tactical error as well. I had peevishly criticized Monsieur Binbonnet for something that must

seem normal both to him and to his concierge; and now the concierge would report that a pig of an American had arrived with a
preposterous complaint, and my man would be prejudiced against
me. Why had I to be so unwise, and at the very beginning of my mission? Why hadn't I conquered my impulsiveness in the first place
and written him instead of coming unannounced? My impatience
to impress Al and Jim with an immediate report had got in the way
of my common sense. Would I continue to botch things like this? At
least, I must from now on restrain my tongue.

As we crossed the sidewalk, my taxi-driver apologized to me for
the behavior of the concierge. "All concierges are —s," he said, using
his favorite word again, "but this one is the queen of the —s. She
and her kind make a bad impression on foreigners, Monsieur," and
so on and so on, a very handsome apology for something that was
in no way his own fault. I was a little surprised that he should talk
this way, for in general Parisians are pretty stoical in the face of
the often vituperative behavior of other Parisians, accepting it
themselves and not commiserating unduly with a stranger who is
aggrieved by it. But then I'm generally liked by taxi-drivers, either
despite or because of the hard service I put them to getting me
in and out of their cabs; this man's apologies were probably just
another example of that, or else the concierge had been even worse
than I'd realized!

At any rate, the driver and I abused the old woman to our hearts'
content as we drove back to the hotel, and there in my room I spent
the rest of the morning and afternoon and early evening by myself,
reading and surprising myself a little by wishing there was somebody who might drop in for a cocktail. At seven I dined beside my
fire. No message arrived from Monsieur Binbonnet, and at 8.30 I
put on my braces again and went downstairs for the second time that
day to take a taxi to 404 Rue Saint-Martin. I wondered whether my
broker would prove any more agreeable than his concierge.

# CHAPTER 4

The street was now still and deserted. There were none of the trucks that had been rumbling through it in the morning, the shop-fronts were shut up tight and lights shone only in the upper windows. Oddly enough, there was a kind of nocturnal charm about the Rue Saint-Martin, so unlovely by day. Its rows of tall old houses formed a dark but light-dotted hedge that seemed to go straight on into the heart of the night. It was impressive, the long, narrow, silent street.

This time Monsieur Binbonnet's street-door was locked and after pressing the bell I waited a long time for the answering click. Then began a new ascent—on the arm of another clumsy but willing taxi-driver—of those breath-destroying stairs. When we were half-way up I heard the concierge's door rattle open and she appeared above in the dim light and silently watched our slow approach.

"Where is Monsieur Binbonnet's office?"

"Next floor, right."

I felt grateful even to that harpy for not saying "Two floors up" or "Three floors up." She watched us go up the second flight of stairs, which was just as steep and uncompromising as the first; then I heard her glass door bang closed. At the head of the stairs were two doors, one bearing Monsieur Binbonnet's name. After waiting two or three minutes for my breath to return I rang, asking the driver to wait for me there where he was. I heard footsteps immediately. The door was opened. "Good evening, Monsieur Weavair! Achille Binbonnet, at your service!"

I stared.

This morning I had suspected that Monsieur Binbonnet would prove to be a typical smaller French businessman. But as far as appearance, at least, was concerned, I was only partially right. Monsieur Binbonnet did look very French. Of a certain particular variety of Frenchman, in fact, he was almost a caricature. But he didn't look like any kind of a French businessman. It was his loudness that was so unexpected.

That he should be short and slight, olive-skinned and dark-eyed, with coal-black hair and a coal-black beard was scarcely surprising. But I confess that I was surprised by the extreme slickness of his pomaded hair, by the number of rings on his hands, the profusion of gold chain across his narrow chest, and the loudness of his striped suit. It was one of those intensely Gallic striped suits that come so near to spoiling the streets of Paris for visiting Americans and English, and it fitted Monsieur Binbonnet so tightly, especially around the waist and down the legs, as to appear a fancy outer skin. It was tight, in fact, everywhere except at the shoulders, where fantastic amounts of padding did their best to give the little man the look of a fullback. Monsieur Binbonnet's letters, at least up until recently, had been so respectable! Why did he look like this?

He too, I perceived, was doing his share of staring. Not only at my crutches—they, I knew, would be stared at as they always were— but also at me, at my face. And quickly I realized that there was one quality of traditional Frenchness that Monsieur Binbonnet lacked, at least in his outward manner: vivacity. His gaze was somber. His large dark eyes had a look even of sadness. For a moment that realization gave me a feeling of strangeness. One so often saw, on the streets of Paris, this olive skin and black hair and these large dark eyes, and one often saw these natural features combined with rings and chains and brilliantine and loud wasp-waisted striped suits. But when they were so combined they usually belonged to someone young and with a jaunty air, someone who was talking gaily with a companion, gesturing, or humming a tune or making love; it was a kind of lower-middle-class French dandy type. But Monsieur Binbonnet was neither gay nor young. Due to his gaudy get-up, he appeared on first glance to be youngish; but a look into his face revealed that he was as old as I, at least. And he was the first somber

dandy I had ever seen. That was what seemed odd. The loud handkerchief in his upper pocket and the stickpin in his tie contrasted
queerly with his serious, even solemn mien.

Such was the first, instantaneous impression.

Then we shook hands, and I launched conscientiously into the
stream of compliments I knew was expected, and—also as I expected—my stream was quickly lost in the Gallic torrent of his. What
with the conventional floweriness of the language, and the jerking
of the black beard and the glittering of the rings and pin and gold
chains, even an illusion of vivacity was achieved. And immediately remarkable—particularly so—was the way the man talked. Such
a beautiful French is rarely heard among men of his station—and
certainly rarely heard coming from wearers of such clothes. The
voice and the intonation were things of beauty. I was no match for a
stream of conventional French phrases of welcome uttered in such
remarkable tones as those. Murmuring only an occasional monosyl-
lable, I allowed Monsieur Binbonnet to draw me into his vestibule,
divest me of my things, and then lead me farther down a short hall
and finally, with ceremonious gestures, into his office.

This was an odd, cluttered little room, one which gave the impression of having started, at some remote time, as a living room,
and of still being used as such during non-business hours. There
was an upright piano, closed and bare of music, and a small sofa
piled with cushions, among which I saw, curled up, a tortoise shell
cat which was purring loudly. But chief among the room's furnish-
ings were the huge business-like desk, well-littered, the dusty and
disheveled display of maps and charts on the walls, and everywhere
else, particularly on the mantelpiece, a collection of test-tubes, spec-
imens of ore, dried grasses, bits of wood and stone and sponges,
glass jars of white and colored powders. The whole thing added up
to the most crowded little interior imaginable; heavy draperies over
the windows, a violently colored false Oriental on the floor, a French
flag somewhere, and everything lit by one blinding electric light bulb
hanging unshaded on a cord from the middle of the ceiling.

I took this all in as minutely as I could, as I sat there smoking
the cigarette I had been offered, for it was my hope never to be in
that room again. I hoped that in the future I might avoid climbing

the steps of 404 Rue Saint-Martin, and that any interviews with Monsieur Binbonnet would be in places chosen by me. So I stared at everything. This task of examination was made easy for me by my host, who was by now under full sail on the sea of polite preliminary French conversation; my monosyllabic replies were more than adequate (with an occasional full sentence or suggestion thrown in for the sake of variety)—particularly because he was conversing, in his soft beautiful voice, on the very topics which I had prepared myself. The beauty of the weather; the chilliness, however, of the nights; the imminence of winter; the alarming international situation—on all these I had my answers ready. There were inquiries as to the health of Al and Jim, as to whether I had ever been in Paris before, etc., etc. It was all very easy.

My examination of the room completed, I turned my attention back to Binbonnet, trying to pierce beneath his surprising surface, trying to fathom his character. Here, uttering banalities with exquisite enunciation, was the man who had written those remarkable letters to Pearce Brothers. What was he like? Overnight he had changed the tone of his letters from one of friendly cooperation to one of defiance. Why? In the briefcase I had with me were copies of those letters—full of belligerent disclaimers of responsibility, grossly simulated astonishment that Pearce Brothers should complain at all. What would this gaudy, somber little man say were I to show them to him and request an explanation? "You come from Touraine, do you not, Monsieur Binbonnet?" I heard myself asking.

"From the city of Tours itself, Monsieur."

I had suddenly remembered a phrase in one of his letters—one of the early ones, in which with great courtesy he had begged to be excused for a slight delay in replying to a letter from Pearce Brothers; "detained at Tours on family business" was the phrase I recalled. That, of course, was the explanation of one thing about the man—his beautiful French, which many of even the humble speak in that region of France, the château country. There the common speech has a beauty envied and imitated by actors and academicians.

I murmured my admiration for his language, and made a few remarks about my own travels among the châteaux. He made suitable replies, and then quite abruptly let me know that preliminaries were at an end. "My letter from Pearce Brothers," he said, in slightly louder voice—and I could see the Pearce Brothers letterhead on the desk in front of him—"tells me that you have come to Europe to call on all their European suppliers. How interesting!"

What was interesting about it, particularly, unless he suspected that statement of being the lie it was? But— "Yes, a general visit to all our European friends, in the interests of closer personal cooperation," I confirmed. "Most American business is conducted on such a vast, impersonal scale . . ."

"I know, I know." Monsieur Binbonnet waved that aside. Then he looked at me closely, and still speaking in his louder tone, said, "It relieves me, Monsieur, to be assured that your immense journey was undertaken for many purposes. It would sadden me to think that you took it solely for the sake of our little matter, solely for the sake of iodine. Any difficulties that may exist there are not worth mentioning, and when I think of the time and exertion expended by you . . . Though I confess I should be flattered, Monsieur, could I think it was iodine alone that brought you."

A laugh, I thought, would most effectively indicate that this was an absurdity, so I laughed gaily. "France is only my first stop. My next is Holland," I said, inwardly groaning as I spoke, for having said that I was going to Holland I should now probably have to go—whatever I might do when I got there. He was malicious as well as odd, Monsieur Binbonnet!

"Then I am flattered that you should come to France first," he quickly replied, quite unsmiling and regarding me still closely. "And you must allow me to be flattered also that you pay me the honor of a visit in the evening. I am complimented. And I confess also that I am intrigued. Iodine is a daytime interest with many of us over here; we give much of our time to it. But in the evening—it takes an American, Monsieur, to be interested in iodine in the evening! Or am I too general? Is it merely you personally, perhaps, who have so keen an interest in iodine as to discuss it at night?"

This time what I did inwardly was to curse. Had anyone ever bungled as I had? "You know how we Americans are, Monsieur Binbonnet," I said, laughing again in a kind of desperation. "Surely you know our saying, 'Time is money!' That explains me, I guess. I'm sorry if I have interfered with any evening plans you had; I hoped you would telephone if you didn't want me to come."

And as I parried his thrusts I looked at my host with increased curiosity, for his very malice was of a strange kind. Most people, when their words are urbanely insulting, look joyous, display a real or pretended smile, have a gleam of satisfaction in their eyes. But not so Monsieur Binbonnet. These most sarcastic remarks were made with the most somber and unchanged expression; sadness seemed to well out of his eyes as he kept ironically pricking me. And why did he now think it necessary to speak so loudly?

With another wave of his hand, he dismissed the topic he himself had so cannily introduced. "It is nothing," he said. "My evening is at your disposal." But then, as though seeming to recollect something, he murmured, as though to himself, the word "Telephone." Again I cursed inwardly. What an actor he was! "Monsieur Weavair," he suddenly boomed, "my concierge tells me that my lack of a telephone appears to have caused you some inconvenience. This I deeply regret, Monsieur. But here in France . . ." And there followed the little talk I so richly deserved—French poverty, French conservatism, French leisure, French individualism. The ease of sending special delivery letters and telegrams was also mentioned. Monsieur Binbonnet's voice continued loud. Never had I heard such beautiful French diction as in this lesson in manners, clearly aimed to make me feel ashamed of myself.

And ashamed of myself it did make me feel, though not in the way Binbonnet intended. I sat quietly while the lecture lasted, and during it something happened to me. Eagerness to impress Al and Jim with an early report that could only be incomplete. The unannounced visit. Irritability at the rudeness of the concierge. Petulance about the telephone. Those were mistakes. And by the time Binbonnet's little talk ended I knew I should not repeat them. To discipline myself, I didn't even retort to his speech, though his was certainly a superior tone for a commission broker to take with his customer. "In short, Monsieur, I am sorry that I am too poor to have a telephone in my business," was his closing sentence, and I let a moment of silence elapse before I spoke.

When I finally did speak my voice was cold. "I confess that I am eager to get this little matter of iodine cleared up as quickly as possible, so that I can go to Holland and attend to some really important matters."

He bowed imperturbably. "I shall cooperate with all my power."

Then came a strange interruption, a scene I shall always remember.

I was seated in a chair beside Binbonnet's desk, facing him and facing the wall adorned with maps and charts that was behind him. And as Binbonnet uttered the word "cooperate," part of the wall began to move. I realized instantly, of course, that the moving portion was a door, though its surface so resembled the rest of the wall, what with its load of tacked-on paraphernalia, that I had not previously recognized it as such. Not that it was a deliberately concealed door—merely an inconspicuous one. The door moved, and through the resultant opening, which was away from me and which I could not see, there emerged a large head. It was so large, and so sagacious, and yet so unhuman, that for a moment I couldn't imagine to what kind of body it belonged; then the door swung wider, and into the room stalked the hugest dog I have ever seen in my life. I knew the breed. It was a Great Dane, and surely the greatest Great Dane of them all. Its head was close to five feet above the ground, and its enormous brown body extended from the door to the desk. Typically, it had areas of darker color, almost black, and on the head and face darkest of all; it seemed to be these splotches, and the deep lines in the skin below the eyes, which made the beast look so venerable. He stood there, staring at me; his entry had been noiseless; and the angle of the door, though it was now open a foot, still concealed from me what was beyond. Looking at the dog, in my surprise, I made no immediate reply to Binbonnet; and he, glancing up, saw my gaze and turned around. And as he turned, the dog began to growl.

It was a blood-freezing sound, like a warning of intense danger, coming as it did from a beast superbly powerful, invincible; and it dispelled all illusion of venerable sagacity.

This was a menacing beast, not a creature of wisdom. Binbonnet leapt to his feet. As he did so the dog made a twitch of his tail which effortlessly swung the door open still wider, and through it I saw, indistinctly, the movement of some form, brown-clad, darting instantly out of range of my eyes. Then Binbonnet slammed the door shut. And it was when he did that, and the dog continued to make its terrifying sound, looking not at Binbonnet and no longer at me, that I knew its hostility was directed at neither of us. I followed its gaze and saw—the sofa.

The cat, previously a purring furry ball, was standing on its cushions in the classic position of fury and terror: back highly arched, every hair on end, tail erect, eyes glaring. And at every deep growl a tremor shook it. I looked at my host, to see what he would do, and what was my astonishment to see, on his face, the emotion of the cat equaled if not surpassed! What an expression of hatred was there! He was staring at the dog as though he desired to tear its throat, to pull its great body into bloody pieces, to torture it, do it all possible violence. "Act quickly, if you'd save the cat," I almost cried out to him, for he appeared to be literally paralyzed by rage and hate.

But there was no need, as it happened, for me to speak; for with a sudden return of movement Binbonnet rushed across the room, seized the cat and, opening the other door, the hall-door through which I had come, thrust it out and closed the door upon it. For a moment he stood there, breathing deeply and glaring fiercely at the dog, whose growls were now changing to disappointed, frustrated combinations of growl and whine; then seeming deliberately to collect himself, he changed his expression and began talking to it in winning, soothing words. "Faust" was the name I heard him repeat, over and over again, in falsely affectionate phrases, holding out his hand, gradually approaching the beast and then patting and fondling him. Faust responded. The cries ceased, the tail began slowly to move. Two or three minutes later, when Binbonnet opened the door in the wall, glancing at me, I thought, as he did so, the great dog obediently padded back through the opening, back to where he had come from. Binbonnet closed the door securely and sank down in his chair. His forehead, I noticed, was covered with sweat. This surprised me, until I discovered that my own was, too. It had been a bad scare. The dog was so huge. The growls had been so deep.

We sat in silence for a moment, using our handkerchiefs in identical gestures. I attempted to smile, but rage had left a sternness on Binbonnet's somber face, and he did not respond. Suddenly he rose, opened the hall door, and returned bearing the cat, now also pacified. He sat there at his desk, stroking her. Was there, perhaps, I found myself wondering, a dog-loving and domineering Madame Binbonnet? Was it she who, clad in brown, had been briefly visible in the next room? But that was scarcely likely, for I had glanced with curiosity at Monsieur Binbonnet's many rings, and there was not a wedding ring amongst them. What French married man would be wedding-ringless, particularly when wearing rings of other kinds? But none of this was any of my business, and no one knew this better than I—except, evidently, Monsieur Binbonnet. He made no comment whatever on the episode. There was silence a little longer, more dabbing with the handkerchief. And then, sitting in his desk-chair with his cat in his arms, Monsieur Binbonnet cleared his throat and said: "As I was saying, Monsieur Weavair, I shall cooperate with you to the best of my ability."

It took me an instant to swing back to our business as completely as that.

"Oh, very good. Then look here," I replied, after the involuntary pause. "Here I have copies of the correspondence," I said, reaching for my briefcase, "copies of some of the letters . . ."

That was as far as I got. To my surprise, Monsieur Binbonnet held up his hand. What? Was he going to refuse to talk about this subject, the very subject I had crossed the ocean to discuss and straighten out? An overbearing broker indeed! And yet, when he spoke I found myself listening to him.

"Monsieur Weavair, do not disarrange your papers, I beg of you. Of my share in the correspondence, I confess I am not proud; to go over it now would be futile. Listen to me, Monsieur."

And he proceeded to tell me the story of his relations with Pearce Brothers and Gerard et Compagnie in detail and with complete accuracy, acknowledging all faults, expressing complete comprehension of Pearce Brothers' annoyance and distress. His narrative was sane—totally unlike his later letters, totally unlike his own personal peculiarities. He was speaking loudly again, and with never a smile, but what he said put him on our side.

"From now on, the situation will return to normal. The October shipment, which should be arriving in New York about now, will, I regret to say, be found of inferior quality. But the shipment of

November first, and all future shipments, will be excellent. What more can I do for you? What more do you desire?"

What more *could* I desire? But how could I have confidence in his mere word, when his recent acts had been so outrageous? "I find it strange," I told him, "that you should offer no explanations for past behavior."

"Explanations, Monsieur? As you say, that behavior is past; let me assure you that it will not recur, and let us try to forget it. When the November shipment arrives in New York you will be in Holland or elsewhere in Europe. If your partners inform you that it is not satisfactory, then come to me for explanations and you shall have them, Monsieur. But you will not have to come. The shipment will be satisfactory. Remember how excellent our service was in the past; I swear that from now on it will be like that again."

The man spoke earnestly. It was a cool proposition, this refusal to discuss and this large promise, but I saw no reason to spurn it entirely. After all, Binbonnet and Gerard had been excellent—perfect—in the past; why shouldn't they be so again? Monsieur Binbonnet's proposal amounted to a postponement for one month—with the possibility of postponing it forever—of the showdown I had come prepared to have. To accept would be an anticlimax—but had I not learned, this very evening, not to be proud? Cancellation of the discussion which I had traveled three thousand miles to have was unexpected, to say the least—as surprising as the personality of my broker, as unlooked for as the appearance he now presented, sitting there in dandy's clothes, his cat in his lap. But I decided to accept his proposition—to take for one trial month, so to speak, the hand that Monsieur Binbonnet was stretching out to me. My chief reason, frankly, was that I had as yet no very clear idea of what else to do. To wait and see for a month seemed a harmless procedure. Binbonnet might keep his promise. And if he did not, I might by that time have discovered some effective course of action.

He saw my decision in my face. "You can trust me," he said impressively, and we shook hands.

So brief was our iodine discussion. Should I have insisted on making it fuller? Only time would tell.

I looked at my watch. It said a few minutes before ten. There was no hurry, but I knew that courtesy demands farewells in France to be as leisurely as preliminaries, and I thought I'd start to make mine.

"I hope," I said, "soon to make the acquaintance of Monsieur Antoine Gerard, of Gerard et Compagnie."

"Monsieur Gerard? Unfortunately, he rarely comes to Paris. He has just been here and gone, and will probably not come again until the spring. What a shame, Monsieur. Had you but arrived a few days earlier . . ."

"I mean that I intend to go to Brest to see him."

"To Brest! Ah, Monsieur, let me do everything in my power to dissuade you!"

I looked at Monsieur Binbonnet in surprise. Why on earth should I not go to Brest? Was not Gerard more important to us even than Binbonnet himself?

"You are evidently unfamiliar, Monsieur, with that part of France—the Breton seacoast. It is there that French families go in summer, for the coolness of the air—but woe, even in that season, to the delicate! Many a delicate child has fallen into tuberculosis in Brittany in midsummer, Monsieur: judge for yourself what the climate is now that summer is past. Promptly with the end of August the summer visitors leave, so early comes the cold. You are delicate, Monsieur Weavair—pardon me, but I can see that; you would suffer in Brittany, believe me. And what would it profit you to go, Monsieur?"

All this was most considerate, but it was also preposterous. Half of my reason for crossing the Atlantic was to see Gerard; to omit seeing him was unthinkable.

"First," I replied precisely, "I should meet Monsieur Gerard. I look forward to doing so, and he would have every reason to feel offended if in my tour of our European friends I omitted to call upon him."

"Listen, Monsieur." Binbonnet stepped nearer, but his voice remained loud. "Monsieur Gerard is a fine fellow, a man of excellent character, but—how shall I say?—he is—between ourselves—archaic, crude, learned in nothing but the burning of seaweed, a successful workman, Monsieur, not a businessman. Almost a peasant, Monsieur. His establishment is a mere shed. Gerard and his kind could not exist without businessmen like us; it is my role to sell, yours to use, his product. Do not take that fatiguing journey, Monsieur; your courteous intentions toward Monsieur Gerard are admirable, but they are too chivalrous, Monsieur, useless. I have confessed today that I have been remiss in the past; how much more remiss should I be now, were I to allow you to visit, in this season, that primitive, sea-swept part of France!"

"Second, I wish to inspect the factory. Perhaps I could even suggest some improvements which would aid my firm."

There was a moment's silence; I heard a clock somewhere strike ten.

"I see that you are determined to go, Monsieur," Binbonnet then said, with an air of resignation. "Believe me, it is for your sake that I have attempted to dissuade you. You will find Brittany a rude, cold place, Monsieur Weavair. Dress warmly when you go there."

I thanked him and rose. Inside myself I smiled: it was possible, I supposed, that Al or Jim might urge a customer to bundle up well when setting out for Chicago or Detroit, but the thought amused me.

It had not been merely for conversational purposes that I had mentioned Monsieur Gerard and his establishment at Brest. In his detailed resume of Pearce Brothers' iodine transactions Monsieur Binbonnet had of course made repeated mention of Gerard et Compagnie. But nearly all mention of them had been in the past. Only his characterization of Gerard as a near-peasant and his lament that he had just recently been in Paris could be called present-tense references to the iodine manufacturer. And as to the future—as to the part that Gerard was to play in the grand promised revival—there was no reference whatever, no definite mention of cooperation between manufacturer and broker. This struck me as strange. Was this not meager mention of Gerard, who was so integral a part of our business?

"Your relations with Gerard are, I trust, always close and satisfactory?" I thought it wise to ask.

My host seemed surprised at my question. "But of course, Monsieur Weavair!"

Well—a month would tell me everything. In the meantime I must not let strangeness of manner affect me too strongly. "Then au revoir, Monsieur Binbonnet," I said. "In one month I will let you know the verdict of New York. Until then, my best wishes."

He thanked me.

And then I discovered that my efforts to say farewell, like my feeble attempts at preliminary conversation on my arrival, were as nothing beside the stream of banal and courteous closing commentary which Binbonnet now effortlessly let flow. We were both standing, and the room was filled with the polite, grave torrent of his trivialities. Great justice was done to the weather; it was discussed from every conceivable angle. On and on went his beautiful voice.

Finally with determination I said I must be going.

He followed me to his door, put down his cat, and helped me on with my coat.

Outside in the hall the taxi-driver was sitting at the top of the stairs, surrounded by a ring of cigarette stubs. Monsieur Binbonnet and I shook hands in farewell. "Dress warmly when you go to Brittany," he reminded me. "They are making you comfortable at the Clarence?"

"Very comfortable, thank you."

He nodded, we bowed and Monsieur Binbonnet turned away.

His door was closing behind him and the driver and I were just about to start down the stairs, when the shrill sound came—came right out of Monsieur Binbonnet's apartment. I turned around in amazement, and there in the doorway I saw that Binbonnet had turned around, too, to see if I had heard it.

Our eyes met. Then without a word he slammed the door behind him. He knew that I had heard it. He knew that I had heard his telephone ring, and he knew that I knew he knew it.

# CHAPTER 5

So—what was I to think?

But it was so very baffling, and seemed so puzzlingly unnecessary, Binbonnet's suddenly revealed lie about his telephone, that for the moment I refused to think about it at all, and during the descent of the two flights of stairs I merely tried to keep from slipping and indulged my feeling of relief that the interview was ended and that I had gone through with it. What a funk I had been in before it—for weeks before it, in fact! And now that I had fought it through, how much less of an ordeal future intercourse with strangers promised to be! I had certainly benefited from this long-dreaded bit of parleying, whether or not Pearce Brothers had.

My next thought was: now that I was able to send a letter off to Al and Jim by the *Normandie* the next morning, what did I have, after all, to put into it? And twenty minutes later, in my room at the Clarence, I put writing materials on the night-table, got into bed, and meditated some more. Did I have anything at all, so far, to write Al and Jim?

Just as Binbonnet's brazen letters to Pearce Brothers had outraged my brothers-in-law, so his brazen lying about the telephone was now outraging me. And, as was so often the case, I was outraged at myself as well. Why hadn't I cried out, or pounded on Binbonnet's door, challenged him at once, demanded an immediate explanation? Why hadn't I had the thing cleared up instantly? I could think, though, of two excuses for my conduct. First, I had been taken by surprise. And second, the thing was so outrageous as to make me feel that it was not easily explicable.

Those were excuses for my own conduct. Could I think of any for Binbonnet's?

I conjured up the image of Monsieur Binbonnet. What a Gallic image it was! I saw his beard, his olive skin, his slick hair, his striped suit. I saw his watch-chain, his gaudy handkerchief. And I saw, as I looked at it steadily with my mind's eye, that the whole thing made up into something just a little out of date. It was his beard, first of all, that was noticeable. There are still thousands of beards in France. But there are, too, thousands of Frenchmen, among them the most progressive and modern-minded, who now laugh at beards, call them old-fashioned and unsanitary and think of them as we do—comic and anachronistic except on the aged. His beard alone put Binbonnet outside the number of the most modern Frenchmen, so to speak. And his stickpin and chain and handkerchief and striped suit—all those were clues that pointed in the same direction: one sees them on the boulevards every day, and yet—a "modern" French-man would have none of them.

So, apart from the notable sobriety of his natural expression, which in the present calculation seemed to be beside the point, I thus found Binbonnet's appearance to be notable for two things: intense Frenchness and decided lack of contemporary tone. Now, if these qualities were carried over into business, what would they indicate about Binbonnet there? What, indeed, unless that he was incorrigibly old-fashioned? And, being old-fashioned, what was more natural than that he should not have a telephone?

That was where I got, in my thoughts, when I started laughing at myself.

What a fiasco!

Starting out to find an excuse for Binbonnet's having a telephone and concealing it, the best I could do was to find a beautiful excuse for his having no telephone at all! Was this what my iodine mission was going to lead me into—situations so crazy that all I could do was laugh helplessly? And then there occurred to me one other thing that I might do. Suppose I didn't find an explanation for Binbonnet's lie. What of it? What of it, so long as I could find one other thing—his telephone number?

For, sometime in the not too distant future, I'd be wanting to get in touch with Binbonnet again, and my antipathy to climbing his stairs was stronger than ever, now that I knew he had a phone. And what American likes even to write notes or telegrams, when he knows he can telephone? Some day, I decided, when I wanted to talk to Monsieur Binbonnet, I'd have him telephone me, and then when I had him on the wire I'd say, quite casually, "Do give me your telephone number, Monsieur Binbonnet—it will make everything so much easier." Having seen me, he would understand my peculiar physical reasons for the request, and give me the number. And possessing the number, I could do without an explanation of his conduct. After all was said and done, why should I have to know why he lied? Why should I care that he lied at all?

That is, about telephones. One thing, of course, I should most definitely be interested in discovering: whether he lied in promising a restoration of good iodine shipments. Whether or not Binbonnet would keep his promise about iodine was my most important concern.

And iodine was of course the only thing to write about if I was to send a letter to Al and Jim. No reason to tell them about Binbonnet's telephone oddity, or about his striped suit, or about his love for his cat, or about the interruption of the Great Dane. (How paradoxically French, by the way, to call a dog by the German name Faust! Gounod's opera is the most popular in France, and just that morning, on my first futile visit to the Rue Saint-Martin, I had passed the Opera House and seen a performance of *Faust* advertised as usual on the great yellow posters.) No reason to write Al and Jim about those things. And yet, what was there to write to them, except one bit of news which they might very well not welcome: that my only action so far was a postponement of any showdown with Monsieur Binbonnet, further reliance on the word of the man whose very duplicity had necessitated my mission? It would be better, I decided, not to write at all, and in the end I cabled, instead, telephoning the message downstairs to the night-porter. "Progress slow but promising. Going Brittany this week." That would tell them at least that I'd arrived and was on the job.

Then I turned out the light and fell asleep more quickly than I had in a long time. Not only was nothing facing me the next day, but I had on this day actually done something. For what previous day in the last ten years had I been able to say the same?

I did have one odd dream. I dreamed that when I went to Brest I found that Monsieur Gerard had been murdered by a crony of Binbonnet's and his business confiscated and continued by the crony and Binbonnet together. That was why Binbonnet hadn't wanted me to go to Brest. That was all there was to it—the dream didn't go any further, and it didn't disturb my rest. I awoke refreshed, and immediately after breakfast telephoned downstairs a telegram to be sent off to Monsieur Gerard in Brest, asking him what day during the week it would be convenient for him to receive me.

It was another beautiful fall day, and before lunch I taxied to a café and sat there in the sun for an hour, wrapped in a heavy overcoat, watching the people go by. I wished I knew some of them. That was the second time I had wished for company in two days—a strange sensation for me. For so long my chief desire had been to be by myself.

Back at the hotel I found Gerard's reply. Friday, he said, would suit him very well. Accordingly I told the porter to get me a round trip ticket and sleeping accommodations on the Brest train leaving Thursday night. It got in, I discovered, at seven in the morning; I knew in what a wretched physical state I'd be on arrival, but at least I'd have time for two or three hours of rest before the interview. "Arriving Friday morning," I wired Gerard. Then I went to my room and tried to rest in advance. For a while I sat on my balcony in the sun, then inside reading, and then immediately after dinner I went to bed. Perhaps, if I could rest strenuously like this today and all of the next day as well, I'd be so fortified that a train trip wouldn't wreak its usual havoc. Already I was dreading the jolting and the veering.

I'd just turned off the light, hoping for a long sleep, when the telephone rang.

It was the only person it could have been. "I do not disturb you, I trust, Monsieur Weavair? You see, I am endeavoring to suit your preference for evening conferences."

That superior tone! How vividly it brought back my visit of the day before!

"Are you telephoning from your own telephoneless office, Monsieur Binbonnet?" I was tempted to ask. Undoubtedly he was doing just that—talking to me from the very instrument he had told me he did not possess; the thought amused me. "You have some news for me, Monsieur Binbonnet?" I inquired.

Not very much, it seemed. He had written to Gerard, he said, telling him that we had conferred and that from now on all should be smooth. Did not such a letter from *him* remove the necessity of the long journey to Brest by *me?* He wanted to spare me, etc., etc.

Perhaps I was a trifle short in my reiteration that I must go and in my revelation that the date of my going was set; but Monsieur Binbonnet showed no offense. He immediately offered another suggestion for my comfort. Since I felt I had to go to Brest, why should I not go more easily than was possible by train? The peculiar schedule and equipment of the Paris-Brest service, he said, made it one of the most fatiguing journeys in France. Through an acquaintance, he had heard of an excellent chauffeur with a luxurious car—a smart-looking sport model, he queerly specified—who would drive me to Brest and back for little more than the railroad fare—for much less than the rate of car-hire usually charged. The journey could be made in leisurely style, two days each way, stopping at excellent inns. That would be more comfortable than the train, he submitted.

Now it so happens that if there is anything that wearies me more than a train ride, it is a long ride in an automobile. For several years, after a certain incident, I couldn't bear to ride in an auto at all; and I suppose that a certain amount of that psychological distaste will always remain. But apart from that, a long automobile ride is physically hard for me. The long-continued motion, at times even more violent than that of a train; the cramped quarters, the inability to stretch out or recline! Those things I detest. The very thought of that "leisurely two-day ride" to Brest filled me with discomfort.

Monsieur Binbonnet was regretful, even a trifle reproachful. He had made the suggestion with special consideration of my nationality. "Are there really then some Americans who prefer to travel in trains? Is it untrue that all the American railroads are in bank-ruptcy?" We had quite a little conversation about the place of the car and the train in American life, and Monsieur Binbonnet seemed interested when I went into considerable detail about the physical reasons behind my own preference. "*Tiens!*" he kept saying. "*Tiens! Most interesting!*" And when I ended by saying, "So you see I don't really enjoy riding in automobiles," he retorted in his familiar way, "But you, after all, are not typical of America." I could only reply that he was correct. I, typical of America! My poor country, if that was the case!

Then I thanked Monsieur Binbonnet many times for his kind-ness, and he assured me it was the *moindre des chases* and told me that though I wouldn't allow him to do me the services he'd most like to, I couldn't prevent him from sending me something as a token of his esteem. A sample of France's "liquid speciality," as he put it, which he hoped I would enjoy. I said I'd be delighted to receive it.

And it was right in the midst of my thanks for the promised present that I brashly said what I had determined to say. "Do give me your telephone number, Monsieur Binbonnet," I requested. "It will make everything so much easier."

"Au revoir, Monsieur Weavair," came the reply. "I hope you have a good journey. I hope that you find Monsieur Gerard well and that . . ."

"Do give me your telephone number, Monsieur Binbonnet; it will make everything so much easier."

"Au revoir, Monsieur Weavair! Bon voyage!"

His instrument clicked. I could only hang up.

It was crazy.


Binbonnet's present, which arrived during the next day, was a bottle of Vouvray and a flask of brandy. It was accompanied by his floridly engraved personal card, which I glanced at and slipped into my pocket. It was a delicate attention, this present. In the first place, I knew that French businessmen don't practice, at least to the Amer-ican extent, the custom of regaling visiting customers with gifts and attentions, and Binbonnet had evidently spread himself a little in my case. And secondly, the inclusion of a bottle of Vouvray in the gift was subtly personal and complimentary, for I knew that that wine was a product of Touraine, Binbonnet's native province. And yet, as I contemplated the handsome bottles, I found myself thinking of the old saw—"The gift without the giver is bare." I had the wine, but I certainly did not "have" Monsieur Binbonnet. I didn't have, so to speak, his number. And I should rather have had that than the brandy—much as I like brandy. And I should much rather have had his number than the wine. For wine I never drink. I hate the stuff.

I had another chat with my waiter-friend, Pierre, at the moment of the delivery of Monsieur Binbonnet's gift. It was he who brought it in, and after we had chatted about nothing for a moment or two he allowed himself to ask: "Monsieur is also a veteran of the World War?"

That is the question, of course, that every American of a certain age-appearance is asked when he travels abroad. I'd been asked it ever since Lucille and I had started coming to Europe, and during my days of picture-buying in Paris my easy "Yes, indeed!" and a few anecdotes from my store of experience in the military hospital had invariably smoothed my way. Now, however, I had to follow my "Yes, indeed!" with disappointing replies to questions about the reason for my crutches, and the waiter seemed somewhat crestfallen. "Monsieur is like me," he said, after a moment—a statement I didn't understand, but accepted as a probable compliment. "I mean that I too escaped from the war unwounded and regret that I can point to no scars," he explained, seeing my incomplete comprehension.

This made me glance at him with a certain interest, for such a statement could be made only by a crackpot. Even in European countries, where chauvinism is so rampant, normal men do not regret—or even pretend to regret—that they haven't lost a limb or suffered a wound in their country's service; and in France especially, that country of intelligence and realism, an intact emergence from the horrors of 1914-18 is cause for frank self-congratulation. So my waiter was a crackpot—a crackpot, at least, on the subject of *la patrie*. His appearance gave no indication that there was anything wrong with him—there was no strange look in his eye, nothing to betray even a slight lunacy. He must have been a mere child when he served in Alsace-Lorraine, for he was still fairly youthful-looking, debonair and smart in his absurd white tie and tails; well groomed, and as a waiter, well trained. He told me that he was a member of several ultra-patriotic ex-servicemen's organizations. "We hunt the enemies of France," he ominously said, in his courteous way.

It suddenly occurred to me that I might secure special consideration, with perhaps resultant benefits in the way of service, were I to tell this patriot that I had come from New York to consummate a business deal which would bring prosperity to an important French industry. This I recounted, and I need scarcely say that in his reply the man expressed flowery gratitude, presuming almost to do so in the name of his country, for the perennial Franco-American friendship as exemplified, at the moment, in me.

So grateful did he profess himself to be that I had no hesitation whatever in asking him to do my packing for Brest. To my gratification he appeared delighted with the idea, and in no time at all enough things for two nights and a day were being laid into a small valise—and being arranged with far greater smartness than any servant I'd ever had would have done it. While packing, he expressed again his gratitude that I should have come to France "to aid French industry," and I gravely accepted his thanks. Then he said something that positively startled me. "I expect that within a few days I shall have received my permit to carry a revolver, Monsieur," he informed me.

"A revolver!" I cried. "What on earth for?" For a revolver in the hands of a maniac like this didn't strike me as a pleasing thought, and for an instant I had a wild impulse to change my hotel at once. Even as a child on the Fourth of July I'd always disliked explosives.

Pierre shrugged his shoulders, lifted his eyebrows and hands. "Who knows, Monsieur? But in such times as these one must be ready."

I stared at him a moment, then away. Something to do with one or another of his crazy patriotic organizations, I supposed. But I thought it far preferable not to request any clarification. "Is it easy to get a revolver permit in Paris?" I inquired instead, purely conversationally.

"Ah, no, Monsieur. An unsupported request is seldom granted. One must have friends or acquaintances in official posts. It has taken me many weeks, but I am now assured that I shall receive the license any day."

"In the meantime," it occurred to me to say with a smile, "I hope you don't carry a revolver anyway."

"Oh, no, Monsieur."

That relieved me. No reason to move right away at least! "I'd be interested to learn when you do get it, Pierre."

"I shall inform you at once, Monsieur."

"That would be very kind of you."

I succeeded in keeping irony out of those last words, I think. But I most decidedly did want to know when my room-waiter started carrying a gun. "The war was a great experience for you, Pierre, wasn't it?" I asked.

"Ah, Monsieur!" And the gleam that came into his eyes gave me my answer and more than my answer. It gave me complete assurance that when Pierre had a gun I'd be more comfortable elsewhere, much as I should doubtless miss him as an otherwise excellent servant. There wouldn't be any danger to me in his having a gun. It was the "enemies of France" that he was hunting, I remembered from his own words; and not only was I no such enemy but I doubted that the Clarence sheltered anyone who was. However, I'm a man of peace, and that's the way I felt.

This conversation with Pierre, which was terminated by the completion of the neatest job of packing that my valise had ever seen, left me brooding over the Balkan-like behavior of Europe, that crazy continent. Since I had left New York, I knew, an international crisis had begun to brew: unpleasant things were happening in most of the countries. How very much must be going on beneath the surface if even I, man of peace on a mere iodine mission, felt repercussions in the quiet of my hotel room!

A mad place, Europe.

I'm not one who cares for European life. I have never cared for it: what I've seen of it has never attracted me. It has always been looking at *things* that I have enjoyed in Europe. I enjoy being an American traveling there. For me—to quote the steamship company's advertisement—"The true Europe is the Europe of the tourist": the glimpses and tastes I have had of daily life as Europeans live it have not pleased me. Family and business life there have always seemed to me more constricted, more combative and difficult, less genial and cooperative, than in America, and national and political life repulsive.

Take for instance the small happening that I had witnessed on board the *Normandie*, a few days before. It was a slight thing, particularly when placed against the present European background, but it impressed me, and it exemplifies the aspect of Europe that has always most revolted me, an aspect which has become increasingly prominent of late years.

I seldom went on deck during the trip. The sea was too rough, the going too difficult for me over the high door-sills. Most of my time I spent in the lounge. On the last day, however, rough though the ocean continued to be, I suddenly felt a need for fresh air; and in the middle of the afternoon, when everyone else was at the movies, I had the steward give me his arm and install me in a deck-chair. Except for mine and one other, all the chairs were empty.

I'd been sitting there for a few minutes, enjoying the air, when I saw a group of people coming toward me from the right, along the vast promenade deck. As they approached and passed, I saw that they were passengers from the third class being guided on a tour of the ship by one of their stewards; several of the women wore kerchiefs on their heads, several of the men wore black hats and beards. Visiting aliens returning home, or citizens revisiting the old country. The last one of the group to pass before me in my chair was an elderly kerchiefed woman who clearly should not have set out with the others at all. She was several yards behind the nearest of her companions, and she advanced painfully, clutching the ship's rail, staggering as the ship rolled and pitched: it was all she could do to keep that close to the others. She seemed uncomfortable, almost panting, in her effort. I kept watching her as she passed, and when she had gone about twenty feet the disaster I'd been fearing for her took place. The ship gave a sudden, severe lurch, she lost her hold on the rail, and was flung in toward the row of deck-chairs.

At that spot, due to an outward curve in the wall of the ship's big salon, the deck-chairs extended further out toward the rail than elsewhere along the deck, and I could see the ends of them without being seen. The very chair on which the woman seemed about to fall was the only occupied chair in sight, and to my astonishment I saw the foot of its occupant rise swiftly into the air, catch the tossing woman in the side, and shoot her violently back across the deck, where she collapsed against the side with a wail. Her party at once turned around, exclaimed, and ran to help her. She stood, supported by them, looking about as though in a daze and murmuring replies to their questions, and then with them she moved slowly off. Clearly she knew only that the ship had lurched and that she had twice been propelled; she did not know that she had been kicked, and kicked hard.

The foot, meanwhile, had been quickly withdrawn. The kick had been rapidly and efficiently executed; the man must have been watching the old woman in her fall toward him, and repelled her instantly. No one else had seen this brutal little by-play: it was so incredible that amazement delayed my indignation and dulled my understanding. It was several moments before it occurred to me that the old woman had Semitic features. Only then did I understand what I had witnessed. I could see the foot—a gray-shod foot—resting at ease on its chair, but I could not see its owner. I kept watching it, however, with growing anger, and in half an hour I was rewarded. Its owner rose and came toward me.

He was a handsome, well-dressed European. As he came near me I determined to ascertain whether I had actually seen what I had seemed to see; I distrust my own imagination sometimes, and the action had been almost too brutal to be believed. Surely, however, it was one of the fine gray shoes approaching me that I had seen in the air! "Was that poor old woman hurt?" I baldly inquired, in a conversational tone, when the man was before me.

He paused, looked at me with an expression of surprise, then bowed politely, murmured in French a regret that he understood no English, and moved on.

"But I speak French," I called in that language, furious now. "Was that poor old woman hurt?"

He gave me the coolest of stares. "Not at all hurt, Monsieur. Very kind of you to inquire, I'm sure." Then he disappeared inside the ship.

It was a long time before my rage cooled. What made me as hot and as angry as the cruelty of the thing was the thought that I had had to let the man go untouched, that I was unable to stand and knock down such a cad. In a situation like that, to be unable to act! The realization was sickening.

I never set eyes on the face of that brute again, I'm glad to say; if I had I should have recognized him. His disgusting action was not a thing one expected to see on a French boat. On other boats, and in other countries, it would have been less surprising. But nationals of those countries weren't traveling on French boats, and there he was. Even in my own country, I knew, there are men capable of kicking an old woman because of her features; of course there must be some in France too.

The thing typified for me the underlying conflict and brutality that I had always sensed almost everywhere in Europe, and which had greatly increased during the years since my last trip abroad. I was sorry that my conversation with Pierre, the room waiter at the Clarence, should remind me of such things as this; he seemed a kind, thoughtful chap apart from his mania, and certainly he was taking good care of me. The fantastic behavior of Monsieur Binbonnet, too: was that not perhaps in line with the mad behavior of Europe as a continent? If one traveled internationally nowadays, evidently, one had to be prepared to see more crazily unpleasant behavior than ever. Worse things than ever. Decidedly, this did not promise to be a pleasure trip. I felt that I didn't want to have anything to do with Europe, except with its iodine!

The discomfort of that night journey to Brest was hideous.

Binbonnet had been quite right. His mention of the "peculiar equipment" on the Paris-Brest line hadn't caught my attention, par-ticularly, when he'd made it, but I hadn't been on the train a minute before I remembered it and knew what he'd been talking about. The fact that the hall-porter at the hotel had charged me considerably less for my tickets than I had expected to pay was also immediately explained. There were no real sleeping cars on the train at all. No beds. What I found myself the possessor of was half a compartment equipped with a primitive, thinly upholstered upper and lower shelf arrangement, called a *couchette*; bedclothes, and only one pillow, which was but a trifle less hard than the boardlike structure of the couchette itself. Fortunately no one came in to share the place with me, and I lay down at once on the lower shelf and covered myself with my overcoat. Comfort and sleep seemed equally remote.

No sooner had we left Paris than the cold of which Binbonnet had warned me began to make itself felt, and the conductor confirmed my suspicion that the heating apparatus was not in working order. After all, as he said, it was only October. My overcoat proving inadequate for warmth, I decided to have recourse to Binbonnet's brandy, which I had brought along for just such emergencies; I uncorked the flask, raised it to my lips—and a sudden terrific lurch of the train caused it to fly from my hand and shatter to bits against the steel wall of the compartment. The conductor, not overjoyed to be appealed to once more, said he had no time to clean up the mess of broken glass; it would be attended to by the regular cleaners at the end of the run. The result was that all night, as the train rattled, quivered and lurched, the pieces of broken glass tinkled loudly and merrily beside me, and what with the cold, the jolting, the hardness and the music, sleep did not come.

Add to that, arrival in Brest shortly before seven on a chill, foggy morning. It was so foggy that it would have been impossible to know whether it was before or after dawn, had I not risen to freshen myself a bit about half an hour earlier and out of the window seen an idyllic, autumnal, upland countryside of rolling fields, yellow and ruddy woods and small stone cottages, all bathed in the first, level rays of a pale sun. The city of Brest, situated on the shore of the Atlantic, was covered, or rather filled, with the kind of thick fog that gets into your throat and makes you cough. When I found myself, after a taxi ride, drinking wretched coffee in the unheated breakfast-room of what the hall-porter of the Clarence had assured me was Brest's best hotel, I felt sorry for myself indeed, and wished hard that I could have allowed myself to follow Binbonnet's advice and stayed in Paris.

It was a quarter to eight when I finished breakfast, and I asked the manageress for a room in which I might *faire ma toilette* and take a few hours' rest. The first part of the request was evidently normal—many traveling salesmen from Paris, it seemed, were in the habit of coming to Brest by the night train and after breakfast taking rooms in which to shave and put themselves to rights before beginning their round of calls. But my saying that I intended to take a few hours' rest appeared to make the manageress suspicious. "You mean that you intend to unmake the bed and get into it?" she demanded, looking at me unpleasantly. "In that case I should have to charge you more than if you were merely to lie down briefly upon it, which is what most of the gentlemen from Paris do here in the morning."

I told her I was willing to pay extra—it turned out to be five francs extra—for the privilege of getting all the way into one of her beds, and that I did, and actually got warm and slept for two hours.

At eleven I went downstairs and asked for a taxi to take me to Gerard et Compagnie. I wasn't in a funk this time, but I didn't feel very merry, either. I was still tired, for one thing, and before going out I stopped in the hotel bar, since I had broken Binbonnet's flask, and gulped down a glass of brandy that was undoubtedly far inferior to his. That made me feel better.

# CHAPTER 6

The fog was thinning as my taxi bore me off from Brest's best, and the same pale, autumnal variety of sunlight that I had seen over the Breton countryside earlier in the morning was filtering down into the city streets. I looked about me with interest, for I had been in Brest once before. I had landed there in 1917, and had barely caught a glimpse of the place. The ship, a camp outside the town, and then northern France: such had been our rapid progress. Now I saw what I had missed: a busy, unattractive city, a large, complex port, a draw-bridge, a navy yard filled with gray ships. And something, pointed out to me by the driver, that had not been there in 1917—a monument partly in my honor. A none too beautiful piece of sculpture, standing beside a kind of boulevard overlooking the sea, commemorating the landing of the first American troops. It moved me, briefly—a bit of America standing there where we had all debarked; and then the taxi plunged into a commercial quarter, a long dull street much like a provincial Rue Saint-Martin, and drew up in front of a building that looked like all the others. I confess to a slight return of my tumbril-feeling when I realized that the moment of a new encounter had come. The driver crossed the sidewalk with me and opened the door. Then all other feelings were drowned in one of surprise.

What a modern-looking office! A large, clean room; immediately inside the door a fenced-in square bordered with benches for callers; beyond the fence, half a dozen desks for stenographers, clerks, bookkeepers; directly facing the door, a telephone girl at a standard. Was I in the right place? I inquired at once and found that I was. Binbonnet's words—"Just a shed"—came back to me with force.

But that was nothing. I was immediately ushered through a gate in the fence, past the desks, into a smaller room. There was a man holding out his hand to me. It was Monsieur Antoine Gerard—the "peasant," as Binbonnet had called him. What a peasant! And what a welcome!

The peasant was a looming, well-tailored figure, one of those immensely big Frenchmen who seem to be taller and broader than men anywhere else, as though to compensate for the more usual undersize of their fellow-countrymen; about my own age, a florid, handsome, aquiline face, a few gray hairs amid waving chestnut, a smile, a double-breasted gray flannel suit, a slight Breton intonation—imposing, prosperous-appearing. Most surprising of all was his welcome; he appeared nothing short of overjoyed to see me. An iron grip, a long pumping of the hand; "I cannot tell you," he said, several times, "the happiness your arrival gives me," and he seemed to take delight in my assurance that I was "the brother-in-law of Messieurs Pearce"—an assurance he twice asked for. Certainly striking, all this, in a man who had corresponded with the firm as he had.

And what did all this make of Monsieur Binbonnet? Why had he lied about Gerard, too?

But there was little time for speculation just then; in a comfortable leather chair, smoking one of Gerard's fragrant cigarettes, I answered his effusive questions about the health and prosperity of my brothers-in-law, whom he longed to meet, my own well-being, my comfort while traveling—and finally, that question inevitable. "Are you a veteran of the World War, Monsieur Weavair?" Today the usual disappointment at my answer to the next question, about my wounds, turned to delight when I quickly added that Al and Jim and I had all, at different times during 1917, disembarked at Brest. At this Gerard seemed enchanted, almost transported. He rose to his feet, gripped my hand solemnly, made Lafayette-like utterances and with beaming face assured me once more of his delight in my presence and of his intense desire to meet my brothers-in-law. Then: "I have the welfare and embellishment of the city of Brest very close to my heart, Monsieur Weavair," he disclosed. "You have seen our beautiful monument commemorating the arrival of the Americans?" I complimented him upon it. "Would that we had more such things," he said. "Things that are artistic, and yet modern. The spirit of this city is very smug, Monsieur Weavair, very small; desired improvements have to be gone at carefully, almost secretly." I offered sympathy and some American parallels. Gradually we approached, and then embarked upon, business matters.

As we talked, I could hear the clatter of typewriters, the hum of clerks' voices. At one point a door slammed. At another, I heard a dog bark twice, seemingly quite near; this reminded me of the growls that had interrupted my last business conference. And as we talked I became increasingly aware that there was a restlessness about Monsieur Gerard.

Something fundamentally restless, almost agitated; realization of this had been growing in me since we had begun to discuss matters of business. In fact, we had barely left behind us mention of general world conditions in business and mentioned iodine only a few times, when Gerard jumped up and said I must see his plant.

I looked at him in astonishment. "What? Now?" I almost exclaimed, and was tempted to plead fatigue—it would have been a sincere protest against something that seemed to me decidedly silly. Why should we interrupt, just as we were beginning it, the business talk I had come to Brest to have?

But I had to see the plant, Gerard said, and for some reason this was the best time to do it. So we went out to buildings behind the offices and I watched the operations. I saw trucks arriving with seaweed; I saw the drying rooms, modern, efficient and clean; and I had even a brief glimpse of the blackened, odorous burning chambers, though since the burning and purifying processes were the secrets of the superiority of Gerard iodine I was not allowed any detailed examination. Then there were the packing and shipping departments, where I was able to make a few suggestions. A fatiguing tour. And when we returned to the office, Gerard told me that his wife was expecting me to lunch, and that we should leave almost at once.

"But before we go," he said, "let us clear up the matter in which we are both so interested. It is simple, I think."

He had seemed at his ease throughout the tour, but no sooner had we returned to the office than his restlessness became once more apparent.

"What more can I promise you than this?" he began, with a self-conscious look. And to my indignation he proceeded to say to me, almost word for word, what Binbonnet had said to me two days before. He even said that he was not proud of his part of the more recent correspondence, and suggested that I judge him by future, rather than recently past, performance. He offered no explanation for past behavior. It was fairly easy for me to imagine most of the contents of the letter Binbonnet had told me he'd sent him! Was Gerard as completely under Binbonnet's thumb as would appear from this? And yet, once again, not seeing quite what else there was to do, I agreed to his proposal of a month's trial, as I had agreed to Binbonnet's. We shook hands.

And as we were shaking hands, I again heard, very near, a dog bark—one bark only, this time. Once again this put me in mind of that terrifying growling of the Great Dane in Binbonnet's office two days before; and chiefly as a device to cover any signs of displeasure over the general situation that might be apparent on my face or in my manner, conversationally I told Gerard about Faust and the cat.

He expressed polite interest as I began my tale, but evidently to him it seemed merely pointless, and I could see that he was waiting with ill-concealed nervous impatience for the end. So I brought it to a hurried and lame conclusion, making it sound even less interesting as a happening than it actually was; and then, his relief scarcely better concealed than his impatience, Gerard rose and said we should be going.

We left the office by the front door and got into his car.

The jerkiness which had beset him at the first mention of iodine and which had returned with our return to the office now once again disappeared as if by magic, and, business matters evidently put quite out of his mind, he was spirited and charming. He didn't fail to drive me by way of the monument in commemoration of the Americans, and to stop his car in front of it, to be quite sure that I should give it the attention it deserved—but that, I suppose, was only to be expected. His car was a Packard, which in France means big money. He told me that he was at my disposal for the entire afternoon, and hoped I'd allow him to show me some of the surrounding country and seacoast. "Shall we see just a bit of iodine seaweed?" I asked maliciously, wondering if even that slight mention of business would make him jerk. But he cheerfully agreed. Evidently it was only in his own office that he was for some reason nervous. And instead of my taking the night train back to Paris, as I told him I planned to, he urged me to spend the night with him and Madame Gerard and return by the next day's train. They were having some people to dinner to meet me, and I should travel better after a good night's rest. This was a kind invitation, but I declined it; my night on the train would probably be sleepless again, but at least I'd be able to stretch out, a luxury almost impossible by day. Then I could really rest up in Paris. I was impressed by the courtesy of a dinner party in my honor.

But Binbonnet seemed to have been right about the futility of my trip. He had certainly coached Gerard in what to say. Could I have any confidence in either of them? And why on earth had Binbonnet described Gerard and his establishment as he had? A peasant! A shed! That mystery alone reconciled me, in a way, to having made my long journey. Had I not come, I might have thought that Binbonnet lied only about telephones!

The Gerard house was a good-sized, attractive, old-fashioned house in the suburbs, and once inside it Gerard was instantly transformed from a businessman into a doting husband and father. His wife was pretty and received me graciously, and his daughter of six was adorable. Clearly Gerard was not a man who was bored in his own home. He followed his wife and daughter with worshiping eyes. At every movement of Madame Gerard, at every little remark made by Louisette, he looked at me and beamed.

He had no idea of what he was doing to me, of course. No idea of the shock the sight of his daughter had given me. The Gerard family trio almost did me in, that afternoon. Clearly wife and daughter meant everything to Gerard; I knew how he felt and how I had once felt; I could barely stand it. After all, it was the first bit of family life I had seen since . . .

I kept fighting back tears.

At one moment I saw Louisette whispering to her mother while looking at me. I knew immediately what she was asking, and calling her over, despite Madame Gerard's protests that she was a rude little girl, I let her examine my crutches and showed her how my braces fit into my shoes and how they clicked shut when I wanted to stand up. She showed a deep interest. "You are lucky to have such things to walk with, aren't you?" she said.

I agreed that I was.

"But it would be even luckier if you didn't have to have them, wouldn't it?"

I agreed with that, too.

Louisette was very friendly with me from then on. That made it even harder.

When she consented to sing to us, after lunch, I was pretty sure I'd give myself away, break down completely. Were it not for her choice of song I probably should have. But fortunately she sang, of all things, the *Marseillaise*, and it didn't touch me the way a child's song would have. She sang gravely and fearlessly, her mother playing the piano, and after she finished she came over to me to be complimented and we had another little talk. Formerly she'd sung only children's songs, she told me, but lately her father had had her learn the *Marseillaise* and she sang it for him almost every day. The international situation was graver than ever, I knew; the papers continued to be full of terrifying indefiniteness; perhaps a Frenchman did well to have his daughter sing to keep his patriotic spirits up.

How much Frenchness I had seen, of late! More concentrated, more pure and violent, than most of the Americanism ordinarily seen at home, it seemed to me. Good reason, too, I supposed, what with neighbors, frontiers and dangers. The expressions of this nationalism differed. Pierre the waiter was deliberately chauvinistic almost to the point of lunacy. Binbonnet expressed his nationality with unrivalled intensity in his appearance. Gerard kept listening to his six-year-old daughter singing the national anthem. To me, as an American looking on, it was all—to use an American adjective—"interesting." Louisette insisted on kissing me when she left us to take her nap. That was more than interesting, but I survived it. I'd forgotten what a child's kiss was like.

We sat about, drinking coffee and brandy, and then Gerard said we might as well start. "Will I see Louisette this evening?" I found myself asking Madame Gerard as her husband and I set out. And when she smilingly said that I would, I knew I had asked hopefully, not fearfully.

It was somewhat of a shock, after that, to have Gerard drive me to the first point of interest he had chosen to show me, and to discover that it was a sordid street lined with brothels.

"We're not going to the country after all?" I asked, as he stopped the car at the corner of the wretched pace.

"Oh, yes, but I just wanted to show you this. For sailors, mostly. Picturesque, isn't it?"

To me it seemed merely dirty and indescribably depressing, and I expressed but little interest.

After giving me ample time for a longer look at the dismal sight than I desired, Gerard drove off. There was a silence, then a clearing of the throat; then: "You go, occasionally, Monsieur, to places such as those?"

I looked at him in amazement. A surprising, discourteous question, I thought. And besides, the whole thing made me conscious of every drop of New England blood I had. "No," I said, a little more coldly than one should. "I have never desired to go to such a place."

"But, Monsieur, so often the desire is born after one enters."

"As to that," I said, "of course I don't know."

The result of that prim statement I should have foreseen. Seeing that I needed enlightenment, Gerard proceeded to enlighten me. We were out driving, that afternoon, from two and a half to three hours. It is no exaggeration, I think, to say that for fully two of those hours Gerard pursued his work of enlightenment. It was astonishing.

We drove through the city, Gerard bowing to acquaintances right and left—his father and grandfather and great-grandfather had lived in Brest before him, he told me, and he knew everyone. We drove out of the city into a still-green countryside dotted with stone, slate-roofed villages with names like Ploualmezeau, Aber-Warch, Pro-Poder, Laber-il-Dut. There were hills and hedgerows, rolling fields, glimpses of the ocean. There were old countrywomen in lace caps, and Gerard even knew some of them. There was a spectacular cliff, sheer above the sea, crowned with a ruined abbey and a lighthouse; we stopped there a while, looking out at the vast panorama of the Atlantic and jutting headlands. Against all these settings my enlightenment continued.

I learned a lot of things I didn't care about knowing.

And during the afternoon I managed to learn a little—just a little—about iodine. Gerard drove the car down onto a beach, almost into the sea, and we watched gatherers coming home on the tide with their boatloads of seaweed. The best iodine, I learned, comes from the weeds that grow the furthest out, so that the best time for gathering is at dead-low tide. The lower the tide, the further out from shore the weeds on the bottom can be cut with the only implement that has ever been invented for the purpose: a sickle-shaped knife primitively fastened on the end of a long pole. Some peasants even wade out and cut, Gerard said. That made me smile, as I recalled one of Binbonnet's earliest letters to Pearce Brothers, in which he had described a phase of his conscientious personal search for the high-quality iodine they wanted. Day after day during his summer vacation, he had written, he had waded far out into the sea at different points along the coast, bending down now and then to cut sprays of weed from the bottom. Now that I had met Binbonnet it was worth thinking about: I pictured the *démodé* dandy, clad perhaps in an old-fashioned bathing dress with little sleeves, dipping conscientiously down into the sea, streaming brine from his beard, as he rose, like some Triton. A comic picture; and yet, it was more, for some mysterious reason, than the broker would do for Pearce Brothers now!

Most good-quality weed, Gerard said, is sold to the better factories, where it is dried and then either burned to ash or treated by secret processes. Only good deepwater seaweed, gathered in summer when it is in its best natural condition, scientifically dried and scientifically burned or treated, results in the most concentrated, highest-quality iodine ash; and nowhere else in the world does there grow such good weed as along this Breton coast. We saw poorer kinds of weed, that had been gathered in shallow water or cut from rocks or even picked up on the beach, being burned by peasants in pits dug out of the sand; a wasteful procedure even for the poorest weed, as in open-air burning much of the strength evaporates. We visited two or three small factories on the seashore where weed of medium grade was being semi-scientifically dried and burned, and Gerard presented me to these unimportant competitors of his: rough, simple men with names to match their villages, names like Lambezellec, Abervrack, Loctudy, and who quite apparently looked upon Gerard as the king of their trade.

I even learned that the element iodine was first discovered in 1812—in Scotland, I think Gerard said, where even today a little iodine is gathered; that nowadays the bulk of the commercial product comes from Chile and Japan, but that the best French ash remains the most concentrated in the world; that a quarter of all European iodine comes from France and that for its manufacture only a dozen or so of the hundreds of species of native seaweed are used. That some manufacturers make and sell only the ash; that others add water and acids and other chemicals to make the final tincture.

That much I learned. I could have learned ten times as much had my mentor been anyone else. But not much more than a barely decent amount of time was being devoted to iodine that afternoon by Gerard. We spent one long stretch of time, I remember, in a café in one of the seaside villages over aperitifs, and there particularly was iodine ignored and the other work of enlightenment pursued. Addresses in Paris were forced upon me. The differences between various types of establishments were analyzed. Even their architecture and decoration were gone into. The beauty of women was ecstatically described. I said practically nothing—either in the café or during the drive back to Brest. It would have been a pity to interrupt Gerard: he so enjoyed doing the talking, on that subject.

What was wrong with Gerard? Something, certainly; and what it was I thought I could guess. If I was right, it must have happened comparatively recently, and for some reason that I couldn't conceive of. A man with a wife and child like Madame Gerard and Louisette doesn't go on and on and on about such a subject as brothels unless there's been a breakdown somewhere. Was I right in my guess as to what it was? I kept looking at Gerard carefully, as much as I could without seeming odd. He was virile-looking and acting, even though occasionally nervous; and apart from the betrayal of this mania, evidently happily married. One child. Could I be right? If so, I was sorry for him, despite his sordid fixation. And—poor Madame Gerard! That is, if she cared for him, and I was sure she did.

It was almost dark when we returned to the house. Gerard kept talking about his subject until we had stopped in front of his door.

He considerately asked me if I might not enjoy a rest before dinner, and I stretched out on a sofa in the library. My thoughts were whirling around the subject of my host and his tragedy—for that was not too strong a word for it—and also around the subject of Binbonnet and his lies. But I dropped off to sleep for a little while anyway. Then there was a fire in the living-room fireplace, the arrival of the guests, and dinner.

Oh, that dinner!

There were four other guests. A Madame and Monsieur Leblanc, and a Madame and Monsieur Dutuit.

Oh, those people!

Pillars, I gathered at once, of the high bourgeois society of Brest; prominent, prosperous in business, one of them in lace, the other in ships. Ponderous people—ponderous in any country, but made super-ponderous to an American by the complication of their manners and their mode of speech. To be the master of French etiquette, to have at one's command all the resources of the French language, can make one the most delightful, spirited company in the world—and that is what many French people are—but to be the victim of that etiquette, the slave of that language, is to be—well, like the Leblancs and the Dutuits. They were, clearly, close friends of the Gerards; somewhat older people, but intimate, and those evidently whom Gerard had thought best to have with me. Everyone called everyone but me by his first name—Gerard was just Antoine, Madame Gerard was "*chère Marguérite*." The conversation, when it included me, was composed of generalities; when it did not include me, and concerned other people, unknown to me and referred to also by first names, it was composed of trivialities. It was a collection of shirts stuffed to the bursting point.

Even the Gerards. Madame Gerard was a gracious woman, and if what I suspected about her husband was true she was a courageous one; Gerard himself could be pleasant company when he wasn't jittery or tiresome; but what a light this dinner party cast upon the Gerards' conception of social life! Whatever they might be in private, clearly in society they and their friends were pillars and admirers of dullness.

After the soup little Louisette came in to say a brief word to everyone and then bid us all good night. One of the ponderous at once demanded that she sing, a demand quickly seconded, and then and there she rendered once more the *Marseillaise*. It was that, I think, that conferred upon me, personally, a greater benefit than any other single happening of the past ten years—even of the past few weeks.

Earlier that day, surprised by my reception into a domestic circle such as I had long not seen, I had been moved nearly to tears; the whole circle had seemed charming, attractive, lovable; the kiss of the child had softened me, and I was thrilled by the thought that now I could see my own nephews and nieces. Those first hours with the Gerards had done much to make me conscious that I could become, was becoming, more normal—though as I look back on myself now I see that the process had begun before that. My very decision not to take a servant with me to Europe, I think, was an indication that something was happening. But during the dinner party, just because I was more normal than I had been earlier in the day, I could look upon the scene more coolly. This was a domestic circle, yes, and I was grateful to it for what it had done for me—but had Lucille and I ever given a dinner party as colossally stupid as this? Louisette was a pretty child—but had we ever had Caroline stand up before a tableful of guests and sing? Particularly—would we ever have dreamed of entertaining our guests by having our daughter sing the national anthem?

First the achievement of having sought out and conversed with Binbonnet. Then exposure to the domesticity of the Gerards. And then Louisette's public performance and the ability to appraise that domesticity. Such was my progress. Other symptoms had been my loneliness in Paris, my desire for company. I recognized this is as progress myself, and I confess that I derived a little solace from feelings of pride about it during that wearisome evening.

And during that evening, too, I kept staring at Gerard and Madame Gerard as continuously and as surreptitiously as I had stared at Gerard alone during the afternoon. Was their relationship the tragedy I suspected it to be? Since sometime following the birth of Louisette had their lives been carefully built up to hide the secret that I thought I had discovered? How I longed to be able to converse with Madame Gerard alone, ask her clever questions which would, without alarming her or apprising her of my suspicions, give me the assurance I wanted. For I found myself decidedly curious concerning the cause of the brothel mania. After all, it concerned me. Gerard's interest in brothels quite evidently eclipsed his interest in iodine. If the cause of the mania was what I thought it was, I knew that his ailment could probably be cured. I'm American, and believe in cures. And crazy though it may sound, it occurred to me that if Gerard could be cured of his mania, his iodine performance might improve. A remote possibility, I knew; but, there it was.

Since my train back to Paris was to leave about eleven, I had to quit the party before the others. Gerard insisted on quitting it himself, temporarily, and driving me to the station. I said my farewells and my thanks, we stopped by at the hotel for my valise, and then— my host drove me once again past the brothel street.

Once again we stopped at the corner and looked in. The place was perhaps a trifle less dreary by night. Outside each house hung a fancy illuminated sign, bearing a large number and some figure— there was a huge electric crescent, I remember, over one doorway, a star over another, and over a third some kind of a face with eyes which kept blinking. There were a few men in evidence, entering the places or leaving them or strolling past, most of them the sailors Gerard had told me were the habitués, and sitting or standing in the doorways were motherly-looking women in coats and shawls.

"Of course," Gerard said, reminding me of some of his lecture earlier in the day, "places of a higher class are not like this. No colored lights. No one outside urging you to come in. No display. On the exterior, completely discreet; and inside, either completely discreet also or—the opposite."

I nodded. I wished he would drive on. I was beginning to worry about my train, and I was getting cold, and besides I was beginning to think that after all this place looked even drearier at night, when it tried to look gay, than it looked by day.

Gerard started the car. "I will show you a house of the other kind," he said, as though he had made the decision after long reflection. "There's one between here and the station."

We drove through the city, along a dark, sober, respectable-seeming boulevard, and without stopping he pointed out the place to me as we passed. It was a house like all the others; only the number seemed to be carefully lighted.

"Doesn't look particularly inviting," I said, disagreeably.

"That's what makes such places piquant," I was at once informed. "The contrast between the sobriety outside and the . . . that which is to be seen within."

I nodded. So be it.

At the station, where we arrived with plenty of time after all, I picked up my reservation and a flask of brandy, and hauled myself up into the train. Gerard followed me into the compartment, and there he surprised me by voluntarily mentioning business. "You can count on me," he said. "Besides, I hope soon to see you in Paris."

"Oh, you will be coming up?" I asked, quite without thinking.

"Yes, indeed; I must. I have not been there since before the summer. I have much to do there. Until recently we have all been living in our summer home, fifty kilometers south of Brest; I have been driving back and forth every day and have been unable to come to Paris. But I must come up soon."

Now I was all attention. "You get to Paris often?"

"Except in summer, once a month at least."

This was finally too much; this must be challenged. "But Monsieur Binbonnet told me the opposite," I cried. "The very opposite. He said you *had* been up this fall, quite recently, and that you wouldn't be back till spring. You tell me you have not been there recently and will be coming often. I am bewildered, Monsieur Gerard. I confess it."

"It is bewildering indeed, Monsieur Weavair. Monsieur Binbonnet told you *that?*"

I nodded. "He told me that most clearly." I repressed, with difficulty, mention of Binbonnet's other mis-statements.

Nervousness had once again come over Gerard; and puzzlement—or what looked like it—was on his face. "Why should he say that?" he demanded.

"How should I know, Monsieur Gerard?"

"Oh, I was not asking you, Monsieur; I was asking myself, aloud. I ask myself again: Why should Monsieur Binbonnet say that?"

I was sitting on my *couchette*; Gerard was standing before me. We stared at each other. We couldn't go on doing that forever. "I'll see you when you come to Paris, Monsieur Gerard," I said, a trifle wearily. "There's a reason for everything. Meanwhile, I shall have confidence in you." That last was a lie, of course.

He looked at me and said nothing more. We shook hands, and he left me. A moment later my name was called from outside. I peered out the window; there he was, beside the train on the platform, motioning me to lower the window. I did. It was almost incredible that already he should have abandoned all thought—or at least all mention—of iodine in favor of the subject he preferred. And yet such was evidently the case. "I hope you will grant me the privilege of escorting you around Paris, Monsieur Weavair," was all he had to say. "I know I can show you many interesting things."

"Perhaps," I replied uncordially. "But I shall be going to Holland for a while now." We nodded farewell again, and I drew the window up.

I felt exhausted. This iodine expedition was turning out to be a trip for a mystery-story writer, not a businessman or even a businessman's brother-in-law. What the hell was the matter with everybody?

Once again my night was almost sleepless, and chilly despite frequent swigs of brandy. I was pretty much all in when I got back to Paris, and I went to bed and stayed there, fighting off a cold with the aid of more brandy and the solicitude of Pierre, who kept me well provided with hot-water bags.

I slept a good deal. During the afternoon I was awakened from a doze by the ringing of my telephone, but I didn't feel a bit like having any immediate conversation with that liar Binbonnet, who was the only person it could be, and I didn't answer. Later I phoned the operator downstairs and asked if there was a message, but there wasn't. Binbonnet hadn't even left his name.

Later I was to wonder just what would have happened to me—what would have happened to me almost immediately—if I had answered my telephone that afternoon!

# CHAPTER 7

As it was, spent the evening in bed, trying to think things out.

In the first place, I reminded myself that my instructions from Al and Jim had been twofold. First, I was to get satisfaction out of Binbonnet and Gerard if it proved possible to do so. Second, I was otherwise to try to find a new source of iodine. And it seemed to me now that it was instruction No. 2 that I should set about obeying.

For everything about Gerard and Binbonnet—the latter particularly—was so odd, so close to sinister, that prospects of success with them appeared indeed remote. I'd wait a month to see whether their promises of reformation were worth anything; that was what I'd told them I'd do and the only thing I could think of doing. But why, during that month of waiting, should I sit idle? Why shouldn't I immediately set about seeking other iodine? The various American banks in Paris, the American consul, the American Chamber of Commerce—I'd go to all those places and hope for fruitful leads.

But there were two things to be done first.

I had to go to Holland—if only briefly. I had told both Binbonnet and Gerard that important business called me there, so I had to go. I definitely did not want them to think that I had come to Europe solely on their account. And before leaving for Holland I had to get in touch with Binbonnet to let him know that I was going—and, incidentally, to thank him for his present.

Then, back from Holland, I would swing into action. I would pay no more attention to Binbonnet and Gerard. If they kept their new promises in thirty days, well and good. If they didn't, as they probably wouldn't, I hoped by that time to be well on the way to finding

satisfactory substitutes. If Binbonnet and Gerard were depend-
able suppliers of iodine, I knew that Al and Jim, as well as myself,
wouldn't give a damn that one of them was a liar and the other erot-
ically suspect; no—it was their wretched recent record that made
these discoveries of mine important and worthy of consideration.
Each man, evidently, had something that he preferred to the iodine
welfare of Pearce Brothers. One of them lied to conceal his preference, whatever it might be. The other flaunted his preference openly.

It was my reflections on such points as that, I think, that gave me
the idea of looking once more into the correspondence to see what
I could find. Nothing, it seemed to me, could be quite as irrational
or as inexplicable as the lying of Binbonnet appeared on the surface
to be. Something in the letter might give me a clue—a clue or a cue.
I opened my briefcase and began to glance through the papers. Was
there some thread that I might follow?

One of the most strongly stressed points in the earlier letters
from Binbonnet to Pearce Brothers, I noticed soon after I began to
read, was the close cooperation existing between him and Gerard et
Compagnie. It was mentioned in almost every letter, and at times
when it was not mentioned it was often implied in Binbonnet's use
of the word "we" to mean the team composed of himself and the
supplier. In fact this use of the word "we" became more and more
frequent as time went on. This was when Pearce Brothers had been
getting its best deliveries, when the affair was running at its smooth-
est. "We" was a kind of symbol of the golden age.

Now, I had heard no talk of "we" since arriving in France. Binbonnet had barely mentioned Gerard et Compagnie during our first
interview, except to lie about them and urge me not to go to Brest
once I had brought up the subject myself. Gerard had had little or
nothing to say about Binbonnet and had been—or appeared—astonished by the one lie of his I had disclosed. What had happened to the
team of "we"?

I returned to the letters. How interesting, now, to discover that
all mention of "we" had stopped the instant bad shipments had been
substituted for good! Even before the first bad shipment had been received, I found, but just when it was being sent, Binbonnet had quite
suddenly begun to speak for himself alone. "*I* have done so-and-so."

"Trusting that my cordial relations with Pearce Brothers may continue." And so forth. No mention of "we" from the very beginning of the big change. And only one mention of cooperation between him and Gerard: in the impudent letter replying to Pearce Brothers' suggestion that he seek another producer. There—and there alone—"complete loyalty to Gerard et Compagnie" was expressed.

And yet—most interesting, perhaps, of all!—the same change was not noticeable in the letters from Gerard et Compagnie. There had never been a vast correspondence between Pearce Brothers and Gerard et Compagnie. Most writing had been done to and by Binbonnet, as broker. But there had been a few letters directly to and from Brest—mostly on matters of packing and shipping—and these had followed the same course, in the matter of "cooperation" and "we." Except that in the later letters "we" had not been abandoned. In the very latest letters it was still there, clearly referring to the combination of producer and broker. Gerard, then, did not consider that the team had been broken up, whereas Binbonnet did. Such was the logical inference, it seemed to me.

And what would the inference indicate? For one thing, it would support the possibility that Gerard had actually been sincere in his astonishment when I had told him of Binbonnet's strange statement. It would clearly place him in the role of victim, or tool, of Binbonnet, ignorant of some of Binbonnet's actions or even purposes. It would suggest that for reasons of his own Binbonnet had engineered the break with Pearce Brothers and no longer considered a state of cooperation to exist between himself and Gerard, although allowing Gerard to continue to consider that it did. How strange this was, that the broker—a mere kind of agent—should have got the upper hand over the producer! Normally Gerard was by far the more important man of the two; if there was an upper hand, why should Gerard not have it?

A mystery still, but a faint trifle less baffling, I thought, than before. At least it was now fairly clear that there were differences of some kind between broker and supplier—differences known, perhaps, only to the broker. In fact I felt pretty sure that the words "differences between broker and supplier" should be changed to read "continual lying by broker."

If these "differences" could be resolved, Pearce Brothers' iodine difficulties might be removed. But—how to get at the bottom of Binbonnet's behavior? That was what was so baffling, so improbable of achievement—more improbable even than the improbably fruitful cure I had conceived for Gerard! That was what made me feel, now more strongly than ever, that my instruction No. 2—the search for new iodine—was what I should pursue on my return from Holland.

I thought a little about Gerard's brothel mania, too, as I sat there with the briefcase on my lap. I thought that it was the kind of thing that was more likely to be found remarkable by an American than by a Frenchman, and that therefore, in thinking more about it, an American would be more likely to suspect its cause. Psychoanalysis and its jargon are so rife among us that we have developed eagle-eyes for neuroses, and pounce gleefully upon peculiarities which the Latin countries, especially, take quite for granted and in the causes of which they remain uninterested. I refer to ordinary individuals, of course— not scientists. I felt sorry for Gerard. He could be such a likable chap, and he and his wife must be so unhappy. Even apart from the benefit which it conceivably might confer on Pearce Brothers, I began to wonder whether I couldn't somehow indicate to him that there was a good possibility of a cure if he'd go about it in the right way.

Finally my meditations were finished and my mind was made up.

I telephoned downstairs to the hall-porter and reserved a place on the ten o'clock plane the next morning to The Hague, and also dictated a telegram to Binbonnet, asking him to phone me before nine-thirty. I'd get away without seeing him, the villain. And when I got back I wouldn't call him up till the agreed month was out.

Once again Pierre packed my valise—a slightly larger valise this time, for I should be away a day or two longer. "No revolver yet, Pierre?" I inquired.

"Not yet, Monsieur. But any day now the permit will arrive. Bon voyage, Monsieur. I wish Monsieur luck in all his undertakings."

"Thank you, Pierre."

Then I had a good night's sleep.

Binbonnet phoned at nine. He had not telephoned me the previous day, he said. That was a lie, of course. His voice was smooth and full of concern. "Your health is good, Monsieur? The cold of Brittany was not too cruel? The long journey not too fatiguing?"

Had he added "And the trip was really worth making?" I should perhaps have replied with a mysteriously-toned affirmative, hoping to make him ponder, but he did not, and I thanked him, instead, for the comfort he had given me in liquid form. "The brandy was delicious," I courteously lied. "Some of the best I've tasted, a real experience for an American. I congratulate you on your taste, Monsieur."

"You really enjoyed it, Monsieur Weavair?"

"Every drop, Monsieur Binbonnet."

"Ah." And he expressed satisfaction that that should be so. The wine was not mentioned. "You will now be in Paris a while?" he inquired. "Would you be in, by any chance, this morning so that I might return your kind visit?"

I smiled with pleasure at the success of my stratagem. "Unfortunately I am even now on the point of leaving for Holland," I revealed in a tone of false regret. "As I told you, I have important business to transact there; and it has become urgent that I go at once."

"And how long will you be away, Monsieur Weavair?"

"I cannot tell, Monsieur Binbonnet. Two weeks at the very least, I should think. There are important things to be done."

"I deeply regret, Monsieur, that I shall not have the pleasure of seeing you before you leave."

"I too regret, Monsieur. Remember, I am counting on you. We shall have interesting things to discuss when I return."

"We shall indeed, Monsieur Weavair. Au revoir, Monsieur, and bon voyage."

"Au revoir, Monsieur Binbonnet."

Not a single mention of Monsieur Gerard! Not a single mention of the man on whom the entire business depended, and whom he knew I had just made a round-trip of 800 miles to see!

Indeed instruction No. 2 was the one to follow!

The trip to Holland was a mere interlude as far as the iodine business was concerned, even though for me personally it proved to be something more than that.

Due to bad weather the plane didn't fly, and I took the best train, the *Etoile du Nord*, a de luxe Pullman affair. I held on tight as it sped and swayed through pouring rain, and talked with the young man in the seat facing mine. The talk was interesting. Not particularly for its content—we talked about travel and scenery and Europe and America the way casual fellow-travelers do—but for a reason connected with the language we used. We spoke in French, and after a time, when the young man hadn't told me what part of France he came from, as almost every Frenchman does at once, I asked him. I learned to my surprise that he wasn't French at all, but German—a young attaché of the embassy in Brussels. His French had not only been flawless, but *French*—as beautiful and natural as Binbonnet's—and after smiling at my surprise he proceeded to speak just as perfectly in English. His utterances were no more profound than they had been before, but his intonation and colloquialisms were just as deceptive. At Brussels he bade me farewell.

After he had left I had another interesting conversation, with a Frenchman across the aisle—a real Frenchman, this time, Legion of Honor and all—whom I had noticed listening to my previous talk. He confirmed my opinion that the young diplomat's French had been perfect, and smiled when I asked whether it wasn't remarkable that it should be so.

"You don't find it true in your country, Monsieur, that one must beware of perfectionists with whom one is unacquainted?" he inquired. "You do not tend to think of them as—possibly suspicious characters?" And when I admitted that that wouldn't be my instinct, he said, "In France we are perhaps absurdly cautious in these times—but an unknown individual who speaks our language so perfectly as to be French beyond suspicion is automatically an object of suspicion to some of us. With such a person, for example, I think I should hesitate to allow myself to be drawn into conversation—as I am conversing with you, Monsieur."

We both smiled at that, and I think I said something about having found a reason at last to be grateful to the imperfection of my French, but he went on. "Such an unknown might of course prove to be a member of the French Academy. On the other hand, he might prove to be, like the young man who caused you such surprise . . .

Ah, Monsieur! *Ces allemands!* It is sad to become suspicious of a people to a morbid degree—but if only their diplomats did not speak the most beautiful French in the world!"

I had a humorous suggestion. "Such an unknown might prove to be something else. He might prove to be simply a native of Touraine, where everyone speaks French beautifully."

Intense scepticism was expressed. "There is certainly good French in Touraine, Monsieur. But of course anyone can learn his French there. Touraine is full of foreigners learning French, learning suspiciously beautiful French. When you meet someone unknown, Monsieur, and he tells you he comes from Touraine . . ." He raised a warning forefinger.

I enjoyed this touch of international gossip, this illusion that I was feeling the breath of danger. It amused me to think of Binbonnet as an object of this man's suspicion, to think that if I were to describe him he would doubtless say it was quite possible that he wasn't a Frenchman at all! Binbonnet, riddle though he was, not French! That was a comic thought!

There was a peculiar happiness about the few days in Holland. The weather turned sunny and mild, my hotel was a good one, and I discovered that I enjoyed enormously the sight of the Rembrandts and the Vermeers that I hadn't seen for so long. Enjoyment! Enjoyment of pictures! Enjoyment of anything! Difficult to express how novel the sensation was, and what a delight it was to recapture it. Attendants detailed by the galleries pushed me about in a wheel-chair from room to room, from picture to picture. Those pictures! When a blind man recovers his sight, they say, he sees gloriously. Well, my sight was coming back. That was what the few days in Holland told me.

I took a plane back to Paris on Wednesday, all set to start carrying out Instruction No. 2.

I had scarcely entered my room at the Clarence when the phone rang, and answering it rather wonderingly, for I knew it wouldn't be Binbonnet and didn't know who else it could be, I found that it was Gerard, up from Brest and asking me to go out with him for dinner. He was at the Clarence, he said—in fact he was calling from the room just next to mine. And indeed I could hear a voice talking vaguely through the wall as the same voice came clearly to me over the wire.

Explaining that I had just that moment returned from a trip, I asked him to dine with me in my room instead, and he accepted. Would I be able to ask him, as a favor to me, to keep the news of my early return from Binbonnet, who thought me absent for two weeks at least and whom I had no wish to see?

On my table I found a cable from Pearce Brothers that had arrived just a few hours before. It told me what I knew already—that the October shipment was unsatisfactory—and added that Pearce Brothers were refusing payment.

And I found four identical telephone messages. "Brest called." Gerard had telephoned me every day I had been away? Why? I'd find out soon enough.

Gerard knocked on my door at eight.

# CHAPTER 8

He was in good spirits, Monsieur Gerard. So good that the moment I saw him I realized that the iodine business was not on his agenda for the evening but that something else decidedly was; that he had come to see me for social reasons and reasons connected with his campaign of enlightenment; and that the word iodine would probably not be even mentioned unless I mentioned it myself. His preliminaries were jovial and of the usual length. In the middle of them I remember thinking that this was probably why the French use the telephone so much more sparingly than we; after all, such obligatory preliminaries take time, and must add appreciably to phone bills. He was particularly insistent on knowing the degree of my comfort on the return from Brest and on both parts of the Dutch round-trip; difficult to imagine Al or Jim being concerned about the comfort of a customer just in from Ashtabula! His four phone calls, he said, had been made merely for the purpose of fixing a rendezvous with me. He had decided to come to Paris, but wanted the pleasure of having me there at the same time, if possible.

Then, the opening scene gracefully brought to a close, Gerard got down to business—business consisting of much hand-rubbing and beaming, with a peculiar expression on the face. "You will join me this evening, I hope, Monsieur Weavair? After dinner I hope for the pleasure of your company—may I have it? I am confident that I can show you some interesting things—some things which according to you are not to be seen in New York."

"Oh, no, that I never said," I protested quickly. "For all I know, everything in the world can be seen in New York. All I said was that I didn't frequent them there—or anywhere else."

"You will see them tonight, Monsieur Weavair, if you come with me!" And he continued to rub his hands and beam with so intense a pleasure that it was possible to read on his face the things he intended to see and impossible to imagine that the sight of them would please him more than his thinking of them.

I rang for Pierre and had him bring the bill of fare. I had left my gift-bottle of wine with him when I went off to Holland, and now I asked him to serve it with dinner. "You'll drink some of Monsieur Binbonnet's Vouvray, I hope?" I said to Gerard, thinking thus perhaps to guide him in his choice of dishes. For an instant, before assenting, he looked at me in positive alarm; I could barely keep from smiling. "Never fear," I felt tempted to say. "I'll not utter the word iodine until you do."

Dinner was served in front of the fire I'd had made in the pseudo-Louis XV white marble fireplace. The Clarence was a good hotel, and there was plenty of steam in the radiators, but during the day the rain had returned and could now be heard spattering against the windows; and wet autumn weather in Paris is so excessively wet and penetrating that only the sound of a fire can really conquer it. Pierre served us with great style. While he was in the room, Gerard maintained a decent silence or a decent flow of conversation, but things were otherwise when Pierre was absent.

It was a curious meal.

It was strange to see this imposing, virile-looking man, so respectable and mature in appearance, given over to a kind of frenzy that most men leave behind them with their teens or early twenties. I had known a few who had preserved it into later years—but they hadn't been gentlemen like Gerard, possessed also of a charming wife and child and devoted to them. *Their* lives had been all of a piece; given the other circumstances of their existence, skirt-chasing had been an inevitable accompaniment. But Gerard's obsession contrasted so oddly with the other visible circumstances of his life!

He offered me a choice of addresses. "Shall we go to 44 Rue de Provence? Or do you think you would prefer 4 Rue Hanovre?"

"But, Monsieur Gerard—how can *I* have any idea as to which I'd prefer?"

"But, Monsieur Weavair! I described both these establishments to you in detail when you were in Brest! Do you not remember—I said that whereas the first—"

And so on—and on and on. It was clearly astonishing to him that I should have forgotten those details. He gave them all to me again, interrupting himself only as Pierre periodically appeared. When he had finished I said that I'd delay my decision until just before we were to set out, since each place appeared to have so many advantages. He readily agreed. It was astonishing to me to see how he believed I was giving the matter the most careful consideration.

As the meal ended I was looking forward to a quiet half-hour, at least, of cigarettes and coffee beside the fire before setting out on our fools' errand, but in Pierre's presence Gerard suggested that we go out, for our coffee, to a "café." I knew what that meant.

I had drunk about a thimbleful of wine—enough for our mutual toast. Gerard had taken about half the bottle, and I wondered that he should stop there. "It wasn't good?" I asked him, and after some polite feinting he admitted that it was nothing exceptional. It wasn't green, it wasn't sour—it simply wasn't good.

"It came from Monsieur Binbonnet, you say?" he remarked after a pause.

"It did. Why?" I wasn't going to let a voluntary mention of Binbonnet by Gerard pass unencouraged.

"Well . . ."

"Yes?"

"Any wine chosen by Monsieur Binbonnet . . ."

"Would be bad you mean? But he comes from . . ."

"Would be *certain* to be bad, Monsieur Weavair. I cannot imagine him choosing a good wine, having the taste to choose anything good, fine, impeccable. He is a bourgeois, Binbonnet, a bourgeois of the lowest class; virtuous and honest, but . . ."

And Gerard said several snobbish things about Binbonnet—not as a businessman, but as an individual. The broker's every personal trait, he claimed, was so wretchedly petty-bourgeois as to make him incapable of appreciating any of the finer things of life in any category. Wine, cheese, cigars—any of these, for example, chosen by Binbonnet would be certain to be unpalatable. Despite his honesty and commercial enterprise, he was just that kind of man. "And take . . . take *maisons closes*," Gerard went on, almost passionately, scarcely to my surprise. "Would Binbonnet enjoy the quaintness, the often charming simplicity and intimacy of the little sailors' places I showed you in Brest? No, indeed—to him they would be poor, proletarian, unthinkable. And on the other hand he would be intimidated by the true splendor and luxuriousness of such places as I shall show you tonight, and unwilling to spend the sums justly demanded by those establishments. I know men like Binbonnet! Special places exist for them, forlorn, bourgeois houses which pretend to be luxurious and are merely pretentious, where the girls lack the naïveté of those in the simple places and the éclat of the girls we shall see. His is a petty spirit, Monsieur Weavair. The instant you told me your wine came from him . . ."

"That was why you looked alarmed? I thought it was because . . ."

"Because why, Monsieur Weavair?" Now he looked alarmed again.

"Because you thought I was going to speak of Binbonnet and business."

Silence fell on Gerard.

"You'll admit we have much to talk about, there, Monsieur Gerard. All kinds of strange things, some of which I've never mentioned to you, but some of which I have mentioned, and about which you've been most queerly silent. Your analysis of Binbonnet's spirit is interesting, but it is our business with him that . . ."

"Please, Monsieur Weavair."

"I beg your pardon?"

How pleading his voice had suddenly become!

"Please, Monsieur Weavair. We had agreed, I think, to leave all discussion of business for one month—by which time I assure you there will be no reason for it. I admit that things are not normal for the moment. But they soon will be. Shall we not hold to our agreement?"

Outrageous!

"Despite all your scorn for Binbonnet as a petty-bourgeois, you say he is honest," I cried. "*Honest!* Binbonnet honest! How can I listen . . . ?"

"Binbonnet is honest, Monsieur Weavair. That is one thing he unquestionably is. But shall we not hold to our agreement? Please, Monsieur Weavair!"

There did seem little use going on. There was a silence.

"If I do hold to it you swear that all will be well in a month?" I lamely demanded.

"I swear it, Monsieur Weavair."

I didn't believe it, of course. But certainly Gerard was right in saying that the discussion was useless. It was useless because he wouldn't discuss. I was merely ruffled and indignant; I had gained nothing by my mention of things I had determined not to mention.

"If you don't mind, Monsieur Gerard," I said, "we'll take our coffee here beside the fire after all. I'm fatigued after my journey from The Hague."

That was only partially true. I felt surprisingly little fatigue considering the active life I'd been leading—a sign, evidently, that my progress was physical as well as mental, or perhaps that some of my fatigue in the past had had psychic causes. But at least it gave me a kind of revenge, for I knew that Gerard was eager to get to those addresses. And it gave me time to recompose myself. Gerard was now very meek.

The Lord knows I didn't want to go out with Gerard at all that night, in the rain and to such places. But it seemed to me an excellent opportunity—perhaps the only opportunity I'd ever have—to obtain proof that my suspicions concerning the cause of his mania were correct. Though I was forced to wonder what I'd do with such proof even if I did get it. For by now I was more than ever convinced that Pearce Brothers' business was something that would never be discussed by Gerard and me. Instruction No. 2 seemed more than ever urgent.

In the taxi Gerard once more gave me a choice of addresses. Once more I had forgotten his lesson, but I chose at random—I think the Rue de Provence. We skidded on the glistening pavements. In twenty minutes I was for the first time in my life inside what I'd once heard my mother call blushingly a "naughty house."

It was a palace indeed, but it and its kind have been painted and described so often that I don't need to give a description here.

Change some but not all of the costumes in some of the bigger Tou-
louse-Lautrecs, add here and there rooms done in ultra-modern
style while keeping elsewhere the cachet of the old, and you have
it. The first room we entered was exactly like a large luxurious café,
except for the costumes of the girls. Men, some of them unaccompanied, were sitting at tables. It was there that we sat first, and it was
from there that we set out, after a consultation with the manageress,
on our tour of the other parts of the establishment.

For that is what we did—tour—and it didn't take me long to see
that my suspicions concerning Gerard were well-founded indeed.

I had told him, on our arrival, that he must proceed exactly as
though I was not there, must not let my presence and unfamiliarity
and tastes hamper him, and he had thanked me and said he knew I
meant it and that he would do so. "There will perhaps be some moments, Monsieur, when you will not care to accompany me," he had
said, and I thought that this might well prove to be the case. As it
happened, however, he at no time suggested that I leave him, asking
me merely once or twice whether I cared to stay with him; I replied
that I did, and not once during the evening did I quit his side, so that
I knew what he did. And the point is, he didn't do—he *looked*. He
made use of exactly one of his senses during our disgusting tour of
the establishment's many rooms: his sense of sight. And he kept asking the manageress, as we ran into her here and there, if there wasn't
"something new" since he'd last been there, some *nouveau truc* that
he could see. It was always novelties which he seemed most eager
to be shown, though few of them, once witnessed, appeared to win
his approval as much as some of the more standardized features of
which even I had previously heard. And in addition to these sights,
each one of which had an entrance price of its own, Gerard showed
the keenest interest in the free sights—the architecture and decoration of the place. He kept exclaiming over this or that alteration
which had been made since his last visit. "*Le dernier cri!*" he kept
exclaiming, and "*Très, très modern!*" I thought it rather provincial
of him, myself, though I was grateful to him for proving me so completely right. Gerard was a voyeur. He was fascinated by the sights
provided by such establishments as the one we were in. And if the

amount of erotic pleasure that he derived from seeing them wasn't very heady (for at no time was he any more excited than he had been at dinner), then it was because he was the victim to an even greater extent than I'd imagined of the malady which I had diagnosed.

I felt pity for him, and once more, now almost entirely for his own sake, my thoughts turned toward the cure I was sure could be effected—if he would go about it properly himself.

Our tour lasted almost an hour, and since it had involved considerable walking and standing I suggested that we sit in the café room and refresh ourselves with a drink before moving on to some other address now being murmured about by Gerard, where he hoped to find additional *nouveaux trucs*. This we did. The café room was now fairly crowded, and to find a table we had to penetrate well into it, and sit down at quite a distance from the door, All around us were men with girls, solitary men (some of them reading newspapers), and men in pairs and groups. We ordered liqueurs. There was even, I noticed, at a table between us and the door, a pair of men who seemed to be immersed in what looked like business papers, spread out over their table. The back of one of the men was toward us; the profile of the other. I looked idly at that profile several times before I realized, with a sudden shock, that I knew it. A grave profile and unmistakable. I had to smile to myself, displeased though I was. The man who adored his cat and lied about telephones and other things! The man I wanted to avoid!

"I've found you out," I said to Gerard, "in a mistake. Monsieur Binbonnet must have some slight endowment of better taste than you credit him with, for he's here."

Gerard started. "What's that?"

"Table with two men over there towards the door. Lots of papers. One man has his back to us—rusty brown suit. Binbonnet's on his right, in profile."

He peered. "With a man in rusty brown?"

"Yes."

"I see a man in rusty brown, but I don't see Binbonnet."

"Beside the rusty brown. Beard. Striped suit."

Gerard looked at me queerly. "That man in the striped suit? But that's not Binbonnet!"

"Not Binbonnet! But it's certainly my Binbonnet, Monsieur Gerard!"

"It's not our Binbonnet, Monsieur Weavair! Not our Binbonnet at all!"

We looked at each other aghast, and then turned once more towards the distant table. At that moment the man in the rusty brown suit twisted around somewhat towards his companion, so that his face, though still invisible to me, could now be seen by Gerard. And instantly, with a start, Gerard clutched my arm and gave a soft cry. On his face was a look of terror. "My God!" he whispered. "We must get out of here!"

And what was so strange was that his terror seemed not to be for himself.

"We must go separately," he was whispering, his face white. "We must not be seen together. That would be fatal—fatal for you."

Fatal! And for me! But *why?*

"Turn away," he whispered. "Don't let them see you as long as you're with me."

"Who is that other man then, Monsieur Gerard? Who are they both?"

"The one you call Binbonnet I've never seen in my life before. But first we must get out of here, Monsieur Weavair. Nothing counts but that."

In whispers, therefore, our faces averted from that table, we planned our exit. "Thank God they missed us as we came in," Gerard breathed. "*You* thank God, Monsieur Weavair."

If I were seen alone, he mysteriously told me, there would be no harm done: no reason for me to fear being seen and greeted by Binbonnet or even by his companion. And he himself could be seen alone by them. But if we were seen together—if those two men realized that the two of us together had seen them together: then—! Gerard made the classic gesture of forefinger across throat: "That for *you*, Monsieur Weavair. For me it would be unpleasant, but not dangerous."

I swallowed hard.

Who should go first? Who should call the waiter and pay? Should I make my slow way out first, allowing Gerard to pay and escape unseen during the conversation which would doubtless take place between Binbonnet and me? In any case it was Gerard who had to make himself invisible. That was more than I could do; I am always noticed, always stared at. That they hadn't seen me come in was miraculous; the doorway had been crowded, I had been among others. Gerard *had* to keep from being seen.

Better therefore that I go first, I thought. Walk slowly towards the door, pretend only then suddenly to see Binbonnet and greet him in cordial surprise, chat a bit if he liked, and then leave, taxiing immediately to the hotel, where Gerard would join me as soon as possible and report his success or failure.

But Gerard wouldn't have it that way. He was getting more and more restless, nervous; every instant he remained with me, he kept whispering, he was endangering my life—not his, but mine. Therefore he must leave, quickly. Besides, he said, he felt ill. He looked it, certainly, and acted it. His jerkiness alarmed me: he was in no state to carry out a ticklish maneuver.

He would leave first, he insisted. I should stay and pay. If he was seen, then the thing for me to do was to stay motionless and invisible in my place until the others left. If he escaped unseen, then I could leave freely. In any case, our meeting-place would be my room at the Clarence.

He insisted that this was the better way. I shrugged agreement. It didn't sound sensible to me. But he was unquestionably ill. He was turning green.

With a final fearful look, and then composing his face, he rose. If only there was another door! He walked rapidly towards the only one there was. As he approached the fatal table, my heart stood still. Would he pass? Binbonnet's head remained in profile. The man in the rusty brown suit was staring down at papers. Now Gerard's tall figure was beside them, between them and the light, casting momentarily a shadow—I was watching every move—a shadow on their papers. The shadow surprised the reader—for Gerard was taller than others who had been passing. The head of the man in the rusty brown suit jerked—jerked upward. And, though I still couldn't see his face, I knew that he saw Gerard. I saw him quickly put his hand on Binbonnet's arm; he said something; Binbonnet's head swung round. Their two faces were fixed on Gerard's retreating back. Then they swung back and looked at each other. Binbonnet was grave as always. On the other face, what expression was there? What face was it? I squirmed and turned, trying to see; then I remembered that now it was I who had to remain invisible, and, unsuccessful in my search, I abandoned it and put my hand to my face. Gerard disappeared through the door without looking back.

And then Binbonnet rose to his feet and began to search the room.

His gaze moved slowly, carefully. It was upon me in a moment, and though my hand was still against my face something else gave me away. Something I forget about when I'm sitting down, and which I'd forgotten about then, but which was there nonetheless, propped up against my chair. My crutches betrayed me instantly, and instantly I knew it. As he recognized me, Binbonnet started and said something. At once his companion jumped up, face still away, and left the room fast.

Well, the game was up, whatever it was. It hadn't lasted long. No use sitting any longer in that place. A waiter approached; I called him and paid. I rose, moved slowly toward the door.

"Monsieur Weavair! Good evening!"

"Ah! Monsieur Binbonnet! Good evening! What a pleasure!"

"You are back from Holland so soon, Monsieur? Things were arranged as easily as that?"

That voice, slightly mocking. The grave face was staring at me searchingly.

We didn't chat. "Now that I am back, Monsieur Binbonnet, do telephone me."

"I will indeed, Monsieur Weavair; I shall not fail to do so. Good evening, Monsieur Weavair."

"Good evening, Monsieur Binbonnet."

Slowly I continued my way out, got my garments from the *vestiaire*, was ushered out onto the sidewalk. "Taxi, Monsieur?" the doorman asked. I nodded. His whistle blew. Then I saw in the rainy darkness by the building a person, a human form, leaning against the wall, making a faint noise. I peered. "The gentleman is ill, Monsieur," the doorman said apologetically. "He is vomiting, Monsieur."

"Gerard?" I called, severely and loudly. "Into the taxi; come; we'll go together."

He retched and moved toward me slowly, like an old man, his tall form bent, hands to his stomach.

As I stood there on the sidewalk, in the rain, waiting for Gerard and the taxi, I noticed that another car was parked just behind the empty space into which the taxi was edging. It was a sport car of some light color—handsome, with canvas top and shiny fittings. And in one of its windows, pressed up against the glass, staring out at us, was a face that I knew. A wise-looking, wrinkled face. "Hello, Faust," I said. "I recognize you." The head jerked; there was a bark—and suddenly I knew that I had last heard Faust's bark more recently than I had seen his face.

The cab had drawn up. I entered. Gerard followed, the doorman aiding us both. The door slammed. "Hotel Clarence." We drove off.

"Was I seen?" Gerard asked faintly. "Was I seen?"

He smelled of vomit. Suddenly I was filled with anger. *He* had spoiled the game. If he had done what I had advised—let me go out first . . . and now this fright—for I was sure that was what it was. "You were seen," I said flatly. "And Binbonnet knows I was with you."

"And the other man. He saw you?"

"I think not. But Binbonnet told him I was there, and he ran out."

"You didn't see his face?"

"No."

"*Pardon*," Gerard said weakly. "*Pardon*. Poor Monsieur Weav-air! My poor friend!"

Hell!

Why hadn't I heeded the warning of the Frenchman in the train to Holland, the warning against people who claim to come from Touraine?

And what was this all about?

# CHAPTER 9

There was no reason, Gerard insisted when we reached the hotel, to send for a doctor. He had merely been badly frightened, he said, corroborating my own diagnosis; his digestion being his weakest part at best, it was there that fear had most naturally done its damage. He evinced no shame at having been scared; on the contrary it was I who felt ashamed—ashamed at having included, even momentarily, his fear among my causes for annoyance; after all, I reminded myself, his fear had been for me! But even so, I remembered his insistence that it be he who leave the café room first, and its evil consequences; and therefore this new insistence, that no doctor be called, I refused to obey. As we went through the lobby and up to our rooms I noticed that he still kept his hand pressed to his stomach and his side. Suppose it was appendicitis, or something of the kind. Suppose the nausea were to return. In any case, there was discomfort, and a doctor could relieve it.

So, upstairs, I told Pierre to summon whatever doctor it was who served the hotel, to give Gerard a hot-water bag, and—having secured Gerard's permission—to unlock and open the doors between our rooms. I could perhaps be of aid to him, and besides—I was beginning to realize that I, too, was not completely without fear. I shouldn't be sorry to know that someone, even Gerard, was near, during the night that now had to be gone through! I was in some danger, some danger grave enough to make this Breton giant ill; the reality of it was only just beginning to seep into my brain.

The doctor arrived in half an hour. He was one of the brisk, self-confident kind.

"What seems to be wrong?"

Gerard answered for himself. "Nausea from fright."

"From *fright?*" He looked at Gerard severely, then severely at me, then went over and pressed, pummeled and otherwise examined the patient. Then he gave me another severe look, took out of his bag, to my astonishment, an apparatus I knew to be a stomach pump, ordered Pierre to aid him, and without any more ado went to work on poor Gerard, to the accompaniment of retchings and gaggings. It didn't take long—there wasn't much left, I suppose, of whatever it was he was after. Then he gave Gerard—now reduced to feebleness—a pill, washed his hands in my bathroom and informed me that the danger was over. I had watched the whole process with considerable bewilderment.

"He will not die," the doctor said. "Though he might have died. Had I not emptied his stomach, other attacks might well have followed."

"Died!" I cried, astonished. "There was a possibility of death? People do die of fright then, sometimes? I mean—apart from heart shocks and such?"

"Die from fright? No, Monsieur." The doctor's tone was condescending. "If this gentleman had died, it would not have been from fright. His vomiting, according to what he himself said, Monsieur, was caused by fright—actually it either was or was not, as the case may be. But previous to the vomiting, Monsieur, what had the patient been eating?" With Pierre's corroboration, I recited our dinner menu. The cuisine of the Clarence is famous. I could see Pierre stiffen at the implication that one of the dishes might have been bad, and when I ended by saying, "With his meal my friend drank half a bottle of Vouvray," Pierre loyally added, with a look of apology toward me, ". . . which did not come, however, from the cellar of this hotel."

"Ah." The doctor pierced me with a look—and all of a sudden I felt dizzy and full of horror. Full of horror and full of suspicion—no: full of certainty. "Dunce!" I shouted inside myself. "To have taken so long to think of that!" But in front of the doctor, I quickly determined, I must not give way: I must not reveal a single one of these terrible things now filling my brain. I disliked this doctor; if eventually I had to reveal my facts and my suspicions, let it be to someone else. For the time being, control, a show of equanimity.

"You mean, Doctor, that the wine may have been bad? Now that I think of it my friend did criticize its taste; I suppose that's why he didn't finish it. Pierre, bring in the rest of that Vouvray, please; the doctor may wish to analyze it." And then, another worry coming too quickly to be disguised except by gruffness: "You didn't drink it up, I hope?"

For that, I knew, I'd have to apologize later. Pierre drew himself up with incredible stiffness; but it was astonishing how courteous he succeeded in keeping his voice. "No, Monsieur."

"You yourself drank none of the wine?" the doctor inquired of me, when we were alone.

"A thimbleful."

"I see."

The atmosphere was easier. Thanks to my mention of the wine's taste, I seemed less under suspicion. But—after the analysis!

"Frankly, Monsieur, I suspect some kind of poisoning. . . ."

He was interrupted by the return of Pierre; I managed a look of shocked incredulity; he held the bottle to the light, examined the fine golden color, then stuffed the whole thing into his bag and became brisk. He had, he said, given the patient a sedative—indeed, Gerard seemed already to be in the last stages of drowsiness. He should remain in bed the next day, for stomach pumping is weakening. He could take some weak tea, toast, *crème de riz*, and should have regular doses of bismuth. He himself would return the next day with his report. He bowed, we shook hands, he strutted out.

I thanked Pierre for his extraordinary services and apologetically explained my seeming rudeness. "I was only afraid that you might suffer like my friend," I said. "There seems to be something wrong with that wine. Probably a touch of arsenic from the vine-spray, as occasionally happens."

Pierre's assurances and expressions of sympathy were so perfect that I was actually soothed into thinking that I had not offended him in the first place. Then I dismissed him. I was half fearful and yet half eager to be alone; eager to look back, to reconstruct. . . . Gerard was sleeping soundly.

I had always kept the door of my room at the Clarence unbolted at night, so that I shouldn't have to get up and open it for the waiter in the morning; and always, wherever I am, I sleep with wide-open windows. But this night in both rooms I locked and fastened the windows and put chairs in front of them, and bolted both hall doors, leaving open only the double-door between the rooms. Since there was danger, why might it not try to strike at once? I resolutely turned out my light and began to ponder.

I am not a habitual reader of detective stories, mystery tales, though I have read a few. Several of my friends, to whom I have at various times told this story of my quite unexpected adventures in France, and who themselves are such habitual readers, have urged me, when I have reached this point with them in my recital, by all means to mention this fact about my reading habits in my written account. Otherwise, they assure me, my obtuseness about the wine will appear well-nigh incredible. They have all said—without undue smugness, merely as a statement of fact—that they were suspicious of "Monsieur Binbonnet's" wine from the moment I first mentioned it. A present of wine, in a story, they say, can mean only one thing.

My excuse, then (which I quickly present, since my friends think I should), can only be, I suppose, that I've never had the habit of regarding my life as a story. And in my life I have more than once received presents of wine, and except as evidences of kindness on the part of well-meaning friends they have had no significance what-ever. Why should I have suspected "Monsieur Binbonnet"? True he was a liar, and in Brest I had learned that his lying wasn't confined merely to the subject of telephones; I knew that he was capable of lying whenever he wished to. But I still can't see why that knowledge should have tipped me off about the wine. To lie about telephones and a man's appearance and habits is lying; to lie about the qual-ity of wine one sends is—or can be—murder; and I insist there's a difference between the two. We've all lied at some time or other, even if only in our childhood; and lying is within the ken of all of us. Attempted murder, on the other hand, is not something with which many of us have dabbled ourselves into familiarity.

No—I'm not ashamed to say that it took Gerard's revelation that "Binbonnet" was not Binbonnet, his warning to me and his terror for my sake, and then the doctor's suspicion besides, to make me think of "Binbonnet," whoever he was, as a would-be killer. Who he might be, why he should want to kill me, when he would next try to, and who and what his companion was, were the things that kept me awake that night. It was ironic, in a way, that Gerard himself should now be deeply sleeping—even snoring—after having so alarmed me; that now for hours I couldn't learn anything beyond those two bare frightening facts: that "Binbonnet" was an impostor and that my life was threatened.

The thing that chiefly occupied me, as I lay there in the dark, was recollection of my receipt of the wine. The mystery of "Binbonnet" was so unfathomable, the identity and role of his companion (whom I now knew I had just glimpsed through the door at the moment of Faust's entrance into "Binbonnet's" office) so inexplicable, the reason for Gerard's fear on my behalf so puzzling, that I kept turning to the thing with which I had had contact myself—the present of wine and brandy. A hundred times I recalled "Binbonnet's" saying that he was sending me a "sample of France's liquid specialty," and more than a hundred times I recalled my gratitude for the brandy, my unscrewing the top of the flask, the lurch of the train, the shattering of the glass and my despair and the intense cold. Death in my sleeping compartment! How satisfactory that would doubtless have been—from "Binbonnet's" point of view! Death alone after a long period of vomiting and suffering such as poor Gerard had begun tonight and had been saved from only by the pump. A wretched death for me before I could contact Gerard, whom "Binbonnet" had so clearly desired me not to see!

And another grisly thought—"Binbonnet's" offer of a "smart sport model" with its chauffeur! What would have happened to me, on that long ride across France? I had grimaced, when he had suggested it, at the discomfort of so long a drive. Discomfort! Ironic word! More than discomfort there certainly would have been. Either in the "smart sport model," which I had myself subsequently seen beside the curb with Faust in its window, or in one of the "comfortable inns," death or attempted death at the hands of the "experienced chauffeur"—who might or might not have been clad in his usual suit of rusty brown. Who was he, that "experienced chauffeur"? And what had he to do with me?

Over and over again I reviewed these two things in my mind—for with them I felt on more familiar terms than with the greater mysteries of which they were doubtless part. I lay wide awake, and after a time I found that I was listening for footsteps, for the sound of fingers on doorknobs or windowpanes. According to Gerard those people were after me. Why shouldn't they come for me now?

My listening grew sharper, more intense, the longer I lay there; so wide awake did I become, so did I quiver, finally, at the slightest sound, that I knew the possibility of a panic was upon me. And a panic was something I couldn't afford, this time. In the past I had allowed myself to be panicked by imaginary dangers, by little fears. It hadn't mattered, really, then, whether I'd had panics or not; I hadn't had anything else to do, much—the panics had simply filled up my empty time. But now—! These dangers were real; these fears well-founded; the next day I must act. Windows and doors were locked, I reminded myself; I could sleep with a good deal of safety if I could get to sleep at all.

On the other hand, of course, if they came and I was in a deep, drugged sleep . . .

But I took a sedative.

Gradually I became drowsy and then drowsier. And it was just when I was very drowsy indeed, just before drowsiness became sleep, that I suddenly remembered something else—something more recent, something I had seen myself but which only now impressed itself upon me. That bottle of Vouvray; Pierre had removed it, after dinner, half empty. And with more courtesy than I had deserved, when I had seemed to suspect him, he had denied drinking it up. But when he had brought the bottle in, and the doctor had held it up to the light—surely the line of its golden yellow was closer to the bottom than it had been! No longer was it half full—of that I was now, in my drowsiness, suddenly sure. Pierre had not, as he had politely said, drunk it *up*; but surely . . .

But that was as far as I went, and sleep took me off, and I didn't remember this vision of my semiconsciousness until sometime later.

They didn't come that night.

When I awoke I didn't feel very refreshed. Lack of air, for one thing. Getting into my clothes I took a look at Gerard and found him still sleeping. I pulled the chairs away from the windows in both rooms and opened them and unbolted both doors. It was another beautiful Indian summer day, and though I was still conscious of mystery and danger, poison and peril seemed less immediately near.

I rang for my breakfast, and was surprised when Pierre appeared with it. "You still here?" I exclaimed. "Is there 24-hour duty now?"

"I thought that under the circumstances I should be here for Monsieur this morning," he said, unsmiling. "And for the other gentleman."

"I appreciate that more than I can say. But such hours—you get no rest."

"It reminds me of the war, Monsieur."

The war! The crackpot spoke more truly than he knew—possibility of surprise attack by the enemy was, after all, a wartime condition. "Well, I am glad you are here," I told him. "But I hope there may be nothing to do; perhaps Monsieur Gerard will sleep on and need no attention."

Even as I spoke, however, there was a sound from the next room. Pierre immediately went to the connecting door. I heard him say, "Bonjour, Monsieur," and he disappeared within. Pushing my breakfast aside, I followed him; Gerard smiled at me, a trifle wanly, from the bed. He started to cover me with thanks, but I stopped him. "You slept well. Do you feel ready for tea and toast?" He said he did. I ordered that some bismuth be prepared for him first; Pierre disappeared. "I shall leave you now for my breakfast, and we shan't talk about anything until you've had yours. Then, if you don't feel like dozing, I'll come back. You're to stay in bed today; the doctor will come in to see you." I went back to my room, finished my breakfast, took up the papers and fell to pondering some more.

What a beautiful day it was! Through the tall windows the soft sunshine poured onto the red hotel carpet and the polished furniture; the sky was Pissarro blue. It gave me a silly thought, the clear beauty of the day after so long a stretch of gray, rainy weather. I thought of it as resembling the change that had just begun to take place in my own life—the first, stirring revival of interest in living after so long a stretch of not caring. And now, with the change just begun, here I was suddenly plunged into a mire of complications and difficulties. It was puerile of me, I know, but as I sat there that morning, waiting to begin unimaginable wrestlings with mysterious difficulties, I was filled with momentary resentment against Al and Jim. It was they who were snatching away from me all the benefits of my finally improving outlook on the world. God only knew what adventures I was in for now, for the sake of Pearce Brothers! Whereas personally I felt that I was just beginning to recover from what might be called the adventure of ten years before, and returning with pleasure and relief to the normalities of life.

It was borne in upon me, too, what sober, practical planning is called for by the most lurid situations. Poisonings and false identities are the stuff nightmares are made of, but now actually confronting me as they were they assumed the guise of other happenings with which I had had to cope as best I could—death of my wife and child as the result of my own collapse; near-fatal illness, incapacity. Poison and murderers were lurid, but perhaps not more lurid than those. I felt irritation too; what a waste of energy it was going to be, having to combat them! It made me think of the crazy continent on which I was, involved in ceaseless strife and presenting to rationally thinking human beings a never-ending spectacle of silliness. But one had to preserve one's self, and one couldn't do that by just being irritable and calling other people silly.

Perhaps I should have felt differently about the whole thing if I knew what I'd done to get myself involved—committed some act for which I could only expect vengeance, interfered in some situation from which I had to be removed. Then I might have continued to be as terror-struck as I had been before taking my sedative. But the whole thing still seemed distant from me because I still felt that *I* was distant from *it*. So accidentally and unwillingly was I involved— if I really was involved—that the affair didn't seem to be my own. Chiefly now, I felt watchful and very curious and determined to find out what the thing was all about. I heard Gerard call me, and I went in.

# CHAPTER 10

He was still pale and weak from the pumping. "The doctor gave me a sedative," he said. "Why did he pump me out so rapidly? What did he find? What did he say?"

"That something you'd eaten had disagreed with you."

"Something I'd eaten?"

"Eaten or drunk."

I thought it better to leave it at that. Better to allow the doctor to be precise, when precise meant lurid.

"And in this hotel," Gerard said. "What is Paris coming to? Frankly," he went on, "if food had anything to do with it I'd think it was the wine—that is if I could still think the wine came from our broker. It would be just like him to choose some low-grade, gut-destroying vintage. But if the wine came from the gentleman we saw last night, it did not come from our broker, Monsieur."

It was only then that remembrance of the whole truth seemed suddenly to return to Gerard. "You must seek safety, Monsieur Weavair!" he cried, in a different voice— a voice that thrilled me despite myself. "You are in danger—grave danger, Monsieur."

"So you told me last night, Monsieur Gerard. But what can I do about it? And how, why, am I in danger?"

"Do you not see?" He raised himself in bed, excitedly. "Do you not see? They know, since they saw you with me, that you must have learned from me that that man is not Binbonnet, as he has pretended to you to be. They know that you must now know that the real Binbonnet has disappeared, that his place has been taken, that he has been put away or done away with. And why should they give you time to notify the police of that discovery, Monsieur? Believe me, they will not give you time. Did no one come during the night?"

"No one." But I confess I felt some goose-flesh to hear my pre-sedative fears so corroborated.

"You see now why I told you we must not be seen together. Had you been seen alone, all would have been well. But since they know you were with me, that you must have pointed out that man to me as being Binbonnet, that I must thereupon have denied that it was he—"

"But you, too, Monsieur Gerard," I said. "They saw you too; they know that you, too, now know that the man who claimed to be Binbonnet is not he; why am I in danger any more than you?"

"Oh, they will make it disagreeable for me, Monsieur," he assured me, his lips curling. "Very disagreeable—never fear. But, unlike you, I am in no real danger because from me they are already getting what they want, and to harm me would be to harm themselves. For you the danger is great. What I saw last night—that impostor in poor Binbonnet's place—has made me realize to what lengths they will go. I was completely terrified for you. I tremble even now at the thought of how unsafe *you* are: how unsafe you are *at this very minute*. You must flee."

"Thank you, but I think I will stay. And I can assure you—and could assure those men—that I have no intention of going to the police. There is nothing I have less intention of doing—unless, of course, they force me to. Couldn't I get in touch now with Monsieur Binbonnet . . ."

"I must remind you, Monsieur: that person is not Monsieur Binbonnet."

Suddenly I was exasperated. "Oh, who is he, then?" I cried. "This is too absurd!"

Gerard lifted his shoulders. "Absurd perhaps. Dangerous certainly. Who that flashy person is I do not know, though what he is I can suspect. He is certainly not Binbonnet. Everything about him is different—his size and his entire allure . . ."

Once again I recalled my conversation on the way to Holland about people who claim to come from Touraine. How clearly it came back!

"Monsieur Gerard," I interrupted with a sudden thought. "Do you know that I have no reason to be completely sure that you are who you claim to be? Do you know that your appearance is entirely different from the description given me before our meeting, that the appearance of your office and establishment was a shock to me after what I'd been told to expect, that your account of your visits to Paris does not agree at all with another account of them I had been given? How do I know that it is not you who are the impostor? After all, we have no photographs of either you or Monsieur Binbonnet in New York."

I was far from being entirely serious in this. Despite the advance description that had been given me by the impostor, Gerard's office in Brest had unquestionably been a bona fide place; his name had been all over it and I had heard him addressed by clerks and stenographers. His name-plate had been on the gate-post of his villa. He had waved greetings to several dozen people in Brest and outside it. Besides, he didn't speak a sufficiently fine French to be suspicious! There was small chance of Gerard's being an impostor, but it had occurred to me that under the circumstances I might as well make the point. Besides, it was as good a way as any of reporting the false "Binbonnet's" lying descriptions. And I was pleased to see Gerard treat the point seriously. Out of the suit hanging beside the bed he took a wallet, and from that a collection of identity papers that would have convinced a thousand banks. "You are quite right, Monsieur, to demand these assurances," he told me, and his lip curled again when I pointed out that now at least he knew what the so-called Binbonnet had been telling me about him. "Never having seen me, so far as I know," he said, "he couldn't know what I looked like. But I should think he might have got a better description from his friend—his friend and agent."

So he was an agent, the man in rusty brown. But I postponed him for the moment. "Binbonnet's impostor made other odd statements, too," I said; and I told Gerard about the telephone.

"Curious, curious."

And I told about the reception accorded me by the concierge.

At that, however, the Breton smiled and shrugged. "A normal reception, I am sorry to say. Nothing suspicious there."

"But even the taxi-driver was indignant and astonished."

"Even taxi-drivers are human beings, Monsieur Weavair. Few Frenchmen will say the same for concierges."

Still, even without his concierge there remained enough of queerness about "Binbonnet." The wine . . .

"Monsieur Gerard," I demanded, to test him out, "was there then no reason for them to seek my death *before* the encounter last night? Before this impostor business came to light?"

"Indeed there was, Monsieur Weavair!"

My heart sank.

"I confess I wonder that something of the kind was not attempted, Monsieur Weavair. Ever since I first learned you had come to France, I have trembled for your wellbeing. When you came to Brest I was overjoyed to see you, for it meant, first, that you were still alive, and, second, that there might be hope for Binbonnet and me. But even then I trembled for you. And I dared not warn you, Monsieur, for while you were there I was being watched."

Yes—I remembered the barking clearly—the barking of Faust. The man in brown had been in an adjoining room, then, in Brest as in Paris?

"But what have they against me, Monsieur Gerard?"

"They want you out of the way, Monsieur Weavair."

"Yes—that's clear, quite clear; but why? Let's get down to brass tacks right here and now, Monsieur Gerard. Just why should they want me out of the way? Exactly why?"

Gerard looked at me, swallowed hard. It was, I could see, a momentary return of his fright. But this time it was on his own account. He was afraid to talk. But he did get it out. "They want all my iodine for themselves." There was sweat on his forehead after he'd said it.

Ah! So that was it! "But isn't it a little drastic, Monsieur Gerard, to resort to murder for a mere matter of iodine?"

"You make me smile, Monsieur Weavair. Murder is nothing to that man, or evidently, to the other—to the impostor, the man he works for."

I didn't understand very well. Binbonnet was merely a broker, and brokers are willing to sell to anyone who pays. "Why should

Binbonnet," I demanded, "a mere broker, be less willing to sell to me than to anyone else?"

At that question, to my surprise, Gerard became as irritated as I had been shortly before, and on the same subject. "You really must try, from now on, Monsieur Weavair, to remember that your Binbonnet is not Binbonnet. You must distinguish between the true and the false—because I assure you there are two. It is of the utmost importance to remember that. At least there should still be two. This one is the false one. God knows what's become of the real one."

I apologized. Still, it seemed to me only natural that Gerard, being a continental, should have less difficulty than I in accepting the grotesque facts. It was difficult for me to remember that "Binbonnet" wasn't Binbonnet, and I remember thinking proudly and absurdly that I was glad I was an American and glad that it was difficult—because it must be a hell of a state of mind to be in, to grasp such devilments instinctively.

"The answer to your question, Monsieur Weavair, is of course that this false Binbonnet isn't a broker at all. The real Binbonnet was a broker and very glad to sell to you, that's probably why he's been removed."

"Then who is this false Binbonnet?"

"The other man's boss, obviously."

"I'm determined to learn what's what," I said after a minute. "Now will you please tell me . . ."

Again the look of fright, the gulping. What was Gerard afraid of? *His* life wasn't in danger—he'd said so himself. And yet his "Go ahead" was more whispered than spoken.

"In the first place, Monsieur Gerard; you have actually seen the real Binbonnet?"

"The real one—many times. But not since about six months ago. On my last visit to Paris, before the summer, I didn't call on him. He was an honest, efficient broker, and things were going so well as to make a visit unnecessary. Besides, he was a poor kind of thing personally, and I wasn't sorry not to see him. Then all summer, as I told you, I didn't come to Paris. This is my first trip of the season. Yesterday afternoon I arrived and telephoned you immediately because you are sympathetic to me, Monsieur. I should probably have called—or tried to call—on Binbonnet today."

"Did you work in close cooperation with Binbonnet?"

"Up until four or five months ago—up until shortly after I last saw him—yes. Were Pearce Brothers not entirely satisfied until about that time?"

"They were. What happened at that time to change everything?"

That was the big question, of course.

I was quite willing to give Gerard a little time to answer it. He sat, looking quite unhappy and undecided, looking at me and away from me and then at me again, thinking something out.

I didn't hurry Gerard. Actually, however, there was, I was now ever increasingly beginning to realize, a need for hurry. Somewhere, at this very moment, two other men were almost certainly talking over these same things, planning what they would do, and how they would do it. And among the things that Gerard was turning over in his mind was probably what they might do to him if he told me what I wanted to know and they found out.

Shouldn't I act to save my own skin while I still could, and put myself under the protection of the police? That was a step of which I should probably not even have thought had Gerard not mentioned its impossibility. But the complications certain to result from it appalled me. And anyway, I wasn't in France on a police matter, but on a business deal. The dealings were proving to be of a pretty surprising kind, but—who could tell? Maybe in some way the surprise element was being exaggerated in an effort to discourage me; maybe by persisting in treating things in as businesslike a way as possible, and by restricting discussion to the parties concerned, I could still win out. Such was my instinct, at least, and in the absence of anything else to go by it seemed to me that I might as well follow it.

But Gerard was finally speaking.

"I confess I am surprised, Monsieur Weavair, that there has been no attempt on your life since your arrival in France. Just before your visit to Brest I was led to think that such an attempt was planned."

Thinking of the poisoned wine, which as yet he knew nothing about, and of the suggested motor trip, I smiled grimly to myself.

"Evidently," he went on, "they hoped that you would withdraw from the field in discouragement, and thus render any such attempt unnecessary. I suspect that the strange behavior, the lies, of Binbonnet's impostor were aimed to bewilder and discourage you, to make you give up your attempts to get my iodine for Pearce Brothers."

And here too I suspected he was right, remembering how hopeless I had become, how convinced I had been that only in Instruction No. 2 was there any hope for Pearce Brothers.

"But now, Monsieur Weavair, since last night, I fear that withdrawal from the iodine field wouldn't save you. You know too much now. You are too dangerous. You must disappear, Monsieur Weavair; not only withdraw from the iodine field, but disappear, leave France. And you must do so quickly, for you have found them out; now they will come after you. Disappear, Monsieur Weavair! Disappear instantly!"

"I have already told you, Monsieur Gerard, that I have no intention of disappearing. Kindly do not warn me, or try to terrify me, again; if you do, I shall begin to suspect that you are as eager as the others to remove me from the field. Tell me honestly, Monsieur Gerard: am I right in thinking that you would like to resume your former relations with Pearce Brothers?"

"You are indeed right."

"Then we are in this thing together, and we must do business together. Forget about my personal danger, remember this is a business matter."

Was this I, talking so boldly? Not a murmur did Gerard make in the face of my bravado; oh, if he could have seen me last night, scarcely daring even to take a pill!

"Answer those of my questions at least which you can without danger to yourself, Monsieur Gerard. Now, then . . ."

"I will tell you everything, Monsieur Weavair, except one or two things. I like you, Monsieur Weavair, and Pearce Brothers are the customers I have longed to have ever since I perfected my iodine process! What do you wish to know first, Monsieur Weavair?"

That was something like it! But to think that it should be I, *I*, inspiring another man with the courage to talk! Irony and pure joy combined to make me almost laugh.

"What happened, then, several months ago, to change every-thing?"

"One morning a young man called at my office, with a letter of introduction from Binbonnet—unquestionably from Binbonnet. He told me that he wished to buy my entire production of first-quality iodine, and offered me unthinkable terms. I declined his proposi-tion, but he forced me to accept it."

"Forced you—how?"

"Blackmail."

"Blackmail!" The word instantly filled my head with ideas. Black-mail on what grounds, I wondered.

"Who was this person?"

"The man in the café last night; the man in brown."

"I have seen him before, you know, Monsieur Gerard. I caught a glimpse of him through a door when his great dog walked into the so-called Binbonnet's office; I didn't see his face, but the color of his suit. And last night the dog was in his car outside the . . . the . . ."

"The café, Monsieur."

"Thank you. And am I wrong in thinking that I heard his dog bark when I was in your office in Brest?"

"No, you are not wrong, Monsieur. He was there, with his dog, just so that his presence would inspire me with obedience. Previous-ly I had heard from him that you might come, though he hoped to prevent it. I thought I knew what that meant, and when you arrived I was filled with joy. Joy and disquietude. Then I heard him arrive; I knew the sound of that car, and I heard his dog bark and knew that he was listening in an adjoining room. He was furious at me for taking you through the factory and on that afternoon auto-ride, where he couldn't follow us; but he needn't have feared—I know and admit that I'm in his power, and I obey him perfectly. He knew that in my home I would be perfectly obedient, for Madame Gerard . . ."

". . . knows nothing about the blackmail?"

"Nothing whatever, Monsieur."

Interesting, that point.

"And then he drove back to Paris?"

"He drove back in his car when you took the train. He told me not to come to Paris for five days, and that then I might come. I

telephoned every day, wanting to warn you; when the operator con-
tinually said that you were "Out of Paris," I feared the worst, even
though you told me you would sometime be going to Holland. Then
yesterday, the fifth day, I came, trembling lest I find that you had
indeed been . . . Had you not gone to Holland when you did go . . ."

Clear as a bell, in my mind, I heard the telephone ring that afternoon when I was lying down exhausted after my return from Brest;
the telephone call I had not answered; the call in which no message
had been left downstairs. Had that been a test? Had they tried to
see whether I was in? And if I had answered, would I have received,
perhaps, a visit? And Binbonnet's cordial request, the next morning,
that he be allowed to pay me a call!

Blood-curdling—but no use dwelling on it now.

I wondered that the man in brown had not forbidden Gerard to
come to Paris at all, considering the discovery of the impostor he
was certain to make when he got there.

"Your iodine went through Binbonnet, as usual?" I pursued.

"Exactly as usual. I knew nothing of what became of my iodine
once it left the factory, though I had my suspicions—was pretty sure
in fact. And through Binbonnet went also that refuse I was ordered
to send to Pearce Brothers for the purpose of discouraging them."
Gerard looked at me guiltily. "How forbearing Pearce Brothers were!
They complained, but they paid me for several wretched shipments
they might well have refused. And I was forced to write such insulting letters."

"When you say that everything went through Binbonnet as usual,
Monsieur Gerard, which Binbonnet do you mean?"

"Ah!" Gerard gestured his uncertainty. "That is what I am trying so hard to calculate—the moment when the true Binbonnet was
replaced by the false. At first I was puzzled by Binbonnet's collusion—for that letter of introduction was unquestionably from him.
Following that, I didn't get any letters from anybody—just telephone
calls from my man in Paris. And then suddenly I got a letter from
Binbonnet that let me know that he wasn't in collusion at all with my
man but evidently acting under compulsion, like me, and struggling
to free himself. It came just before I heard from Pearce Brothers
that you were coming to France—about two weeks before your actual

arrival. It was short, barely one line, absolutely in Binbonnet's hand, written in the faintest pencil, as though at the moment of writing it he wanted to make it as inconspicuous as possible. It said simply that everything would be all right in a month. It wasn't signed. It made me feel that he had some plan, some scheme of putting things back to rights, and that he had thus risked telling me so, knowing as he doubtless did that I too was acting under compulsion. Now, unless that letter was written after poor Binbonnet had already been seized and put away somewhere—and it seems less likely that he should risk such a letter after seizure than before—it would seem to indicate that sometime between the sending of that letter, a week or so before your arrival, and the date of your interview with the impostor, the false Binbonnet was put in the place of the real. That was a space of about a week; just what happened, sometime that week, to poor Binbonnet, Monsieur Weavair? Has he been murdered? Where is our broker?"

"I wish I knew," I said. "I wish I knew." Only now had Gerard finally made me fully realize that I had never met Achille Binbonnet, broker dealing in commodities, and that quite possibly I never should meet him. A pang came over me at the thought of what his plight might be. Blackmailed into retiring in favor of the impostor, undoubtedly; but was there more than blackmail, perhaps? Was Binbonnet alive?

"It is now almost three weeks," Gerard said, "since I received that second letter from Binbonnet, saying that everything would be all right in a month. I confess I have but little hope left, Monsieur Weavair. No word from Binbonnet in three weeks, and just last night the revelation that my blackmailer is working for a man who assumed Binbonnet's place. . . . Little hope, Monsieur Weavair."

Something occurred to me. "But that's exactly what the impostor told me," I said. "That everything would be all right in a month. And as a matter of fact, Monsieur Gerard, that is what you told me, too, in Brest."

He looked guilty again. "That was different, Monsieur Weavair. Before you came to Brest, my man telephoned me and said, as I told you before, that you might be coming down, though he hoped to prevent it. And he said that if you did come, I was to pretend complete repentance and reform, refuse to discuss anything, and say that a month would put everything to rights. Those were his orders to me; little wonder that the impostor said the same thing to you. Binbonnet's mention of a month was quite different, though the statements happen to coincide. That second letter from Binbonnet meant something. I know it. The other statements didn't—they were merely stalls."

That just bewildered me.

"Just who is this man in the brown suit, the blackmailer?" I demanded.

"You think he has told me, Monsieur? I do not even know his name, or any name for him. Binbonnet's letter simply presented' 'a friend interested in iodine'; and in telephone messages from Paris he announces himself by saying, 'You know who this is.' And I always do know."

"Now, Monsieur Gerard, tell me something else. Something that you unquestionably know. Tell me on what grounds you are being blackmailed."

"*Oh, Monsieur!*" Gerard almost shouted, and he sat straight up in bed as though he had been yanked into that position by some exterior force. I was not surprised by his indignation, and I confess that my approach to so brutal a question had been deceptive. But this was in some ways the most important question of all.

"Is it so very terrible, then, what the blackmailer knows?" I said, more gently.

"I myself told you, Monsieur, that I agreed instantly to his demands when he revealed his knowledge of it."

"What would happen to you were he to reveal that knowledge to others?"

"I should be ruined as a man, and my wife and daughter would be ruined. If my friends in Brest were to learn of it . . . That would be the end."

"How could the man in brown have learned of it?"

A lift of the shoulders. "Things of that nature leak out, I suppose."

"Tell me for what you are being blackmailed, Monsieur Gerard."

He shook his head. Obviously he found my demand incredible; he could scarcely believe that I should make it.

I looked at him, pity and exasperation filling me. Poor wretch! I knew what the ground was, of course. The moment he had first used the word blackmail, I had known. It was what I had immediately suspected during my afternoon with him in Brest, what I had become certain of during our evening in Paris. The cause of his brothel mania was the ground for his blackmail. I was sure. I was convinced that actually there was nothing wrong with him, and, once convinced of that himself, by a good psychiatrist, he could tell his blackmailers to go to hell. And with blackmail out of the picture, he could start deliveries of iodine to Pearce Brothers at once. I had to get him to admit to me what it was.

"Tell me, Monsieur Gerard."

"I cannot, Monsieur Weavair."

"Then let me tell you this: I *know* your secret, Monsieur Gerard."

"You know it! Impossible, quite impossible for you to know it, Monsieur."

"I assure you I do indeed know it. And since I know it, why should I not blackmail you myself? Your blackmailer in brown, whoever he is, threatens to reveal it if you don't sell to him. Why shouldn't I threaten to reveal it if you don't sell to *me?*"

He looked so stricken that I feared his convulsions of last night might return; a nervous, impressionable man indeed, Monsieur Gerard. Natural, probably, considering his psychosis and the strain of the blackmail for it. But this was too much like frightening a child. "Obviously I won't blackmail you," I said soothingly. "But tell me, just tell me. The thing can be cured. You can show the world it isn't true. Everything will improve."

He just stared at me. But gradually, slowly, a look stole over his face. He was going to tell!

I didn't feel possessed of any extraordinary insight in having guessed the reason for Gerard's shame. As I said earlier, I gave the credit to my American background, in which a working knowledge of psychology and psychiatry has become to such a degree the common property of all. What chiefly obsessed me was a growing realization of how intolerable Gerard must find the situation. The deficiency from which he was suffering, the cause of his brothel mania and the ground for his blackmail, is of all possible catastrophes the one most abhorrent to any man worthy of the name; or, if there is one catastrophe more abhorrent, it is that this deficiency should become known to others. Particularly in France, it seemed to me, where virility is perhaps more highly prized—and certainly more talked about—than anywhere else, knowledge by others of such a condition would almost drive a man to suicide. "I should be ruined as a man," Gerard had said. "If my friends in Brest were to learn of it . . . ! That would be the end." The thing was such a threat to his respectability. Suppose those people I had met at his house, for example, the Leblancs and the Dutuits, were to learn of his condition. Imagine the snickering, the gossip, the condescension, the false pity. Gerard knew hundreds of people in Brest—suppose they all learned about him, all gossiped and snickered at the mention of his name, at the sight of him! I could well understand that he should pay his black-mailer and dread to disclose the thing even to me. But I would help him.

"Tell me, Monsieur Gerard. After all, you trust me. We are friends."

The look grew.

"Tell me."

The promising look became more intense. All I had to do now was wait—wait a minute, or two, or three. Or would it help were I to start for him the sentence that he would speak, give him the words to use? "Monsieur Weavair," I tentatively drafted within myself, "what the blackmailer knows about me is that I am impo . . ."

I never said those words. And even within myself I broke off in the middle of what would have been the last word. For suddenly the footsteps in the hall, which I had been hearing all morning, now became real footsteps, and someone knocked on my door.

There was a moment of utter silence.

And in that moment I had a flashing, disillusioning, puzzling revelation. That look on Gerard's face. The look that I had read as meaning that he would tell, had been only—curiosity. That became suddenly clear and unquestionable. The most intense curiosity. I had been eager for him to tell, and in my eagerness I had misread his look as I had. Self-delusion; pure wish-fulfillment. The most intense curiosity. Why?

The knock was repeated.

# CHAPTER 11

But though Gerard and I glanced deeply at each other before I finally called a slightly weak "Come in," it was not a deputation come to kill me that entered the room.

It was the doctor; and despite a distinct surge of relief, nevertheless the moment I saw him my dislike returned fourfold. The same briskness, the same bursting self-confidence that had so displeased me the night before. I was sorry for Gerard's sake but not for the doctor's that the patient didn't look more blooming: Gerard appeared decidedly the worse for wear. The doctor gave him a long stare, then catechized me.

"You gave this gentleman, for breakfast, what I ordered?"

"Yes, Doctor."

"What was that?"

"Tea and toast, Doctor."

"No bismuth, Monsieur?"

"Bismuth *before* breakfast, Doctor."

"Ah."

Then he asked Gerard how he felt, to which the poor fellow replied "Tired," and then he kneaded and pummeled and examined him as he had done the night before. "Very satisfactory," he pronounced. "Continue with the bismuth and the present diet for another day or two, then return gradually to normal foods." Whereupon he retired to the bathroom and washed his hands and on re-emerging declared that our need for his services was at an end and that he had the honor to wish us good-day. Gerard, interrupting the rebuttoning of his pyjamas, thanked him, pressed some bills into his hand and bade him farewell. I accompanied him to the door.

I thought, of course, that the doctor was showing discretion. I was even beginning grudgingly to be grateful to him for such tact— such consideration for the patient in not mentioning disturbing matters in his presence. But to my astonishment, when he had opened the door, he merely bade me good-by once more, passed out into the hall and started to leave. It was difficult to believe my senses. "But Doctor," I called, as softly as I could. "Your analysis—after all, what have you discovered to be the cause of my friend's . . . ?"

He stopped and turned towards me. From the expression on his face, it was clear that a deliberate maneuver, a quick get-away, had failed; but the man's coolness in failure was remarkable. "The cause of the patient's attack, you are inquiring about, Monsieur?"

"Yes, Doctor."

"Fright, Monsieur. The patient did have a frightening experience, I think he himself said?"

"Yes, but . . ."

"It is my professional opinion, Monsieur, that the patient's violent attack of indigestion was due to fright." His face had now assumed an expression of professional patience; his voice, too, oozed patience; he was a busy doctor courteously answering foolish questions.

I, too, pretended to be patient. "What did you find to be the condition of the wine, Doctor?"

"An inexpensive, poor-quality wine, Monsieur, if you will forgive me for saying so. You are perhaps not too well acquainted with our French wines, Monsieur? Now in choosing a Vouvray . . ."

I knew, of course, what he was telling me. For many people, doctors included, it is difficult to say "I was mistaken." I know that, because I have known more doctors in my life than most. But for this man not to say "I was mistaken" was evidently a point of honor. He was an alarmist; and full of self-importance. The wine had been all right. He had been wrong. But he wouldn't—couldn't say so in so many words.

And it was at this point that I remembered, for the first time since it had come to me, the flash I had had in bed at the moment of dropping off to sleep. Pierre had drunk some of the wine—quite a little. And Pierre had not been ill. So why had I allowed myself to continue to believe, after the sight of that emptier bottle, something that I then knew could not be true? Besides—Gerard's attack had come so long after he had drunk. I was filled with a fury against myself, with a storm of self-disgust for being so at the mercy of an alarmist. I had allowed a thought which my own brain had given me to disappear into temporary oblivion, whereas had I held tight to it I should never have been the miserable dupe I now saw myself to be. I had not been clear-headed. That realization filled me with rage, and it was this rage against myself, I suppose, that caused my boorish behavior toward that doctor—behavior which to this day makes me blush when I think of it.

"So there was nothing whatever out of the way in the wine, as you yourself were so sure there was?" I brutally demanded, interrupting him. "The suspicion of poison which you voiced and which you put into my mind you now admit to be quite unfounded?"

He darted me a look of contempt for my lack of finesse. He bowed his assent. "And now, Monsieur, I have the honor to bid you . . ."

I uttered the word "Quack" and shut the door in his face.

That was indeed an unworthy reply to such artistic effrontery as his.

And it was a tribute to the justice of the doctor's scorn that I felt a sudden need to be surer than I was. He was quite right: I am not subtle. I am much more comfortable when things are clear. I went back into my own room, passing Gerard in his bed without a word, and rang for Pierre.

"I must ask you a personal question," I said abruptly, when he appeared. "A question on whose answer a certain amount of French welfare depends. You will remember that I told you I was here on a commercial mission, which if successful would enrich a certain French industry. It so happens that by answering the question I have in mind you can help insure that enrichment. To me personally the answer, whether positive or negative, is indifferent. Are you willing to answer it?"

"But of course, Monsieur." He all but saluted.

"Then—remember, I am not asking for personal reasons—did you or did you not drink some of the Vouvray which was left last night?"

It was pitiful to see him flinch, just quiver a bit in his full-dress suit, that uniform of the office which he filled so well. "A small glass, Monsieur. And I gave a small glass to my young colleague, Lavisse, who tends the service elevator and the furnaces at night. Monsieur . . ."

"Pierre, no explanations; the staff of every hotel in the world samples wine—you know that and so do I. And under the circumstances I assure you I am glad you did drink some. Neither you nor Lavisse felt any ill effects?"

"None whatever, Monsieur."

"And by the way—what was your opinion of the wine?"

Hesitancy; then—"We agreed that we had tasted better, Monsieur."

"Thank you, Pierre. You have aided your country by your frankness."

"I am happy to have been of service, Monsieur. Thank you, Monsieur."

The five hundred francs I gave him—to cover also past favors—was as well spent, I felt, as any outlay I had ever made.

And, purely conversationally, to bring the scene to a less abrupt close, I asked him whether this Lavisse, the wine-sharing elevator-man, was his particular friend.

"Yes, I think he might be called that, Monsieur," he replied, just a shade of doubt, however, on his face. "He is not a waiter, of course, not trained in service, not definitely a hotel person at all; rather a laborer, but a good fellow. I seem to have a certain influence on him. It is important, Monsieur, that we instill among young persons of that class the proper ideas, ideas of patriotism to combat the other ideologies which are so insidiously . . ."

He was off again on his hobby-horse. Evidently he had considered that a drop of Vouvray would go a distance in instilling the proper ideas into young Lavisse; too bad, for Pierre's sake, that the wine hadn't been better! I let him talk a bit about his ideologies, and then thanked him again and let him go.

I had to think about the situation which he had helped to clear up, a situation which in these mere five minutes had changed as though from black to white.

How glad I was—was my first thought—that I had not told Gerard the doctor's suspicions, and my resulting certainty! And my second, what an alarmist this new situation made Gerard out to be!

For my sole basis for belief in the murderous parts of his story had been my belief that an attempt had already been made on my life. As long as I had believed the wine to be poisoned, then I had been able to believe in his tales of attempted murder and his warnings of future attempts; but now—! Since the so-called Binbonnet's gift had not been poisoned, evidently I had been in no danger of death whatever in that sleeping-compartment, for example. And as to the ride in that "smart sport model" which I had been offered, the car would doubtless have been driven by the man in brown, and I had no reason to doubt Gerard's statement that that man was a blackmailer; but it is quite possible to ride for many miles with a blackmailer— even further than from Paris to Brest—and not be *murdered*. And though something had certainly happened to our poor broker Binbonnet, there was no indication whatever that he had been killed. Even Gerard had hesitated to be definite about that.

So here I was, back again at my own thought which I had abandoned with cowardice just because of that alarmist doctor. The enormous difference between murder and lying. That enormous difference which had kept me, in the first place, from thinking ill of the gift of wine, like my detective-story-reading friends. From now on I should have to hold tight to that difference; I mustn't forget it again.

The false Binbonnet was a liar—a liar about telephones, a liar about Gerard, and greatest of all a liar about his own identity. But did that make him a murderer?

And there was a difference between murder and other crimes, too. That man in brown—to come back to him—was a blackmailer. Gerard had never known him to commit murder; he had merely interpreted one or two of his remarks as meaning that he was going to commit it.

The fact that I had been seen with Gerard in the "café" didn't mean that I was going to be liquidated.

Murder was out. Out of the picture.

But the idea of murder had become astonishingly imbedded in my gray matter since the night before. I found it hard to eradicate it now. Eradicated, however, I knew it must be, if I was to think straight and act straight in the future; and I set to work on it immediately. "Murder is out," I said to myself severely. "Murder is out. Murder is out." I worked hard at that, sitting there in my room.

What I took as a proof of success, after several moments of this intense anti-murder concentration, was the feeling of relief that began to pervade me—a degree of relief that I had never dreamed anyone could feel. Had I then been as terrified as that, that I should be so relieved now? It was a delicious, precious feeling, and brought with it a calm, warm, prosaic sort of normal confidence that was very different from the bravado I had felt and displayed an hour before. Now, since there was no danger, I could do whatever I liked, without the necessity of being either courageous or afraid.

What *was* there for me to do?

There were three things, it seemed to me. I must get Gerard to defy his blackmailer, by convincing him that it was absurd to continue to suffer persecution for a malady that could be cured. I must find the broker Binbonnet. After all, he had worked faithfully for Pearce Brothers, and merited immediate alleviation of his lot—if it was not already past alleviation. And I must have a brutal talk with Binbonnet's impostor, tell him what I had learned, and demand a showdown. I must finish with him once and for all, get him and his confusing lies out of my way, though his final defeat seemed to depend on my success in my two other tasks.

Unfortunately I could not go about those two tasks first. Gerard was at present quite unwilling to talk about the grounds of his blackmail. Despite my wishful thinking, he had given no indication that he would talk, every indication that he would not. And I had no idea of how to set about tracing the whereabouts of Binbonnet, except by getting in touch with the police—a step I preferred not to take.

So it was my third task that must be undertaken first. I must go to the Rue Saint-Martin—disagreeable and fantastic though the visit would probably be—and see what I could find out. Gerard I must leave till later. I could hope to accomplish little concerning him in the Rue Saint-Martin, though it was possible that concerning Bin-bonnet I might learn something there.

I got my hat and coat, and went in to tell Gerard I was going out.

He had been astonishingly patient and considerate since the doctor's departure. My indignant conversation with the quack had been carried on in whispers; but Gerard must have known that it was taking place, and that it could only be about him. He had let me pass through the room, following the conversation, without asking me a thing, and he had let me sit in my own room without a sound for fifteen or twenty minutes. Now I had a pang of pity as I saw him lying in his bed. His condition was undoubtedly unalarming, but it angered me to see him pale and weak as the result of that totally unnecessary stomach-pumping. After his nausea he had felt better. By the time we had reached the hotel, he had doubtless been well on the way to recovery. He would probably have been perfectly well in a few hours had that self-important ass of a doctor not taken him in hand. I felt repentant; it had been I, after all, who had insisted that the doctor come.

"You're all right, or so the doctor says at least," I told him. "At the door I was scolding him for having pumped you out. He needn't have done it. The wine was all right; your upset was a purely nervous affair. He was a fool." I watched him closely, in case by some look or gesture he should indicate that he himself had suspected the wine of being poisoned; but there was no sign that the thought had occurred to him, and I was glad of it. "Now I'm going to do a few errands," I said. "You'll be all right, won't you, till I return?"

"I shall of course be perfectly all right. But you. You forbid me to speak of your personal danger, but . . . You will use every caution, Monsieur Weavair?"

"*Every* caution, thank you, Monsieur Gerard." What was the use of telling him I'd discovered that my "grave danger" did not exist? He would only protest and be alarmed; and besides, why shouldn't I allow him to continue to think of me as full of bravery in the face of peril? I smiled to myself; I enjoyed being so considered even though it was false.

I had an idea, at that point, which made me telephone the hall porter before going downstairs. I was going to. The Rue Saint-Martin, and I might be going there several times during the afternoon and evening; for I was determined to return again and again, if my man should be out, until I found him in. Since I might well be spending considerable time in a car, getting in and out of it, depending on its driver for help, why shouldn't I be as comfortable as possible? Taxi-drivers are generally amiable and willing, but their cabs are rarely comfortable for me and they themselves rarely skilled at assisting me; a hired car and chauffeur would make things easier. So I telephoned downstairs my request that a car and driver be sent for; someone who would be obliging and helpful, I specified, with a comfortable machine. The porter said he would get a car at once. At that moment I was particularly glad that I no longer had within me that dreadful vision of death in a smart sport car, speeding across France, at the hands of a chauffeur in brown. Had I still thought of that as an actual danger which I had escaped, I should probably not have dared hire a car at all, and should have worn myself out in a series of taxis. On the subject of automobile disasters I was even after ten years somewhat—well, suggestible.

I sat chatting with Gerard a while, talking about nothing that was in any way connected with our affairs, and continuing to enjoy the knowledge that he was thinking of me as a man of courage. Finally the phone rang and the porter said the car was there. I went downstairs. I wasn't yet totally convinced that Instruction No. 2 wasn't Pearce Brothers' only hope, but I was determined to give Instruction No. 1 a good final try. This coming interview with the Rue Saint-Martin ought to be pretty lurid.

I was downstairs and on the sidewalk waiting for the car to approach, when it struck me that I'd neglected to ask Gerard one question which was of potential importance, to put it mildly. He had said, during the course of our conversation, that he had had a pretty good idea of where his iodine had gone—the iodine that he had sold at such a ridiculous price to man in brown and his boss. Where had that iodine gone? Where was it still going? In other words—at least I thought the two questions were probably identical—just who were the man in brown and the man in the striped suit? Who were they or whom did they represent? Who, in short, needed iodine?

Disgusted with myself for being so careless, for being precipitous as usual and not bringing sufficient common sense to an important job, I was on the point of going back upstairs, or telephoning Gerard in guarded language from the porter's desk in the lobby. But at that minute the car drew up, and also it occurred to me that Gerard had no knowledge of these things. Suspicions were all he had claimed to have, and I knew how worthless some of his other suspicions had been.

If my man in the Rue Saint-Martin was out, I decided, I would come back and ask Gerard these things; but now I would proceed without doing so. I got into the car and drove off.

# CHAPTER 12

It was a comfortable car—a big Lincoln, or Cadillac, or I something of the kind. An American make, at any rate. It seemed to be of a more recent vintage than the usual hired automobile, and from toe bursts of speed that the driver now and then gave it on the way to the Rue Saint-Martin it was evidently capable of fast action. The driver was smartly attired; this day's hacking would doubtless loom large on my Pearce Brothers' expense account! But I was frankly delighted by the comfort of the upholstery and springs and the warmth of the rug covering my lap and legs; this was better than a taxi, certainly. After all, I had been leading, of late, a life of a degree of activity to which I was scarcely accustomed: across the Atlantic, train to Paris, flights of stairs, train to Brest, auto trip through the countryside, train back to Paris, a touch of night life—to say nothing of incidental emotions. I hoped that from now on, though in a sense my task had just begun, I could take things more quietly. The business to be transacted promised to be difficult and dramatic, but I hoped that the manner of its transaction would be less strenuous. As we entered the Rue Saint-Martin and proceeded slowly amid the morning rumble of its trucks I hoped that our progress at that particular moment might symbolize the remainder of my stay in Paris: comfort amid turmoil. Certainly turmoil was the word to describe the state of the iodine business. And comfort was what I wanted and hoped to have.

As we pulled up in front of No. 404, however, I gave a dreary groan, for I saw at a glance that the very first of the new plans I had conceived for my own greater ease was already destroyed. I had planned to send the driver upstairs, with a request that "Monsieur

Binbonnet" descend and converse with me in the car, hoping in this way to avoid not only the long climb but also any contact with that watchdog of a concierge. But to my disgust there was the harpy herself down on the sidewalk, standing between the tape-and-braid shop and the nameplate that said "A. Binbonnet," deep in conversation with a young woman. I had had sufficient dealing with her to know that of eluding her there was no question; there wasn't a person in the world—to say nothing of a uniformed chauffeur—who could sneak through that door and up those stairs without her seeing him, no matter how steadily she might be talking to someone else. So, when the car had stopped, I sent the chauffeur over to her, to ask her to step over to me.

Suspicion and ferocity were registered from the beginning, I could see; she glared at the chauffeur and peered horridly toward the car, and when she came over it was with the air of hostility that I remembered so well. The chauffeur trailed her, looking discomfited.

"Bonjour, Madame. Monsieur Binbonnet is at home?"

"No."

"When do you expect him?"

A shrug.

"When was he last at home?"

"You ask me too much," she fairly barked.

But today I was in a mood to persist. "I think not, Madame. You are the concierge. Surely you keep track of your tenants."

No reply. A steady glare.

"How long have you been concierge of this building, Madame?" For suddenly I had an idea about the woman. Same response.

This seemed pretty hopeless. There appeared to be nothing to do but send the chauffeur upstairs, despite the shrill protests that such an action would doubtless evoke, to see whether "Binbonnet" actually was at home. For offhand I could think of no reason for believing that the crone was telling the truth. Probably it would be even better for me to go up myself. "Binbonnet" was quite capable of opening the door, blandly telling the chauffeur that Monsieur Binbonnet was not in, and then just sitting quietly within and refusing to open when I came up myself after hearing from the chauffeur about his reception. Or he might well have his man in brown—if he happened to be there—open the door for him, make the same reply, and follow the same course if I were then to go up.

"Monsieur Binbonnet's friend, the gentleman with the dog, is perhaps in?" I asked.

"No."

To hell with her. I called the chauffeur, and, ignoring the woman, who stood brazenly by, told him that I was going to climb to the third floor, and began to give instructions as to how he might best help me out of the car and up the stairs. He interrupted me, however. "Pardon me, Monsieur. But I overheard the name of the person for whom Monsieur asked; Monsieur wishes to see a Monsieur Binbonnet, I believe?"

"Yes."

"Then if Monsieur will forgive me, I will suggest that Monsieur can save himself the effort of climbing two flights of stairs. For Monsieur Binbonnet appears indeed to be out. This person appears to be telling the truth."

One could almost hear the words "strangely enough" tacked on to his final sentence, such was the look of dislike that he cast upon the concierge who had received him so gruffly and who stood there listening to his every word.

"How do you know that Monsieur Binbonnet is out?"

He was pleased to be of use to me so early in his employment. "Because that young lady is very disappointed not to find him in."

I followed his gesture, over toward Achille Binbonnet's door. The young woman with whom the concierge had been talking was still standing there, a small and inconspicuous figure in black, but she was staring most intently at us. She couldn't hear us—she was too far away for that—but our presence, our procedure, our every move, seemed to interest her vitally. "Would you be so good as to come here, Mademoiselle?" I impulsively called. And as the girl stepped swiftly over, the concierge uttered a sound that expressed anger if anger was ever expressed. She darted me a glance of hate that I thought must prelude an indignant turning of the back and stalking away; but she continued defiantly to stand where she was. At my call across the sidewalk, a few passers-by had turned to stare—such hailing, I quickly remembered, is unheard of in Paris—but they passed on, and now there was no one in the immediate vicinity but our foursome. The young woman was beside the car.

She was a pale, undistinguished-looking young thing, dressed in sensible but not too dowdy black. Girls like her pour by the thousand out of Paris office buildings at noon and again at six. She was no more individual-looking than the usual office girl in New York, though more soberly dressed, as is the custom abroad. One thing, however, did distinguish her. She had been crying. Her eyes were red, and in one hand she still held a handkerchief.

"Forgive my impoliteness in calling you that way, Mademoiselle," I said. She could see, through the window, my crutches lying on the floor of the car. "You are a friend of Monsieur Achille Binbonnet?" I inquired.

"I am his fiancée, Monsieur."

"Indeed! Then it is possible that you have heard him mention me—Mr. Weaver of New York. Or if not me, then my firm—Pearce Brothers."

"You are from Pearce Brothers? You have come to France to see Monsieur Binbonnet? Have you seen him?"

No lack of interest, at least!

"Why do you not come in here with me, Mademoiselle, and sit beside me? Then we could have a conversation. I should like to converse with you very much." How very much, she could scarcely know.

"Very willingly, Monsieur."

The driver opened the door for her, and she entered and sat down. Then, when the door was closed, I raised the glasses in all the windows. I couldn't resist taking a look at the concierge, to see how she liked my move. Powerless, outside looking in, she betrayed her rage; now she did twist furiously away, with a final glare and a toss of her head. She didn't go far, however. Just across the sidewalk, over to where the girl had been. There she stood, staring at us as intently as the girl had stared before.

"How long has that person been concierge of this building?" I demanded, abruptly. It was something I was eager to know.

"Oh, for a long time, Monsieur. Several years, at least."

Then I was right; the concierge must be in on the thing too! For as recently as a month before, Gerard had told me, the real Binbonnet was almost certainly still in Paris. The concierge must know of the replacement of the real by the false. And, knowing, and being hostile to those seeking the real Binbonnet, she must be on the side of the false!

But this girl beside me, how much did she know? If she was really the fiancée of the real Binbonnet, and didn't know that he had been replaced, far be it from me to tell her such frightening news. It is easy for me to make gaffes. When the girl had first said she was Binbonnet's fiancée, I had in fact almost demanded, "The fiancée of which Binbonnet?" How cruel that would have been! And now she was weeping again, even without my having said anything out of the way.

"I have already told you my name, Mademoiselle," I said, carefully. "Now suppose you tell me yours."

"My name is Denise Richard, Monsieur."

"And you have known Achille Binbonnet a long time?"

"Several years, Monsieur."

"And engaged to him a long time too?"

"A year, Monsieur."

"And where is Monsieur Binbonnet now?"

"Oh, that is what I wish I knew!" And the tears welled out, the handkerchief was desperately used, and there were even some sobs.

"Come, come, Mademoiselle," I scolded her. "I have traveled across the Atlantic Ocean to see Monsieur Binbonnet, and have considerable business to do with him. You can imagine that I'm most eager to see him. But what good would it do if I were to weep because I can't find him? I appreciate your feelings, Mademoiselle, don't think I don't, but you and I can help each other much better, I am sure, if we don't weep."

That evidently struck Mademoiselle Denise as an odd speech, for she stopped her sobbing at once and stared at me, from welling eyes, with a somewhat stupid expression.

"You had better be sure of my identity," I went on, taking out one of my Pearce Brothers cards and giving it to her. "Because I want you to tell me as much as possible about Monsieur Binbonnet, and I want you to feel confident that you are telling it to someone who is every bit as deeply concerned for him as you are."

"But I am his fiancée, Monsieur!"

"And I am an American businessman who has matters to discuss with him. Do you not know, Mademoiselle, that we Americans consider business the most important thing in the world, and that being American I can feel as deeply attached to Monsieur Binbonnet for business reasons as you can feel because you are his fiancée?"

Was it unkind of me, to take this semi-whimsical line to impress her? But impress her it did, and that was what I wanted; I wanted her to stop weeping and to tell me all she could. It was my original hail across the sidewalk, which I had quickly recognized as being strange to a Parisian, that had given me my cue as to what line to take. She seemed a simple, impressionable soul. What with my crutches and my queer outlook on life she clearly found me bizarre, and as a result she herself became more poised. "I will tell you what I can, Monsieur," she said, almost primly, "since I do believe that you are concerned for poor Achille. What is it that . . . ?"

But I interrupted her with simulated surprise. "'Poor' Achille? Why should you call Monsieur Binbonnet 'poor'? He has been doing an excellent business with us, and I can assure you that any difficulties and interruptions did not originate on our side. What is poor about Monsieur Binbonnet?"

"Oh, but he is such an *unhappy* man, Monsieur!"

"Unhappy? With a steady American customer like Pearce Brothers and a fiancée like you, Mademoiselle? What in the world is he unhappy about?"

The urge to laugh at me, and her chagrin, struggled for expression on the face of Mademoiselle Denise.

"Something—I don't know what—came up and suddenly made him frightfully unhappy," she said, sadness winning. "So unhappy that it changed everything between us. Changed it temporarily, I mean, of course, Monsieur. He told me that I mustn't try to see him again or write to him until he let me know that the thing had been straightened out."

"You mean you have not seen your fiancé for some time?"

"Not for three months."

"But despite his command you have been trying to see him, like today?"

"Oh, no. Up until today I haven't tried to see him or write to him at all. Today . . ."

"One moment, Mademoiselle. You never wrote to him, you say. But did he write to you?"

"Once only, Monsieur—a note that I received just after I had left for my vacation, a month ago."

"Mademoiselle—would it be too much if I were to ask you to let me see it, that note? You probably have it with you, I imagine, haven't you?"

She considered a moment, then decided she had and opened her bag, and found and gave me a little envelope. It was addressed to her in pencil, and the note it contained was also in pencil, the faintest pencil. Gerard, I recalled, had received a similar note at the same time—so faintly written, he had said, as to make it seem that Binbonnet had wanted to make his writing as inconspicuous as possible. That was the impression this one gave. It was a mere line, unsigned. "Act as arranged. All should be well in a month." That same message again. In a month. In other words, just about now.

I thanked Mademoiselle Denise, and gave her back her note. "And why did you try to see Monsieur Binbonnet today, after obeying him for so long?"

"Because of the newspapers, Monsieur. All through my vacation the news grew worse and worse. I returned to Paris last night. This morning the situation seems so bad, Monsieur, I was afraid that Achille might have been . . ." More tears.

"Been what, Mademoiselle?"

"Been mobilized, Monsieur." Dabbing with handkerchief. Then: "And besides, the month mentioned in the note is so nearly up, Monsieur. I thought that he might perhaps have written to me that everything was all right and I might have missed his letter because of my train journey yesterday."

"But this morning you found that he was not there?"

"I knocked and rang, Monsieur. There was no answer."

I thought a moment. There were some things I wanted to learn. "Mademoiselle, up until three months ago, you say, everything was normal with you and Monsieur Binbonnet?"

"Oh, no, Monsieur. Not entirely normal toward the end. Even a little earlier than three months ago he had begun to act strangely. I knew that something was on his mind. It was three months ago that he told me we mustn't see each other until things straightened out."

"Now as to the concierge. First of all: you sometimes saw Monsieur Binbonnet here, at his office?"

"Very often, Monsieur. I am a stenographer by profession, and evenings I frequently came and helped Achille with his correspondence."

"Perhaps it was you, then, Mademoiselle, who typed out some of the letters from Monsieur Binbonnet to Pearce Brothers that I read in New York?"

"I typed many of them, Monsieur."

"They were most beautifully typed, Mademoiselle. I remember what unusually good letters they were. Monsieur Binbonnet expressed himself well, and the letters presented a very neat, expert appearance."

"Thank you, Monsieur." There was a slight smile; it was clear that even my compliments seemed quaint to Mademoiselle Denise.

"So three months ago you stopped coming here. At that time you were acquainted with this concierge, no doubt?"

"Of course, Monsieur."

"And was she always as amiable as she is today?"

"Oh, Monsieur! Today she has been unbearable! Insulting! She told me I had no business coming, that Achille wasn't in, that she knew nothing about him whatever; and when I insisted on going upstairs she shouted at me. I did go up, and I rang, and there was no answer. When I came down again she followed me right down to the street, evidently to see that I went away. I began to cry, and begged her to tell me something about Achille. . . ."

"But what I want particularly to know, Mademoiselle, is whether the concierge has always been like this."

"Oh, no, indeed, Monsieur. People often have to put up with a great deal in a concierge, but never with anything as outrageous as this. She was never an amiable woman, Monsieur, but today I was aghast at her behavior, outraged. When she lived downstairs she was never . . ."

"When she lived where, Mademoiselle?"

"Downstairs, Monsieur, on the street, like other concierges. That was before the building was remodeled, before the tape-and-braid shop was enlarged and the concierge moved upstairs."

At last I felt that we were getting some place.

"And when did this remodeling and moving take place?"

"It had just begun the last time I was here, three months ago, the day Achille told me I must not come again."

"Indeed." I remembered my first visit to 404 Rue Saint-Martin. I had been struck by the location of the concierge's quarters, and had facetiously wondered whether her surliness might be due to her isolation. That her behavior and her location were related I now had no doubt. It wasn't the fact that she was deprived of her former street-view that made her ferocious—even now I couldn't seriously think that—but her move upstairs and her increased savagery were certainly in some way connected. In just what way? She had been in the building for years. What had come over her? Had she been bought by the false Binbonnet, the man who was doubtless upstairs at this very moment, perhaps even peering down upon us from his window? That seemed the most obvious explanation. And what was the role of the tape-and-braid shop?

I glanced out, across the sidewalk. There was the tape-and-braid shop—not shop, really, but wholesale establishment. There was the concierge, standing staring at us. And there was the sign "A. Binbonnet" beside the door leading to the stairs. Three elements. How were they inter-related? The tape-and-braid shop, especially, so dreary and unremarkable-looking: what connection did it have with the concierge and with A. Binbonnet, whether the true or the false?

"You and the concierge were talking when I arrived here this morning, Mademoiselle. Could I ask you to tell me what you were talking about?"

"I was begging her to tell me something about Achille, and she was pretending that she knew nothing about him. That was what was so outrageous—pretending to know nothing about him! If you had not arrived, Monsieur, I think I should have gone to the police, even though I know I oughtn't."

I jumped on her, at that.

"But why oughtn't you, Mademoiselle? That is why the police exist, supposedly, to help people unjustly distressed by the behavior of others. Why shouldn't you go to the police, Mademoiselle?"

There was a shrug, but no other answer.

"Why not, Mademoiselle?"

I knew, I thought. She "oughtn't" to go to the police because Binbonnet had ordered her not to go. And since there was blackmail in this iodine mess, and since Binbonnet evidently dreaded the police, it seemed to me clearer than ever that he had been blackmailed into disappearing in favor of his impostor.

"Why shouldn't you go to the police, Mademoiselle?"

A shrug again.

"I have reason to believe that your fiancé is being persecuted by blackmailers, and I suspect that you know this, and that you know that is why Monsieur Binbonnet ordered you not to go to the police under any circumstances. Am I right?"

"I do not know, Monsieur." She could be very prim, Mademoiselle Denise. Very prim and very stupid.

"Remember that I represent Monsieur Binbonnet's best customer. I seek only his good. His well-being is of great importance to me. Remember that you can trust me. Now I ask you again: Why shouldn't you go to the police, Mademoiselle?"

"Achille would not want me to answer your question, Monsieur."

Now it was I who shrugged. "Well, if you don't want to help me try to find Monsieur Binbonnet . . ."

"Oh, but I do, Monsieur! There are things I cannot tell you, but I will do everything I can, Monsieur, to help you find him."

"But perhaps the only way you can help find is by telling. Can you tell me this, for instance: have you any idea of where Monsieur Binbonnet might be? Or, if not that, then is there any place where he might be known about, any place where you've been with him, for instance, where some information about him might be forthcoming?"

She appeared to consider that a most strikingly brilliant question, the dunce. "Why, yes, Monsieur, I do," she replied, wide-eyed as though with discovery, after a moment's reflection.

"Then let us go there at once," I said. "We have to start our search somewhere. I'll call the chauffeur. Where is the place? What is the address?"

"Oh, but it is not in Paris, Monsieur."

"Not in Paris? Then where is it?"

"Quite far away, Monsieur. Achille's mother—in Tours. Perhaps she can tell us something. Perhaps he is even there, with her."

Tours! Binbonnet's native town! "Detained at Tours on family business"—once again I recalled that phrase of apology from one of his letters. How carefully, evidently, the false Binbonnet had learned the facts of the true Binbonnet's life; how glibly he had replied, when I had asked him whether he came from Touraine, "From the city of Tours itself, Monsieur!" And the beauty of his French had made the statement convincing.

"Monsieur Binbonnet has a family in Tours?" I demanded.

"Only his mother."

"You have been there with him and met her?"

"Yes."

"We must go down, Mademoiselle, and talk with her. Will you accompany me to Tours, Mademoiselle? It may be of the utmost benefit to us both. When shall we go? If we went early tomorrow morning by train . . ."

"But I must work tomorrow, Monsieur. Today my vacation ends."

"Tomorrow is Friday. You work Saturday too, Mademoiselle?"

"No."

"For Tours we should start early in the morning, if we are to return the same night. Shall we go Saturday, Mademoiselle? Will you come to Tours with me on Saturday?"

I was all eagerness. To talk with Binbonnet's mother, to investigate the tape-and-braid establishment sometime when the concierge was not about to spy on me as I did so, to return also to 404 Rue Saint-Martin later today with the hope of taking the impostor by surprise: those were now certainly the things to do.

"You make plans quickly, Monsieur," Mademoiselle Denise was saying, when suddenly my attention was drawn to the concierge.

She had been standing motionless there all the time, arms folded, staring straight at us; now she was gazing beyond us, as though out into the street, and her gaze was moving, as though following something. I followed it, but could see nothing of interest. The street was as usual choked with trucks, and trucks lined the curbs; we were parked between two of them, in front of one and behind another.

And as I was searching to see what the concierge was looking at, two things began to happen. The truck in front of us began to move back slowly toward us, as though preparing to draw away from the curb and leave; and simultaneously, with signs of agitation the concierge rushed from where she had been standing to some point on the sidewalk ahead of us which was still hidden by the truck.

I lowered the window quickly. "Where is the concierge going?" I called to the chauffeur, who was standing there beside us. "What is she doing?"

He went to see; as he did, the truck ahead, having by its backward move apparently secured enough space ahead to enable it to pull out, began to do so; slowly it drew out from the curb into the thick traffic of the Rue Saint-Martin. Ahead of us, where the truck had been, was now an empty space; and ahead of that empty space there was another car.

It was the smart sport car, evidently just arrived. It was smart indeed, painted a light cream; one of its doors on the sidewalk side was open, and the concierge was standing beside it, talking with animation to whoever was inside, talking almost violently and gesturing in our direction. The departure of the truck also revealed our chauffeur, who was halfway between our car and the other, standing uncertainly, now watching the concierge, now turning toward us. Then suddenly, after particularly violent gestures, the concierge slammed the door of the sport car, there was a roar from its engine that was heard even above the noises of the street, a puff of blue smoke from its exhaust, and it began to move.

"Chauffeur, come back!" I called out the window. "Come back! Follow that car!"

He rushed back, jumped into his seat; in an instant we were off.

But that instant had given the sport car a good start; it was far ahead, weaving its way in and out among trucks and carts. We tossed and jerked as we hurried after it. "Don't lose it!" I cried. "We must not lose it!" The driver nodded grimly. There was a lucky empty stretch in the street; we roared ahead. If I had had any wonder as to who was in that sport car—any wonder as to the identity of at least one of its occupants, for how many there were I had no way of knowing—it would have been dispelled at that moment. There was a rear window in its canvas top, and peering out through the glass was the sagacious face I had seen the night before peering out another of its windows. From a distance it looked almost like a human face. Faust was looking back at us with a kind of venerable derision as his master sped the car. But then a truck came between; and when once again we caught sight of the car it was farther away.

So it continued.

I shall never forget, I think, that chase across Paris.

All the way up the Rue Saint-Martin to some boulevard; then to the left; then abruptly to the left again, returning south in the direction from which we had come. Past and between trolleys and busses, through the busiest, most commercial section of the city; over the river on a narrow, crowded bridge; through the entire other half of the city and finally out through one of the gates—just which gate I could not tell. We rubbed other cars; we ignored the commands of policemen; fortunately there are few traffic lights in Paris, and the car we were following knew how to choose streets on which there were none.

Most of my attention was given to the sport car far ahead, which our chauffeur was skilled enough to keep always in view. I tried not to notice any other car; I closed my mind to the ones we almost hit. Occasionally I stole a glance at Mademoiselle Denise. She was sitting silent and white. At one particularly bad moment I saw her make the sign of the cross.

"Why are we following that car, Monsieur?"

"Because I want to talk to the man who's driving it."

Out through the suburbs, going sixty and over when we could.

For half an hour we drove with scarcely a word.

Woods and fields began to take the place of houses. Ahead of us the cream-colored car was moving steadily; steadily we kept after it, the distance between us neither lessening nor increasing.

We were still going south.

"Where does this road go?" I finally demanded of the chauffeur.

"But that depends on how far you follow it, Monsieur." The reply would have been impertinent at another time; now it seemed the sensible answer. For following was what we were doing, and there was no telling how far that other car would go.

"What is the first big town, then?"

"Orléans, Monsieur."

"And then?"

"Unless we turn off, Blois."

"And then?" But I knew the answer.

"And then Tours, Monsieur."

Mademoiselle Denise gave a little gasp. I couldn't restrain a laugh at her. So I made my plans quickly, did I? Saturday had seemed a bit soon to go to Tours?

And I thought of Gerard—poor un-virile, persecuted Gerard, now weak from the quack's stomach-pumping, waiting in bed for me to return from my "errands."

And as I clutched the hand-strap of the swaying car I thought with a smile of the schedule for the future which I had so recently determined to adopt. Comfort amid turmoil, indeed! Thank God, at least, it wasn't a taxi I was in.

We drove on and on.

# CHAPTER 13

And the odd thing was that despite all the discomfort of the swaying and the rushing, and the effort I had to expend to keep myself braced and not fall all over the place, I was not finding it unpleasant, this ride. For years a ride in an automobile had been inconceivable; and as recently as a week ago the suggestion that I ride to Brest in the very car which I was now pursuing had filled me with dismay. But now that I found myself so unexpectedly on the highroad, traveling at times sixty-five or seventy, I felt no dismay at all, but a kind of exhilaration. For one thing, this was a chase. I was determined to catch that man in brown and talk to him, or at least to track him to wherever he was going. We were in the midst of doing something; and a taste for doing things was one that I seemed recently to have definitely reacquired. But even apart from that—just the riding it-self; I wouldn't have believed it, but it was good! Good to be driving! Good to be driving so fast!

A qualm did come over me at one point, when it occurred to me to wonder whether this chase might not be another example—even the crowning example—of my impetuousness and headlessness. The moment I had spotted that cream-colored car in front of us, and seen it move off as though in response to the concierge's vigorously ges-tured exhortations, I had determined to go after it. Since he had so fortuitously put in an appearance, it had seemed to me that the man in brown, subordinate though he was, was the man to go after. But was he? Would it have been wiser to wait, to see the false Binbon-net first, and get my showdown over with? That interview, almost certain to be fantastic, would also doubtless be most informative.

It was indispensable. Sometime it must take place. Shouldn't I have hung around the Rue Saint-Martin until I'd cornered my man and investigated the tape-and-braid shop besides, instead of rushing off on this chase?

But as I was wondering, we slowed up for a crossroad and as we slowed I read a sign: Tours 160 kilometres. That was the answer, it seemed to me. The lucky chance that the cream-colored car was almost certainly headed for Tours, where therefore it seemed strongly possible that the real Binbonnet was, justified my sudden decision to pursue it. The man in brown was taking me further away every minute from one of the Binbonnets I wanted to see, but every minute he was taking me nearer to the other one, or so I hoped. And if he was going to Tours, and if that proved the real Binbonnet to be there, why then how was Gerard's alarmism once more discredited! For not only had Gerard said that I was in danger, but he had also indicated his fear that Binbonnet had been done away with.

And the road-sign told me something else: our progress was actually as rapid as the rush of the landscape past the windows had made it seem. I knew that Tours was 150 miles from Paris; we had already gone fifty of them in a little more than an hour, plus however many extra miles it was that we had covered amid the traffic of Paris itself. Quite an average! Soon we'd be coming to Orléans, and there we'd see whether the car we were after turned off the Tours road or kept on it.

We had not been totally silent during that first rushing hour, Mademoiselle Denise and I. That she wasn't a particularly brilliant young woman, any more than an outstandingly attractive one, I had gathered during our conversation in Paris. Had she been brilliant, or even bright, it seemed to me, it would have occurred to her before this that something might be found out about her fiancé in Tours. She would have been there herself long ago. She would have spent her vacation there. That would have been sensible—keeping in touch, if not with her Achille, at least with his mother, to whom like most Frenchmen he was apparently a devoted son. It occurred to me to ask her where she did spend her vacation, and in a tone which showed that she knew I was merely making conversation because we happened to be thrown together she replied, "In Brittany."

"Indeed! What part, Mademoiselle?"

"Not far from Brest, Monsieur. A small village on the seacoast."

She appeared to have no idea that I should find this information in any way extraordinary.

But I did find it so. "It is so cold in Brittany at this time of the year," I said, trying to make my words casual as the car rushed us on. "Why didn't you go to some more temperate place, since your vacation was so late, or else to whatever part of France your parents come from, the way so many young people working in Paris do?"

"But my parents were Parisians, Monsieur." She made the sign of the cross.

"You lost them a long time ago, Mademoiselle?"

"I have been an orphan for many years, Monsieur. I have one brother."

"You are close to your brother?"

"Very close, Monsieur. We live together."

"And yet he let you go to such a dangerously cold place for a late autumn vacation? I'm sure Monsieur Binbonnet wouldn't have approved had you been in touch with him."

I said that banteringly, and the tone worked.

"But it was Monsieur Binbonnet who told me to go there, Monsieur!"

"Indeed?" I concealed my interest as best I could. "Monsieur Binbonnet sent you to Brittany? How did he do that, since you hadn't heard from him during the previous two months?"

"He had told me two months before—the last time I saw him. Told me just where to go, and just what to do."

"Just what did you do in Brittany?"

"Excuse me, Monsieur, but Achille asked me to tell no one."

"But, Mademoiselle! I'm sure it was for Pearce Brothers that you were acting. Monsieur Binbonnet would want me to know."

"That is true, Monsieur, but he will tell you himself."

"When?" I asked brutally. "When will he tell me?"

"Ah, Monsieur . . ." She didn't cry, though I almost hoped she would.

"It was iodine, wasn't it, Mademoiselle?"

"Excuse me, Monsieur, but you must not ask me any more about it."

I submit that it is difficult to keep one's temper with people like Mademoiselle Denise. To tell as much as she had told, and then refuse to tell more! Not to have the wit either to keep still altogether, or else to confide fully in me, since she herself admitted that I was the person most concerned! What could Binbonnet have had her do with iodine down there in Brittany?

"Tell me, Mademoiselle."

I pled with her.

She became more and more prim, her sedateness contrasting absurdly with the jolting and jouncing the car kept giving us both. "You must not ask me. It is business. Business is private."

I asked her about herself, hoping to get somewhere that way, and received another momentary shock when she said that she worked for the police. The shock ended as soon as she described her position; she was one of half a dozen stenographers in the office of the assistant to the department's buyer of materials. Nothing to do with any of the exciting sides of the department, and she said she was glad of it. I admired that. It was normal, and sympathetic to me, such frank pleasure at being distant from excitement that might be dangerous. How different from that kind but crazy waiter Pierre, and his expression of regret that he had received no wounds in his country's cause!

On the subject of herself, Mademoiselle Denise became quite uselessly talkative. The man she worked for, she said, the assistant buyer, was a "real pig." He "made promises and then broke them just to force you to give him something for making them again." If a girl "made the slightest request she always had to give some favor in return." I scarcely listened to her. I wasn't interested in her office gossip. Lots of stenographers have to do favors for their bosses to keep their jobs. A deplorable thing. But I didn't mind a bit that this young woman had to do favors. She wouldn't do any for me. Served her right to have to do them for someone.

I had scarcely noticed Orléans as we had hurried through it, past Joan of Arc's church. I had been pleading with Mademoiselle Denise. "He is keeping on the road to Tours, Monsieur," the chauffeur called back to me, when we'd got through the city.

"Don't lose sight of him for anything. We must follow him."

"I am doing my best, Monsieur."

It was past noon, but there was no question of stopping for lunch. The chauffeur sportingly shared with us the slices of sausage and bread and the red wine he had brought along, passing portions back to us as he drove.

I began to recognize things along the road. Lucille and I had come down here more than once—we had loved the châteaux of the Loire, as I had so naively told the false Binbonnet. One church tower in an old river town I remembered perfectly as we dashed by; and in Blois I peered up at the great castle on the hill. Lucille and I had climbed all through that.

After Blois came Amboise and another chateau, and as we rushed past a little inn on the riverbank I remembered that Lucille and I had stayed there. That was over ten years ago. Not since my arrival in France had I thought so vividly of Lucille; many memories were evoked that afternoon as we sped past one place after another that she and I had visited hand in hand. I won't deny that there was bitterness. And yet I enjoyed seeing these things again.

I was enjoying everything about my ride, except my aches and the prim stupidity of the girl beside me. On and on she went about the girls in the office, the strain of the work, the meagerness of the salary.

"What did you do in Brittany, Mademoiselle? Tell me."

"No, Monsieur."

It reminded me of trying to get Monsieur Gerard to tell his secret. The difference was that this time I didn't know the answer in advance.

And then suddenly, as I was staring out the window at a particularly beautiful, broad stretch of the Loire, paying but little attention to what she was saying, I distinguished new words. "I will tell you something about Monsieur Binbonnet, Monsieur."

I turned quickly. "You will? About what he had you do in Brittany, you mean?"

"Oh, no, Monsieur. Not about that. But . . . I really believe that you have Achille's interests at heart, Monsieur."

"I have indeed, Mademoiselle."

"Achille needs sympathy, Monsieur. He is an unhappy man. He is being . . . At one time he was victimized by a blackmailer, Monsieur."

"Oh?" Maybe coolness would warm her into talking, perverse little fool.

"But of course that was years ago, when he was scarcely more than a boy."

"Indeed!"

"The trouble is . . ."

"Yes?"

"The trouble is that lately the blackmailer has turned up again, Monsieur."

I grimaced politely. "How unpleasant for Monsieur Binbonnet. But does all this concern *me*, Mademoiselle? I can't say . . ."

"But Monsieur! Don't you see . . . ?"

Ah! Was she really going to talk?

"Achille had long thought the thing to be an affair of the past, Monsieur—the distant past: for years he had supposed that the blackmailer was dead. And now suddenly . . . Until lately I knew nothing about it. Only that day when Achille told me we mustn't see each other for the time being did he tell me the story. He said that everything would have to be in a 'state of suspense' until the blackmail business finally and unquestionably did become a matter of the past."

"What was the story that Monsieur Binbonnet told you, Mademoiselle?"

"Oh, Monsieur? I cannot give you particulars. Perhaps I shouldn't have told you even this much, but . . ."

"Tell me the story, Mademoiselle."

"No, Monsieur."

I glared at her. How maddening—how completely maddening—she was! Though I had to admit to myself that even from her irritating brevity I had gained something. I had gained corroboration—corroboration that was bare but certain. It was the blackmailer of Binbonnet, as well as of Gerard, that we were pursuing—a blackmailer who was speeding to see the man whom he had forced, or helped force, to retire. Though of course it wasn't known to Mademoiselle Denise that retirement and replacement had been effected.

"When Monsieur Binbonnet wrote you that all should be well in a month," I asked her, "what did he mean?"

"I have no idea, Monsieur."

"You mean you won't tell me?"

"I honestly don't know, Monsieur. I have wondered myself."

I believed her.

We weren't very far from Tours now. For quite some time I had already been feeling in my muscles and my bones the effect of the long ride. I had shifted from one position to another. I'd crossed my legs, I'd spread them straight out, placed them now apart, now close together. For a time I had let down one of the auxiliary seats and rested my legs across it. Now and again I had thought of taking off my braces. That's always a comfortable thing to do—after sitting a while the straps are apt to become tight and painful. But I hadn't dared to do it; without them it would have been impossible to keep myself in position at all; we were swaying and veering so, at our high speed, that I should have rolled from one side to the other and been flung to the floor at the slightest jerk.

Still, by now my muscles were aching so badly that I had to do something. I took my crutches up from the floor and began to experiment. First I put them under my arms, just as I do when I walk, and put my weight on them, bending forward and bracing the tips against the foot-rest on the floor. That eased some of my back muscles. But the jerking of the car made the crutches dig into my armpits so badly that I had to try something else.

Asking permission of Mademoiselle Denise, who was on my left, and apologizing to her for what she must have thought an additional example of American oddness, I took the crutches and laid them straight across us both—not touching us, but with each end of the crutches resting on one of the arm-rests of the car. They were just long enough to wedge there securely. This gave me a kind of crossbar on which I could lean. I could brace myself on that instead of with my legs. Now, if I wished to, I could take my braces off.

But we were so near Tours that I wondered whether it was worth while to go to the bother of unstrapping them and then soon putting them back on again; and it was as I was trying to decide this that the car slowed down. The highway ahead was closed for repairs. There was a barrier, with a detour sign pointing down a small road to the right. The sport car had followed the arrow, the chauffeur said, so we too turned to the right and proceeded as fast as we could. The road was narrow and poorly paved. For the time being I must keep my braces on, for the additional stability they afforded me.

It was a winding country road, and I kept peering ahead, hoping that the rounding of each turn would bring the sport car back into view. Finally we saw it. After one of the many bends we came upon a straightaway of several hundred yards. In the middle of the straightaway was a railroad crossing. In true French country style the red and white poles were down. One has to honk, in France, when one arrives at such a crossing, and call the attention of the guardian. On the other side of the crossing, parked beside the road, was the sport car.

Why was it parked? A bad tire, perhaps, or engine trouble? Could we now catch it even before getting to Tours? The chauffeur raced ahead, honking loudly for the guardian. And at our very first honk the sport car drove off. If we'd been near enough, I'm sure we should have seen Faust with his superior look staring at us through the rear window.

We honked and honked. No one appeared to raise the barrier. We stopped in front of it, still honking. We were tense, furious. Such a delay is quite common on remote roads in the French country-side. The guardian may be working in his garden, or milking his cow, or eating his dinner; he comes when it suits him. But that it should occur on an obligatory detour from a principal highway was outrageous. The chauffeur was fuming and muttering and honking. This was disastrous. Finally the gatekeeper appeared from around the corner of his little house, staring fixedly away from us as people do at such moments. Slowly he turned the handle. Slowly the poles rose. We dashed through. I glared. The chauffeur called out curses. We sped down the straightaway. Then around a curve. No car in sight, of course. He'd got a good start now. Quite possibly we'd lost him. But why had he waited there at the railroad until we'd come into sight? Why hadn't he taken full advantage of our handicap?

That was what we found out soon enough. After the first curve there was another straightaway, and down that we flew. Sixty, sixty-five, seventy. I peered and peered, hoping for a sight of the cream-colored car. In the distance was another curve. The man in brown must have rounded it, and I was just preparing to relax until we too had done so, since there was no chance of his being seen before that, when I saw the thing happen. I saw every detail.

There were fields on either side of the road, about a yard higher than the pavement; the road was a kind of narrow valley between them, with a ditch on each side. It was along that ill-paved valley that we were rushing, when suddenly, a hundred or so feet ahead, I saw a figure rise up out of the field on the right. Silhouetted against the sky, the figure raised its arm; something flew into the air, across the road. The figure rushed away. But after the missile, stick or stone or whatever it was, another figure leaped straight out of the field in pursuit. A huge, tawny figure, with four legs and a tail. It leaped down from the bank into the road—leaped directly down into us! For we were upon it in an instant. There was a scream of brakes; with a thud the superb leaping body struck our right front wheel; there was one brief, piercing howl. What with our great speed, and the speed and great weight of the catapulting body, the car shot sharply to the left, its two right wheels off the ground. We seemed to be poised, for a minute, in mid-air; and then, on the left of the road, halfway into the ditch, the car collapsed onto its left side.

There was a scream from Mademoiselle Denise, a shout from the chauffeur, the sound of broken glass. I was flung upon the girl. For a moment I didn't know how she was, but I knew that I was unhurt, and I continued to see everything perfectly. I could still look through the windshield. And through it I saw, pulling out of a side road a hundred feet ahead, a lane that came almost invisibly out of the fields, the cream-colored sport car. It pulled out into the road, straightened, and with a puff of blue smoke disappeared around the curve—towards Tours.

# CHAPTER 14

There was nothing miraculous, I suppose, in the fact that none of us was killed or even injured. No car had been coming in the opposite direction. Some chauffeurs are killed in auto accidents because they are pinned behind the wheel; others are protected and saved by the wheel. Ours was protected and saved. And Mademoiselle Denise and I were protected and saved in much the same way—by the firm cross-pole formed by my crutches, which held us back against the seats. The left shoulder of her coat, we discovered later, was torn a little by the broken glass of her window, and her legs were bruised by the metal of my braces. The chauffeur had a few scratches on his left hand. They easily clambered out through the doors—the doors that were now above our heads—though Mademoiselle had to pull herself out from under me to do it. Then together they reached in and pulled out me and my crutches, and got the seat-cushions out too, and laid them beside the road.

We all sat on the cushions for a few minutes. Little was said. There were mutual inquiries. Each one examined himself and the others for possible injuries. Cigarettes were lighted. I conquered a fit of trembling that suddenly attacked me. We were all saved. No human harm was done. Such luck! But why—why couldn't a little of that luck have come my way the last time an automobile . . . It was a surge of bitterness and sorrow and despair. To stop my trembling I clenched my fists, forcing my arms and hands to be still; then I pressed my hands to my face. That controlled it.

The chase was over. We had lost. The closed gate, evidently, had given the man in brown his devilish idea. Had he perhaps even tipped the gatekeeper to open tardily for us? At any rate, he had won. By now he'd be almost in Tours, picking up Binbonnet and taking him someplace where we'd never find him.

Impossible any longer to disbelieve in Gerard's certainty that murder was possible! Murder was not out of the picture. Murder—for a matter of iodine!

The chauffeur was the first to get up from the cushions. He had climbed agilely enough out of the car before, and had helped me beautifully; but now I could see that he had had time to wonder whether he really was all right after all. He stood up as though experimentally, moved carefully. Then, confidence returning, he began to examine the car. It wasn't a pleasant sight. Right front fender, right headlight, radiator and bumper bent and shattered by Faust. Right front tire ruined. And the entire left side, half in the ditch and invisible, probably quite mashed. The extraneous matter was unpleasant, too. Faust was all mixed up with everything. A few parts of him were on the highway, the rest caught up in the car.

No more would Faust threaten the false Binbonnet's cat! And the sight of his mangled body made me feel that the man in brown had been very desirous indeed of getting us—or at least me—out of the way; the deliberate sacrifice of a dog as splendid as Faust was impressive.

We had seen few cars on that country road, and at the moment of the smash there had been none in sight, and none had come since from either direction. I remember wondering at that. But it was a lull in traffic such as is found on any highroad, and on French highroads lulls are more frequent than on ours. Traffic is less heavy in France; there are fewer autos. But now they started coming from both directions. They all stopped, of course. Soon there were a dozen cars and several dozen people about us. Over and over again we were asked what had happened. We were congratulated. The amount of the damage was estimated. That so much could have been done by a dog was marveled at. Faust's weight was guessed at; two hundred pounds was thought to be most likely. Several ladies were indignant that we should have taken the life of such a valuable animal. We must have been going very fast, they said. They were right. Everyone wondered who the owner could be.

Mademoiselle Denise had not seen the thing happen, and the chauffeur, though he had seen the man throw the missile and run off, and the dog leap down in front of us, had not seen the sport car drive away. He didn't know who the thrower was, and I didn't tell him. I had no intention of telling anybody—yet. Someone, we said, had thrown something for the dog to chase, and that person had disappeared. To the chauffeur, to Mademoiselle Denise, and in fact to everyone except me, the story seemed most mysterious.

The car would have to be abandoned for the time being. The chauffeur would have to concern himself in Tours with police and garage matters. He took his papers, his bag of tools and other valuables, and we all climbed into the Citroen of a hospitable traveling salesman who was on his way to Tours. The chauffeur and Mademoiselle Denise repaid our host's courtesy by recounting every detail of the accident they could recall. I said as little as I could, but I wasn't let off entirely; eventually, of course, the salesman asked me all about my braces and crutches. It was only when I found how hard it was to collect myself sufficiently to tell him, that I realized how blurred my mind was, how terribly fatigued my body. For the entire remainder of the day I was as though in a daze.

With enormous effort, I determined a course of action. I decided to waste no time in Tours. Mademoiselle Denise and I would call on Monsieur Binbonnet's mother, if we could find her, and see what she had to say. I was pretty sure of one of the thing's she'd tell us—that her son had been there a few weeks and had just left. And that was probably *all* she'd say. Then we'd take a train back to Paris. With the man in brown and Binbonnet now unavailable, only the work in Paris could be done.

In Tours I asked the salesman to drive to a taxi-stand. Mademoiselle Denise and I transferred to a cab. The chauffeur seemed a little disappointed that I wasn't going to stick by him a little longer, and I didn't blame him. It would have given him at least moral support to have me with him when he made his report to the police; but that was when I particularly didn't want to be with him. He didn't need me for anything else. His company had a representative in Tours, and the matter would be arranged between the car-renting company and the insurance company. I'd get a big bill via the hall-porter of the Clarence—they'd see to that—and the payment of the bill would end the thing as far as I was concerned. I comforted the chauffeur a little out of my wallet and bade him good-by.

In the taxi, Mademoiselle Denise acted almost drunk. The excitement of the accident had apparently made her even more silly in the head than usual. She seemed to be convinced that now we would find her fiancé with his mother and that she would be reunited with him forever. I didn't disillusion her; she'd find out the truth for herself. And maybe the shock of it would induce her to tell me some of the things she had hitherto primly insisted on keeping quiet about.

She couldn't remember exactly, of course, where Madame Binbonnet lived. She knew approximately the part of town, and we cruised round and round, down one street and up another, as she tried to recognize a house-front. My suggestion that she look in the city directory, readily available at any café, she met with the merry assurance that she'd find the house "any minute." Finally, after a fruitless half-hour, I told the driver to go into a café and bring out the addresses of whatever Binbonnets he could find. He returned with one only, that of a Madame Binbonnet who Mademoiselle Denise said was the one we wanted. She laughed—as though she was thus shown to be right—when it proved to be just around the corner. To think that the fiancé of such a woman as Mademoiselle Denise was worth all this effort! I remembered the scorn that Gerard had expressed for Binbonnet's middle-class mentality and the poverty of his personality and taste. Now that I had become acquainted with his favorite, I sympathized with every word of it.

When we drew up in front of the address—a modest apartment house—I refused to get out of the car until I knew how many flights up Madame Binbonnet lived. "If she's up more than one, just visit her yourself, Mademoiselle, and find out what you can. Or else ask her to be good enough to step out here."

"I will bring Achille out to you, Monsieur."

"I hope you'll be able to."

I made myself as comfortable in the taxi as I could. I wasn't tired—I was exhausted. After a little while it became clear that Madame Binbonnet lived up at least two flights. I was glad of it; the effort of climbing even one flight appalled me—particularly since I knew the old lady could have nothing of interest to say. I even dozed off, there in the cab; for about twenty minutes I kept falling asleep and waking up. Finally I was wakened by the opening of the door. There was Mademoiselle Denise, red-eyed.

"Well, where is Monsieur Binbonnet?"

"He is gone, Monsieur! Gone, with that person I feared, barely an hour ago!"

"Then where is his mother?"

"In bed, Monsieur. She is old, Monsieur, and feeble, and distracted, and weeping that that person should have come back for Achille after so many years. She begged . . ."

I interrupted her to tell the driver to take us to the station. Then: "Tell me what Madame Binbonnet said, Mademoiselle."

"She begged that you would excuse her if she did not come out, Monsieur. And she said that it was a cream-colored automobile. . . . Oh, Monsieur, it was that car we were following, that was coming here after Achille?"

"Evidently. That is all she told you, Mademoiselle?"

"That is all, Monsieur. She was weeping so much, and was so distressed, and I wept, and did a few little things for her. She had not seen Achille for so long, and now to have him taken away after only a few hours, and by that person!"

What was this?

"Mademoiselle!"

"Monsieur?"

"What do you mean—'after only a few hours'? Has Monsieur Binbonnet not been staying here for several weeks?"

"Several weeks? Why, no, Monsieur. He arrived only this morning, and now so quickly . . ."

"Only this morning! Where did he come from?"

"From Paris, Monsieur."

"He has been in Paris all the time?"

"It would seem so, Monsieur."

Then his coming to Tours must be connected with something else, I knew instantly—with his scheme, whatever it might be, for clearing things up "in a month"—in other words, about now! That was why he had run from his captors to Tours at this particular time;

in Tours, evidently, he had planned some coup. And he had failed. He had been nabbed a few hours after his arrival and been taken away.

Well, now that ray of hope was gone.

I turned almost savagely to Mademoiselle Denise. "Now do you realize that Binbonnet is in danger? Now do you realize that there is no one to help him but you and me? And now will you tell me some of those things that I must know, if I'm going to be able to help at all? Will you, Mademoiselle?"

"Yes, Monsieur." And very tearful and meek she was.

"Then I'll ask you when we're on the train, and I'll thank you to tell me everything."

"I will tell you, Monsieur."

What a little fool! At the station I bought first-class tickets, so that I might enjoy the luxury of stretching out at full-length.

"Oh, Monsieur, you shouldn't buy a first-class ticket for me! Oh, let me travel third-class, Monsieur! It is quite unnecessary that . . ."

"And how do you propose telling me all the things I want to know, when you're in one class and I'm in another?"

Silence.

The train, due in Paris about eight, left Tours at five.

I ordered dinner almost immediately. We had cold chicken, and salad, and wine and cheese and fruit, all brought into the red-plush compartment and all tasting very good. Then we had coffee. And when that was finally taken away, and I knew we shouldn't be disturbed again, I told Mademoiselle Denise to talk.

First I had her tell me Binbonnet's blackmail story.

And as she told it I realized that for once Mademoiselle Denise couldn't be blamed for reluctance to talk: it was no laughing matter, Binbonnet's trouble.

In the summer of 1914, it seemed, just before the war, my unfortunate broker had graduated, at the age of 18, from the *lycée*, a kind of French junior college, in his native Tours. The course of study in such an institution had been a considerable luxury for him: even today in France the son of a not-too-well-off baker, which is what Binbonnet was, seldom gets that far with his education. To earn money while studying he had tutored fellow-students. He had given

French lessons—as so many people in Tours do—to young foreigners in the *lycée*, and had also tutored in mathematics, for which he had an aptitude. During his last year he had had one steady student in each subject: an intelligent young foreigner in French, and a stupid, rich, wild-living young Parisian in mathematics. The foreigner had passed his final examinations and graduated with his class, but the Parisian, despite Binbonnet's best efforts, had failed to get his degree.

A day or two after commencement there had taken place a traditional celebration—a picnic in a meadow beside the Loire held by the young citizens of Tours who had just taken their bachelors' degrees, and from which all other students—also by tradition—were rigorously excluded. This was Binbonnet's unlucky day. During the festivities he had gone off alone for a stroll into an adjacent wood, and there to his surprise had found lurking his unsuccessful mathematics pupil, not only drunk, but in resentful and belligerent mood. He was coming to the picnic, he asserted, tradition or no tradition, and when Binbonnet tried to dissuade him he burst out into an angry torrent of abuse concerning what he termed his tutor's incompetence and double-crossing. The more he talked, the more violent he became; finally, beside himself, he began to strike. In self-defense Binbonnet struck back; as the result of one of his blows the young drunk staggered and fell. As he dropped there was a dull sound and he lay still; his head had struck a sharp rock; he was dead. Shaken and terrified, Binbonnet returned to his companions, saying not a word about the encounter.

Several days later the young man's body was found; the police published demands that any witnesses come forward. Binbonnet remained silent, and eventually a verdict of accidental death was returned.

But what was Binbonnet's fright, shortly afterwards, to receive a visit from his other pupil, the young foreigner, who showed him a series of photographs of the fight in the wood! In the vicinity because he had determined to snap pictures of the class picnic, even though he himself was excluded from it, before returning to his native land, he had on his way to the picnic happened upon the encounter, and had snapped that instead.

It was a boyish kind of blackmail that he demanded—some spending money that he needed, whatever sum Binbonnet could scrape together. In return for it he seemingly destroyed all proofs and negatives, and the two of them drew up a childish written agreement to the effect that he was to make no future demands upon Binbonnet. The incident left Binbonnet pretty frightened, but it appeared to be closed—particularly when shortly after the foreigner had left France for his own land war broke out between the two countries. Binbonnet served in the French army throughout the war. I gathered from Mademoiselle Denise that he had felt a kind of gratitude to the conflict, and thrown himself into it fiercely: for Achille Binbonnet, at least, the World War had come at the proper time! And he had remained a patriot ever after: he was a member of various ex-servicemen's organizations, his fiancée said. How many men there must be in France—and elsewhere, too—like Binbonnet and Pierre! After the war he hadn't resumed his studies and trained for a profession like most of his classmates. He had chosen the obscure, mathematical, petty-bourgeois career of a broker, and had made his way with honesty and initiative.

For almost 25 years there was no echo of that fight in the wood. And then, suddenly . . .

Of course the young blackmailer hadn't destroyed all the pictures. Even Binbonnet, as time went on, had felt pretty sure of that. But there were so many million men killed in the war! That was the ironic thing: that the young foreigner should turn out not to be one of those millions—just as Binbonnet wasn't one of them either; and when he reappeared, as the man in brown in search of iodine and other commodities, there was no reason why the blackmail shouldn't be resumed—and in more serious fashion than it had been begun. There were the pictures, there was the absurd document which was signed evidence by Binbonnet that he had already once paid to keep the thing quiet. Binbonnet had disobeyed the law in not coming forward in answer to the police call for witnesses. Those photographs were ugly things. A lapse of time doesn't save one from prosecution for murder. Would, therefore, Binbonnet do as the man in brown ordered? Or would he prefer to stand trial and almost certainly lose, in the glare of the publicity that would come, at least the reputation and the business he had so carefully built up? It was indeed no laughing matter.

For six months, now, Mademoiselle Denise told me, he had been miserably doing his blackmailer's bidding, hatefully aiding a foreign country which was now once more the enemy of France. Mademoiselle Denise didn't know, and even now I didn't tell her, that Binbonnet had actually stepped out of his identity and allowed the man for whom the man in brown was working to usurp it.

Such was the story.

Sketchy though it was, it was intensely interesting to me, of course. Not so much for its mention of blackmail—further mention of that I no longer needed—but for its mention of the "young foreigner." He was a middle-aged foreigner, then, our murderous, blackmailing man in brown? I wished more than ever that I had asked Gerard about his suspicions concerning the destination of his iodine. For now I had my suspicions, too. I began to feel I had been somewhat naive in thinking of Faust as a typically French name for a dog.

"What was the nationality of this young foreigner, Mademoiselle?"

She told me what I was already sure of. A French name for a dog, indeed!

Then I made Mademoiselle Denise tell me what it was she had been doing in Brittany.

This she still didn't want to talk about at first, and I was afraid that after all I should have to reveal to her the distressing fact that her fiancé was being impersonated as well as persecuted. I should have done it, too, had it been necessary. But finally a certain amount of cruel emphasis on the danger he was in, on the unscrupulousness of the foreigner, and on her duty to tell me all so that I might do everything possible to save him, brought out her tears and broke down her resistance.

Quite simply, she had been buying up quantities of good iodine with her own savings and money that Binbonnet had given her, and having it stored in the places where she had bought it. Just as things had begun to turn bad, Binbonnet had located several hitherto unknown gatherers of excellent quality iodine. Ordinarily he would have signaled their stock to Gerard, who would have bought it himself and refined it as usual. But he knew that Gerard was affected by the new conditions too, and accordingly he had Denise buy up the stuff and put it aside, so that when things became normal again there would be a supply of good crude iodine on hand to be refined for Pearce Brothers.

"But this is most interesting to me, Mademoiselle, and casts nothing but the most loyal and favorable light on Monsieur Binbonnet. Why on earth couldn't you have told me this before?"

Well, Achille had told her not to.

"But to me, Mademoiselle; I am the most interested party."

"Achille didn't mention you by name, Monsieur. Besides, he wrote that things should be all right in a month—in other words about now. I am sure that he will soon be telling you all this himself."

"But he is in the hands of that foreigner, Mademoiselle!"

"That is true, Monsieur!" And she wept again.

Well, that was that. There was a supply of good iodine ready to be refined as soon as Gerard could release himself, or be released, from his bondage to the foreign blackmailer. Binbonnet was at this very moment in the hands of the blackmailer, and was also being impersonated by the blackmailer's boss. But up until today Binbonnet had thought that about now everything would be settled. What had he counted on to do the settling?

Mademoiselle Denise had told me her tales at considerable length, but such were her narrative powers that I think that even in the compressed form in which I've given them I've omitted nothing of importance. She was the most vapid variety of *raconteuse*; and besides, much of her time was taken up with weeping.

And when she had finally finished, and I was convinced that she had nothing more to tell me, I literally turned my back on her. I pretended to go to sleep. But I didn't sleep. I returned to what seemed these days to be my usual occupation. What to do next?

One thing was sure. It would be impossible for me to do anything very soon. Certainly not tonight, and probably not even tomorrow; for the simple reason that I was half dead as the result of what I had been through. The past weeks had been active; the past twenty-four hours a hallucination; the past twelve hours physical agony. No matter how I lay, on that first-class upholstery, I could not ease the aches that filled my entire body. I was done in.

So the investigation of the tape-and-braid shop would have to wait. And while I waited, why shouldn't I be nicely, quietly, and at last successfully assassinated? As I almost had been today. As I should have been, I now finally knew, had I accepted a ride in that smart sport car to Brest. Why not?

But there was, I thought, a good way out. It couldn't yet be said that murder was out of the picture, perhaps, but I thought I'd found a good way to keep from being murdered nevertheless.

I lay with my back to the irritating Denise until we were nearly in Paris. Then I sat up and told her I hoped she would keep in touch with me. I asked her for her address, and wrote out mine for her on one of my cards and gave it to her and she put it in her bag.

The train was pulling in. 'If you learn anything, Mademoiselle, tell me. Don't keep so much to yourself if you want Monsieur Binbonnet to get out of the mess he's in."

"I merely try to be discreet, Monsieur."

We arrived. I sent a porter for a wheel-chair and had myself rolled to a taxi. I dropped Mademoiselle Denise at her subway and went on to the Clarence. Now I'd astonish Gerard with my news.

# CHAPTER 15

I was so utterly exhausted when I arrived at the hotel, that for the first time I let the doorman bring out the wheel-chair that always stood just inside the front door and let him wheel me in it to my room. On my way I stopped at the hall-porter's desk. The man on duty was not the one who had been there when I had left the hotel in the morning, but he knew about my having rented the car and was all concern at my report of the accident. One of the reception clerks happened to be near, and he too expressed his concern, and before I reached the elevator the other clerks and the cashier had all come up to make sympathetic inquiries and congratulate me on my escape. That feature of life in a good hotel has always amused me. You go out in the morning to a cordial chorus of "good-mornings" from the staff, and you return ten hours later to an equally cordial chorus of "good-evenings" from a totally different set of individuals. The place is the same, but the people in it have all changed. And because they keep changing, they can always be cordial and interested when they see you. If they didn't change, if the same people were there all the time, they'd doubtless be unable to maintain even an appearance of cordiality or even courtesy for any length of time worth mentioning.

I speak of course of the average hotel employee. Not of such paragons of serviceability and indefatigability and courtesy as Pierre.

For that very night, as I came off the elevator at my floor, pushed by the porter, it was to see Pierre coming flying down the corridor to meet me. He had been on duty the night before, welcoming me and unpacking for me on my return from Holland, serving dinner for Gerard and me, and acting as assistant to that quack of a doctor after our return from the "café." He had served us our breakfasts that morning. And here he still was. Pierre, it seemed, was always on duty. They had phoned to him from downstairs, to say that I had had an accident and was on my way up; they had neglected to say that I wasn't hurt, and the breathlessness of Pierre's "Thank Gods" took me somewhat by surprise. Clearly I was a favorite. He took charge of me at once and wheeled me to my room, and on the way didn't fail to apologize formally for his undignified expression of relief. I told him merely what I had told downstairs, that a Great Dane had run into the wheel of the car as we were traveling at high speed. And I asked him to knock on Gerard's door and tell him I had returned and should like to see him.

"But Monsieur Gerard has gone, Monsieur."

"Gone! Gone where?"

"He has returned to his home, Monsieur. Here is the note he left for Monsieur."

I took it and tore it open. "I regret that business demands my return. May I wish you good fortune?" The coward! He considered me to be in the gravest danger, and yet he fled! I knew why he had gone; the length of my absence had alarmed him, and he'd thought it wise to absent himself from the scene of any possible unpleasantness. What a coward! I knew better than he; I was pretty sure that I was not in danger—now. But, believing me to be in peril, he had nonetheless deserted me. A gentleman perhaps, but a lily-livered individual certainly. But it was scarcely surprising, was it? A man who would weakly give in to a blackmailer instead of fighting—?

Well, that was cooperation. Now I should have to proceed quite alone.

I asked Pierre to open a window, pull the curtains and leave me. I took off my braces, but for the first time in my life I didn't manage to get my clothes off and my pyjamas on. I fell fast asleep half-undressed, with the lamp still lighted beside me, and slept uninterruptedly till morning.

And when I awoke, it was to an instantaneous realization of two things. One was that my muscles were still aching so furiously that any immediate activity was out of the question. And the second was

another of those sudden dawnings—results of my poor thinking—
that had recently been bursting on me at incongruous moments.
Like my tardy certainty that Pierre had drunk some of the Vouvray.
Like my remembrance, as I had set out that morning in the hired
car, that I hadn't asked Gerard about his suspicions concerning
the iodine's destination. What now swept over me, the moment I
opened my eyes, was the realization that I didn't know what the real
Binbonnet looked like. I wouldn't know him if I saw him. Probably
Mademoiselle Denise had had a photograph of her fiancé with her.
Certainly Madame Binbonnet possessed one. And I hadn't thought
to ask to see it! It would be well, to put it mildly, to provide myself
with a likeness of the gentleman, in case I were by chance to run into
him. A picture of Binbonnet would be a good thing to have.

Still, there was one thing that I needed far more, at that particular moment, and I knew just what it was—a massage.

I rang for breakfast. What a disappointment, when it came, to
find that Pierre wasn't with it! "Pierre is off duty?" I asked his young
colleague and subordinate. Heaven knew there was every reason
that he should be off duty. I was surprised by the sharpness of my
disappointment at not seeing him.

"He is, Monsieur. He particularly instructed me to tell Monsieur,
if Monsieur asked for him, that he would return by four o'clock this
afternoon at the latest."

A trifle odd, wasn't it, for a floor-waiter, even Pierre, to leave
such a message for a guest in a hotel? On the familiar side? And yet,
I should not have received the message hadn't I asked my question;
if I hadn't inquired, Pierre's colleague wouldn't have spoken. I was
glad to know when Pierre would be back; it was considerate of him
to have made it possible that I should know. And yet—there was
something at the very least . . . unusual. . . . And it was even stranger
what a different place the hotel seemed this morning without Pierre.

I ate my breakfast and read the papers and telephoned down to
the hall-porter and asked him to send up a masseur. He deluged me
with regrets and congratulations on my accident. The masseur came
about eleven. Then I slept some more, and woke feeling less sore,
and lunched in bed, and about two o'clock decided to get up.

I'd tackle the tape-and-braid shop today after all.

By now the tape-and-braid shop was my last hope for Instruction No. 1, and indeed I was almost back at the opinion that Instruction No. 2 was my only course. Whether I'd find anything in the shop was problematic. It had been enlarged at the moment when the concierge had been moved; that was all I knew about it. It was perhaps a perfectly innocent, independent establishment. That was what I wanted to find out.

As to the false Binbonnet, I was decidedly not going to risk seeing him. And I wasn't going to risk being seen by the concierge. Because I didn't want any more murderous attempts to be made upon me.

When, exactly, had the attempts at murder been made? The first one, the attempt to lure me into the sport car, had been made when I had undertaken to go to Brest. And the second, the fiendish sacrifice of Faust, had been made when I had undertaken to follow the sport car to Tours. In other words, they had first tried to kill me before I would see Gerard, and then tried again as a means of keeping me from the true Binbonnet.

It was only when I had made positive efforts to contact my two principals that my enemies had struck.

Therefore, it seemed to me that if I now desisted from such efforts, they would desist from theirs. And it seemed to me that if I let them know that I was desisting, I could live without fear. For instance, if I were to write a letter to Achille Binbonnet, 404 Rue Saint-Martin, saying that I was disappointed and discouraged by the lack of cooperation that I had received from him and Gerard since arriving in France, that Pearce Brothers had no further confidence in them, and that I was definitely breaking off relations and transferring my patronage to other sources, it seemed to me that such a letter would do double duty. It would tell them what above all they must long to hear—that they could go about their business without further interference from me. And, in so informing them, it would assure my safety. There would be no further reason for murder. They wouldn't murder me in cold blood just because I had accidentally learned of the substitution of the false Binbonnet for the true; that was a Gerard exaggeration. Now that I'd lost the chase to Tours I was safe, I felt, until I took another step. But if my next step was to say that I was withdrawing entirely—that I wasn't going to take any more steps—then I'd be safe once and for all.

That was what I had figured out on the train, coming back from Tours. I was in danger just so long as I kept taking positive steps, and no longer.

It meant, of course, not seeing the false Binbonnet—not having my showdown with him. Seeking a showdown might well be construed as a positive step. It meant the abandonment of the true Binbonnet; too bad about him—he'd have to look out for himself. It meant discontinuation of any relations with Gerard, the coward and deserter. It meant, in short, the end of Instruction No. 1.

Except for the one remaining hope: the tape-and-braid shop. A visit there, I thought, could be safely managed. I would drive rapidly past No. 404 in a taxi, looking to see if the harpy was standing out in front or if anyone was in Binbonnet's window. If not, I'd have the taxi turn around, and I'd get out and go into the shop and see what I could see. Even that was dangerous, of course. I'd have to have the taxi waiting for me with its engine running, in case I had to get away in a hurry. I'd stay near the door. And in case I was spotted by the concierge or by the impostor, or in case I felt that the visit would be reported to one or the other of them, I'd hurry home and save my skin by writing the letter and having it delivered immediately.

But before writing the letter I'd try the shop. Something there might just make it unnecessary for me to write the letter at all. Something there might still save Instruction No. 1.

I began to get dressed. And as I did so I realized that the massage had perhaps helped me a little, but had certainly not helped me enough. It was all I could do to get my clothes on. It was so painful to lean over and fasten the laces of my shoes and the straps of my braces that I gave actual cries several times, and when I was finally ready I felt as exhausted as I had the night before. Quite impossible for me to walk to the elevator; I could only hope that getting in and out of the taxi would limber me sufficiently to walk into the shop.

I phoned down for the wheel-chair.

The *bagagiste* who brought it up—not the man who had wheeled me the night before—both commiserated with me and congratulated me on the accident, and down in the lobby the entire daytime staff crowded around me and did the same. Several times I had to tell how the dog jumped; how large he was; how much he must have weighed; the damage he did. I felt more and more fatigued. Finally my sympathizers melted away; in my chair I was being wheeled out toward the front door; and suddenly—well, I realized that I could not go through with it.

I was simply too utterly exhausted. I ached all over. My legs trembled when I thought of using them. My arms trembled when I thought of lifting myself into the taxi. And besides, I was, quite simply, afraid. Afraid to take that last possible step. Suppose I was spotted; there was no doubt what they would try to do, and do quickly, the man in brown, the false Binbonnet, that concierge, the whole merry crew! And this time they might well succeed! Despite all my planning, I could not go. How far was this from my bravado with Gerard and the calm confidence that had followed it!

I told my pusher I had changed my mind. He asked if I wanted to go back to my room. I did not. I felt lonely, lonely for everyone—for the people in New York, both the living and the dead. And absurdly, I felt lonely for Pierre. To sit in my room, all by myself, knowing that Pierre was not there on the floor to serve me—I couldn't bear it. His perfection as a servant, his kindness as a human being, crackpot though he was—those I felt need of. I was weak, exhausted. I wanted to be near someone who could help me if I needed help. But it wasn't four yet, and until four Pierre would be away.

I told the pusher to take me to one of the comfortable chairs in the lounge and to leave me there and have someone bring me writing materials. People were always coming in and out of the lounge, and from my chair I could look out into the busy lobby. The writing materials came. Immediately I began my letter.

And then, for a moment, I interrupted it. Why not the police, after all? Would that not be the intelligent course? But even apart from my disinclination, apart from the incalculable complications that would ensue, it seemed to me it would not be intelligent. For one thing, Binbonnet and Gerard would probably deny that there was any blackmail. Binbonnet might well be instantly assassinated were I to divulge his story. Gerard probably wouldn't be killed—he was too valuable a man; as producer he was necessary, whereas an agent can always be replaced—as indeed Binbonnet had already been replaced. Gerard would certainly deny that there was any blackmail, for the ground of his blackmail was not one to be admitted to the police; it was something to be admitted, if at all, in privacy, to priest or psychiatrist, someone who one felt might be of comfort or assistance. No—the police would not work. And besides, I retained my old objection: I was not in France on a police matter.

I resumed my letter—my letter to Achille Binbonnet, which I knew was not going to Achille Binbonnet at all, but to someone whose name I didn't know and should probably never know. I wrote it, announcing in definite terms that I was breaking off relations, withdrawing from the field. And I had the hall-porter come in, and I gave it to him with instruction to deliver it by hand at once. He promised to send a boy instantly. I told him to have the boy take a taxi if it would be faster; I wanted it delivered right away. And I wanted to be told that it had been delivered. He promised. I felt much better after that. The thing was finished. I had failed completely at Instruction No. 1. But at least I was through with that sinister crowd. And in a day or two, when I felt better, I'd start trying to obey Instruction No. 2.

It had been two o'clock when I'd decided to get up, and by the time I'd sent off my letter it was after three. I wanted to stay in the lounge until Pierre would certainly be upstairs. I had a cup of tea brought in. I looked over some magazines. The chair was comfortable; it was a little like being in a comfortable bar, with people coming and going.

Someone came in and pulled the curtains and turned on the lights; it was one of those early-dark days—night seems to fall faster in Paris, in late fall and winter, than anywhere else. So much overcast sky and mist, I suppose. About four the porter's boy came in and told me the letter had been delivered. I stayed there a little longer. Then I had the man come with the wheel-chair again. As we passed the desk I asked them to phone upstairs as they had the night before, and have Pierre meet me at the elevator. I felt ashamed of this dependence, but I was too tired not to give way to it. We got in the elevator.

# CHAPTER 16

But Pierre did not meet us.

As we emerged from the elevator it was Pierre's young colleague, he who had brought my breakfast and lunch, that came hurrying down the corridor. He was an excellent waiter too, and a pleasant and helpful young fellow, but he was not Pierre. It impressed me even then, and struck me as inexplicably foolish, the way my heart sank at the sight of him. "Pierre is not here?" I demanded.

"No, Monsieur. Pierre's service does not begin until five o'clock."

"But he said he would be here by four at the latest, and now it's after that," I complained petulantly. "You yourself told me he said he would be here by four."

How trying it must be for hotel people when guests are cranky and whining about trifling matters. But the young waiter was perfectly courteous, even apologetic. "That was indeed the message he gave me for Monsieur. But his plans must have changed. His service does not begin until five."

How suspicious I was today! How quickly I had thought it odd that Pierre should have left a message for me in the first place. And now, how definitely I felt there was something not straightforward in what this young waiter was telling me. There had been a look in his eye, for just an instant. . . . But it was absurd, of course. I was half dead with fatigue and upset in my mind over the total collapse of Instruction No. 1. I mustn't begin suspecting everyone I met of being a liar. "Then would you be good enough to take me to my room?" I asked. "I shall rest until Pierre returns." An odd way for me to put it. Why should a guest in a hotel ever have occasion to say that he'd rest until the return of one of the waiters? If others were bizarre, how bizarre was I myself getting to be! But the young waiter gave no indication of finding me queer, and merely took over my chair from the *bagagiste* and wheeled me down the corridor and into my room.

There I had him stand by and help me get into bed; I was afraid that no more than the night before was I capable even of undressing myself. He pulled the curtains and opened the bed; as I took off my clothes he placed them for me on a chair; he handed me my pyjamas. I had dropped my crutches and braces on the floor: "Where shall I place these . . . these . . . *objects*, Monsieur?" he sensibly inquired. That is, it was sensible of him to inquire since he *had* to inquire. Pierre had never had to inquire. I remembered my very first day at the hotel, when without a word he had taken the braces and crutches from where the chambermaid had left them and placed them next to my bed. It was during my first annoyance at Monsieur Binbonnet for having no telephone, I remembered. Now I indicated where the things should go. The young waiter asked me whether there was anything else that I desired. I told him to ask Pierre to come to see me as soon as he came on duty. That would be in about half an hour. He promised to do so, and departed, saying he'd leave the wheel-chair outside in the hall.

I turned out my light and sank back in bed. It had been freshly made up that day, and I remember how delicious the smooth new sheets and pillowcase felt.

I had been crazy, to think of returning to the Rue Saint-Martin and snooping around that tape-and-braid shop. Crazy to think of doing it at all, considering the insoluble mess the whole thing was, the dangerous maze it had been. And particularly crazy to think of doing it today, when I was so weak that I'd been barely able to dress and hadn't even dared undress alone. I was well rid of Instruction No. 1! Little had Al and Jim realized, when they had come to lunch that day and given me their ultimatum, what they were getting me in for; they would turn a bit pale, I imagined, when I told them! Now all that was past, thank God. The letter was sent. Sent and received.

I was in no state to do anything for a few days. Coming as they had on top of all my other activities, the adventures of the trip to Tours had put the quietus on me for some little time to come. And once again I thought ironically of the motto I had chosen for myself as I had begun to luxuriate in that hired car: Comfort amid turmoil. Well, now at least I could discard one half of that motto and keep the other, the good half, for my own: just *comfort*. I was comfortable now, stretched out in the Clarence's excellent bed. And comfortable I intended to remain. Soon Pierre would come in. We'd have a bit of conversation. Perhaps without asking me he would make a fire in the fireplace, or have one made. He would suggest tea. After tea I would rest or read. Then he would return and I'd choose a few dishes for dinner. As he served me we would converse some more. Then I'd read a little longer, if I could, and sleep the clock around. For several days I would rest. And then, at a comfortable pace, I'd set about finding new iodine somewhere—new iodine which could be bought from non-crazy people in a businesslike way.

There was only one thing doubtful in this program, and that was at the very beginning. Would I be able to stay awake until five, when Pierre would be coming? I was so very comfortable, and so very, very tired. . . .

And it was just at that precise moment, when it occurred to me that in half an hour I might well be fast asleep, that something else occurred to me that not only chased every thought of sleep out of my mind, but made me sit bolt upright in bed, my muscles twinging as I did so. I began to tremble. I began immediately to sweat. For—this was the fourth, and the worst—oh, much the worst!—of my flashes that came from my bad thinking: *I was not out of danger at all.*

I had told myself that any attempts against me had been made when I was in the act of taking definite steps. Going to Brest, going to Tours. But no. That simply wasn't so. One other attempt—an attempt all memory of which had left my mind during the turmoil of the last 24 hours—had been made when I was doing nothing—nothing at all.

The telephone call that had come for me, that afternoon following my return from Brest, preceding my departure for Holland. I had known it was "Binbonnet," and hadn't wanted to speak with him, and hadn't answered. And the operator had told me that the caller had left no message, not even his name. And "Binbonnet" had denied having called. But he had called. It had been he. I knew it. In all of Paris there was no one else to call me. He had called *to see if I was in*. And the next morning, when I had talked with him, he had asked to come. The man in brown had ordered Gerard to stay away from Paris for five days. Had I not gone to Holland for those five days an attack would certainly have been made upon me. Made at a time when I was taking no steps whatever, when in fact I had just returned from Brest, where the man in brown and his boss well knew that I had accomplished absolutely nothing!

So that Gerard was, after all, entirely right. Following the discovery that the wine had not been poisoned, I had thought him silly on the subject of murder, a complete alarmist. And then, following the attempt to kill me on the road to Tours, I had had to recognize that he was partially right—that they were capable of trying to kill me when I was taking a step that they didn't want me to take. But now—now that I remembered that telephone call, that effort to discover whether I was in so that a visit might be paid me—now I had to admit that Gerard was utterly right. From the beginning they had simply wanted to get me out of the way. And since my discovery that the man who called himself Binbonnet was an impostor, they must have been more determined than ever to do away with me. My letter of withdrawal, the writing and sending of which had made me feel so much better, would not affect them at all. Why should it? Why should they believe it, for one thing? Why shouldn't they suppose that I had written it as a blind, an attempt to appease them while I continued to carry on my investigations, possibly with the police? Why shouldn't they make another attempt against me, now, at this very minute? How could I have been so stupid as to think that with such men as that against me I could simply retire unscathed from the field?

I sat there in the dark. And now panic did come over me, and enfold me, and put me almost out of touch with my senses. Away at the back of my mind was the thought—a tiny, glowing thought amid all the black terror—that soon Pierre would be coming, that we should be conversing. That I could perhaps tell all this to him, even though he was only a waiter; that he, perhaps, would insist on phoning the police—the police, who would after all afford me security, who were after all, or should be, a refuge for desperate, unhappy, persecuted, hunted men. The thought of Pierre was there. But everything else was confusion, a sort of helpless whirling of the mind.

And then, in the very midst of the whirling, when apart from that steady thought that Pierre would be coming I was unable to put together a single clear reflection or idea, there came the sound that I was waiting for. The knock at my door. The gentle knock that always announced Pierre.

For a moment I could not reply; my mind couldn't find the word to use, the word "*Entrez*" to call out. But no matter; Pierre's gentle knock was always quickly followed by another sound—the sound of his master-key in the lock. And now came that welcome sound, too. The sound of the key in the lock, and the soft sound of the door opening. "*Entrez!*" I finally managed to cry, my whole being bursting with relief and thankfulness. "Pierre, turn on the light, please, I am not asleep!" But there was a silence, and the light was not turned on. "Pierre! Is it you?" I raised my arm to turn on the lamp beside my bed, but before I could reach it the entire room was illuminated. And it was not Pierre that I saw.

Men who know their last moments have come, one hears it said, see their entire lives pass before them in review in their mind's eye. And I have told enough of the life I had lived, before coming to France, to indicate what should have been some, at least, of the things to take shape in my mind when, sitting up there in bed, bathed in the sweat of fright and dazzled by the brightness of the light, I saw standing in my room, side by side, perfectly motionless and perfectly silent, the impersonator of Monsieur Binbonnet and the man in brown.

But I thought of none of the things I should have. I didn't think of my parents, or my childhood, or of the war, or of Lucille, or of Caroline, or of that afternoon on the coast road below Santa Barbara. I thought of one thing: that my panic had disappeared in a flash. "It takes a murder to kill a panic," I remember foolishly thinking. And I thought of the letter I had written barely two hours before. "But I wrote to you," I heard myself saying—in a voice which I confess didn't sound like my own. "You got my letter, didn't you? The letter in which I said I was withdrawing from the field?"

The man in brown pointed to my crutches and braces standing there beside my bed, and said one word. "Binbonnet." And "Binbonnet" came quickly over and took the braces and crutches away, put them far out of my reach. And then the man in brown spoke to me. "Yes, we received your letter, Monsieur Weavair," he said, with a little laugh. "Thank you very much for it. It was your letter, in fact, which told us that we should probably find you in."

"I see." A good idea of mine, that letter!

I could not see the face of the man in brown. It was covered with a white handkerchief. Only his eyes showed, between the handkerchief and the brim of his hat. He was in a brown overcoat, too, and he held his right hand in a way that didn't surprise me; he kept it in his overcoat pocket. I looked at him intently. This was the man I had hitherto only glimpsed. The blur of brown I had seen through the doorway of Binbonnet's office. The brown back I had seen in the "café." The figure I had seen silhouetted against the sky of Touraine, throwing the stick or the stone for Faust to leap after. And now, as before, all I could see was brown. But this time I could hear something. I could hear his voice; and it was a voice that told me things. What a beautiful voice! What pure French! I should have believed this man in brown, had I had converse with him in the past and had he told me that he came from Touraine. For was it not from poor Binbonnet, who was truly from Touraine, that this man had learned to speak? Mademoiselle Denise had told me about that; his voice proved her story true.

And poor Binbonnet was now himself being impersonated by the sleek-haired, loud-cravatted, beringed man standing here beside the man in brown, this impostor who himself spoke such deceptively beautiful French. He wore nothing over his face, this false Binbonnet. Today he didn't even wear that sad, somber expression that had so struck me when last I had seen him, which had contrasted so oddly with the dandyish gaudiness of his allure. Now he appeared nervous, excited. Not his manner—just his expression. His eyes, mostly. His eyes looked eager. And why shouldn't they? They were going to see the last of me, weren't they? That was what my two visitors were here for, wasn't it?

Why didn't they speak again, or move?

Oh, for Pierre! Now, more than ever, oh, for Pierre! It was five o'clock, even a little after; he must have arrived, he must be in his pantry, just a few feet down the hall. So near and yet so far! If only he would come—and, this time, if only he wouldn't knock as he came, just open the door silently and come in. And, as he came in, with his quick wit do something. Something. Anything. Take in the situation at a glance. Rush at the man in brown. Ring a bell. Make a noise. Why had Pierre not come? Was it because he couldn't? My visitors had opened my door with a key. Was it Pierre's key? Had they visited Pierre first? Was Pierre indeed in his pantry—but bound, perhaps, or even—dead?

Now Binbonnet's impostor was looking at the man in brown, looking at him with those eager eyes, the way a dog looks at his master in eager beseeching for an order, for the signal to go. And the man in brown, evidently, judged that the time had come. "*Allez-y*, Binbonnet," he said. "Go to it, Binbonnet."

And "Binbonnet" went to it.

Out of a pocket of his overcoat he took a small glass flask, and uncorked it and held it out to me. I recognized it at once. I had seen one just like it break into a hundred pieces on the floor of my compartment in the night train to Brest. And when he spoke—for the first time—his voice was as eager as his eyes. "Drink, Monsieur." He spoke quite loudly—as loudly as he had spoken to me in his own office.

He held the flask out for me to take. So here was another question finally definitely answered! That brandy had been dangerous! The wine had not, but the brandy had. Why was that? Why should one of those bottles have been dangerous, whereas the other . . . They had arrived together, hadn't they? Both sent by this pretended Binbonnet. . . .

And something else: it was the man in brown who was giving the orders! It was the man in brown who had pointed to my crutches; the man in brown who had said, "Go to it, Binbonnet." And it was the other who had obeyed; certainly it was the man in brown who was the boss, not this person who had received me so oddly in his office, this person who had lied about his telephone and about Gerard. This person was not a boss but an underling; the man in brown was on top!

And still one thing more: the man in brown was calling him Binbonnet. Binbonnet was the name he went under, of course, but wasn't it odd for his confederate to play the game so completely as to *call* him Binbonnet? Call him Binbonnet himself, knowing not only that the man was not Binbonnet but that *I* knew he was not? Was that not a little queer?

This sudden idea that surged over me! Was it possible, was it conceivable, that . . .

But: "Drink, Monsieur Weavair." It was the second command to drink. And this time the eyes were more eager; the facial expression was more strained; the voice was definitely louder.

And at that second command to drink, the strain upon *me* became so intense as to make me wonder whether it was possible for me to bear it.

For as I sat there in my bed, facing the man in brown with the handkerchief over his face and his hand in his pocket, and facing the man who was holding out the bottle of poison and telling me to drink it, a door directly in front of me began noiselessly to open. I saw it from the moment it started to move, for I was staring straight at it. It was the door communicating with the room in which Gerard had slept. The second door—the one controllable from that other room—had been opened noiselessly; the bolt on *this* door, the door controllable from my room, must have been left pushed back, and now it was this door that was swinging open, swinging open into my room, behind the two men who were facing me. And as the door opened, someone came into view. And it was not the sight of the gradually opening door that so moved me as to make it all but impossible for me to control my features and not give the whole thing away. And it was not the sight of the person whom the opening of the door revealed. It was what that person was holding in his hand that worked upon me so excitingly as to make me feel I could only break under the strain.

It was not Gerard who was standing silently in the door. Gerard had fled to Brest when things had begun to look dangerous. No; it was the person whom above all others I had wanted to see. It was Pierre. And Pierre was holding a gun.

Pierre's gun! The permit had come, the permit which had taken so long! It had come, and he had bought the gun—the gun whose purchase had made me so uncomfortable in advance! When it came, I had decided, I should be more comfortable out of this hotel; and Pierre had promised to let me know when he got it. This was his way, evidently, of telling me. But how . . . ? Why . . . ?

He stood there, his face expressionless. Had he gestured toward me, or tried to convey some message with his hands or lips or eyes, all would have been lost. Inevitably I should have responded. But he was not looking at me at all. He was staring fixedly at the back of the man in brown, and it was toward some spot on the back of the man in brown that he was slowly pointing his new gun.

"Drink, Monsieur Weavair!" It was the last warning, I knew. Of such warnings there are conventionally three. This was the third. Now another gun was moving. The gun of the man in brown was out of his pocket, and was moving up so that it pointed at me. I could look straight into the muzzle Strange, to think of something coming rushing right out of that hole, straight into me!

I know that nothing in my life ever has, or ever will, cost me as intense an effort as the thing I did then. I shall never forget the day I first put on my braces, for example, and first locked them and tried to walk in them. That called for effort. But this other thing called for more. I answered the man who was telling me to drink poisoned brandy so that his companion wouldn't have to shoot me. I made the effort of answering because I knew I could no longer continue the even greater effort of controlling myself as I watched Pierre standing there with raised gun.

"Hell, I know that stuff's poison," was what I said. "Do you expect me to commit suicide?"

That was just what they did have some faint expectation of my doing, of course. But even so they were surprised by my words. "Binbonnet" looked up in helpless bewilderment at the man in brown. And the man in brown was surprised for an instant, too. No longer could I look straight down the barrel of his gun. But that was only for a second. He immediately raised his arm again, took deadly aim; he raised his other hand to his face—or rather to the handkerchief that covered it; I flung myself to one side; there was an explosion, deafening and detonating.

But it was from Pierre's gun that wisps of smoke were coming.

The man in brown seemed to have received a violent push from behind. His hat flew off. He stumbled. He flung his arms into the air, tossing his gun away as though carelessly as he did so. He fell forward onto the red carpet. Not flat on his face, but with his head twisted to one side. His handkerchief was not disarranged. Only—it was no longer very white. And the carpet, too, began to darken.

And as he fell, something else fell. The man who had been holding the brandy flask could hold it no longer. He dropped it. It fell softly onto the carpet—a very different fall from the fall in the sleeping compartment! The brandy flowed out darkly, making an almost black stain on the red.

That made two stains.

And the man who couldn't hold the brandy couldn't seem to hold himself. His knees sagged. He sank into a chair, uttering the strangest sigh. For a moment I thought that he had fainted.

But then from his crumpled position Binbonnet sighed again.

For, evidently, "Binbonnet" was Binbonnet, after all.

Pierre was wiping his forehead.

# CHAPTER 17

I had seen the coming of death before. In the hospital in France I had often watched its approach. And at one other time, though I had not seen it, I had been beside it as it came, and I knew its aftermath.

But never before had I seen it come like this.

And even stranger than the fact that I should be seeing it come like this now, was what the sight of it brought.

A visitation of clear-headedness and energy descended upon me. Even as it came I knew it wouldn't last; it was one of those tricks the nerves can play. But, while it was there . . .

I flung the quilt from my bed over the figure on the floor. It was a yellow quilt, I remember, bright yellow sateen. Nice to cover up some of that red, I thought, and to hide one of the spots on the carpet. One hand, however, stuck out beyond the yellow.

"Oh, Monsieur!" Pierre's face and gesture—gun upraised in surprise—were protesting. "The quilt. . . . Indiscreet, Monsieur!"

But I ignored him. I bent over toward the huddled figure in the chair. "If you are really Achille Binbonnet," I said in a loud, stern voice, "show me papers that will prove it, instantly."

Never have I seen such utter astonishment. The man was literally astonished out of semi-collapse. He gave me a long, open-mouthed stare, and then without a word took a wallet out of his pocket and simply handed it to me. It was as convincingly full of identifications as Monsieur Gerard's wallet had been, that morning when . . . God! Was it possible that that had been only *yesterday* morning, my long talk with Gerard?

And then, still with this unnatural clear-headedness, I pursued my advantage. "Are you able to walk, Monsieur Binbonnet? Because I think that for your own good you should go at once."

Again he stared at me. Pierre, too, was looking at me as though I was doing strange, incomprehensible things. Pierre was still standing in the doorway. And it was partially the fact that he was still standing, standing quite erect, that made me feel we could do without Monsieur Binbonnet. Any man who could stand as erect as that, after the scene that had just taken place, didn't need the help of the wretched little dandy in the chair.

"I suggest that you go at once, Monsieur Binbonnet. Disassociate yourself entirely from this scene."

The dark eyes began to have a little light. "You mean, Monsieur, I should go . . . I should not stay to . . ." There was a faint gesture toward the yellow pile on the floor.

"We will take care of that without you, Monsieur Binbonnet. Is that not so, Pierre?"

"Certainly, Monsieur." The perfect servant, as always.

"You see?" I said to Binbonnet. "You may go."

"Oh, Monsieur Weavair." It was like a hymn of thanksgiving; his eyes were glowing. He stood up uncertainly, closed his eyes for a moment, then stood more securely.

"Do only two things, Monsieur Binbonnet. Take this man's gun with you and dispose of it."

I paused. Eagerly, he picked the gun up and put it in his pocket.

"And, Monsieur Binbonnet, kindly give me your telephone number."

At that, I could even smile. But Binbonnet did not. "Archives, 71-083," he merely said.

I looked about for a pencil, a bit of paper. Pierre was watching me. "Do not trouble to write it down, Monsieur. I know the number quite well."

"You know the number, Pierre!"

"Yes, Monsieur."

I allowed myself to look wonderingly at them both for a moment. But that was merely one of the many things that would come later.

"Now go, Monsieur Binbonnet. We are releasing you from any further association with this man, with this entire event. Be in your office tomorrow morning, please."

"Oh, Monsieur Weavair!" He made as though to come over and take my hand. I shook my head. On his way to the door he wrung Pierre's fervently. In a moment he was gone, and I heard the door close behind him.

Nature's little trick was giving out fast. I lay back against the pillows. "Some brandy, Pierre," I ordered.

Probably the most selfish thing I ever said in my life. And the only time Pierre failed me.

"Monsieur would allow me," he said, as though he had not heard what I said, "Monsieur would allow me—to . . . sit down?"

"Pierre! Of course!"

For an instant the force of the reproach made me sit up, filled with concern. Pierre came into my room. He carefully laid the gun on the mantelpiece. And then he sat down. He didn't crumple as Binbonnet had done. He just sat there, erect and impeccable. Only—his eyes were closed. It was equivalent to a sprawling, disorderly swoon in anyone else.

I lay back again and closed my eyes.

Three silent people in my room. Pierre, I, and—who was it, under that quilt? That too I'd find out.

Everything wasn't silent, though. Out in the corridor somewhere a bell was ringing. It had rung several times before. Now it was ringing in a never-ending series of little sharp sounds, ringing, ringing. . . . Somebody was angrily demanding Pierre.

I looked at him, wondering if he heard it. He did hear it. He opened his eyes. "Monsieur . . ."

"Yes, Pierre?"

"Monsieur would forgive me if I went . . ."

He was a crackpot, this man who had saved my life. Still, I almost loved him at that moment. "Pierre, if I could go, I'd go for you, and let you rest."

"Oh, Monsieur!" He was genuinely shocked. He stood up. "I shall not be long, Monsieur."

The door closed behind him, too.

I lay back on the pillows again. Nature's trick gave out entirely. I began to tremble. It wasn't from horror—horror of what had happened, of what was under the quilt on the floor; some of that feeling of horror came later. This, evidently, was mere weakness. I trembled and trembled, feeling cold. And then—I can't conceal it—I shed a few tears, a few tears, lying there by myself—or almost by myself. Weeping, trembling, cold. . . . What a man! And Pierre doing a beautiful bit of room service somewhere!

He was gone a quarter of an hour. And do I have to say that when he returned he was carrying a tray with a glass and a brandy bottle on it? He saw me trembling. He held the glass to my lips. I drank. He brought me a hot-water bag. As he went to and fro he had to make wide detours around, or step over, the yellow mound and the hand. Belatedly, I murmured that he should get a glass from the bathroom and drink some of the brandy himself. He did. And to drink he sat down again.

The hot-water bag did immediate good. I stopped trembling and got warm. I looked at Pierre as he sat in his chair drinking his brandy. He looked at me. "Well, Pierre?"

Were things to be explained to me now, immediately? Evidently not.

"I will prepare the bed for Monsieur in the other room."

I understood. The thing couldn't be moved yet. So he thought it would be nicer for me if I moved. I thought so too. "No hurry, Pierre."

"Thank you, Monsieur."

"But, Pierre—there won't be questions, about my going in there? Shouldn't I telephone downstairs, to the desk . . . ?"

"I have already taken the liberty of engaging the room for Monsieur. I took the liberty of saying that tonight Monsieur would need the two rooms."

I stared at him. It was becoming harder not to ask questions now.

He sat there with his brandy for perhaps ten minutes more. I could see we both felt better. Then he rose, went into the other room, turned on the light. Soon he was before me again. "The bed is ready for Monsieur."

There was no question of putting on my braces and walking into that other room. I couldn't have done it. And clearly Pierre didn't expect me to, or he would have brought the braces and crutches over to me from the distant corner where Binbonnet had put them. I pushed back the bedclothes and prepared to lower myself to the floor. In an instant Pierre was beside me. "Oh, Monsieur, I will bring the wheelchair from the hall."

"But there isn't room in here to move the chair around, now, Pierre. I'll just crawl in . . ."

"Monsieur?"

And before I knew what was happening, Pierre had lifted me and was carrying me. He carried me into the other room and put me on the bed. I was too tired to protest.

"Monsieur must try to sleep."

Sleep! Was he crazy?

"Nothing can be done in that room until nearly midnight. I have dinners to serve now. There will be people arriving from the evening trains. The corridors begin to be empty about eleven. Sometime after that I will come. Monsieur will not be disturbed until then."

"Pierre. It was selfish of me to tell Binbonnet to go. I had my own reasons. I did it for myself. I wanted him to be grateful to me, so that in the future . . . You must get him back, to help. . . ."

"Oh, Monsieur—that is arranged."

"*Arranged*, Pierre? Arranged with whom?"

"With my colleague, Lavisse."

Arranged *already!* Arranged with the wine-tasting elevator- and furnace-man disciple!

"Monsieur will desire dinner?"

"By no means—but some newspapers, Pierre." Something to keep me occupied for part of the six hours of waiting I now had ahead of me.

"Certainly, Monsieur."

He closed the doors between the rooms and went out. He was soon back with papers. "If you want anything you will ring, Monsieur?"

I said I would.

I was alone in my new room.

The newspapers were still full of their talk of war. I read them a bit, then put them down. Then took them up again. Then put them down again.

Well, how *did* it happen that Pierre knew Binbonnet's phone number? And how did it happen that Pierre happened to be there, with his gun? How was it possible that all was arranged? How, for that matter, did it happen that Pierre knew Binbonnet at all?

That last, I thought I had the answer for. Mademoiselle Denise had indicated, hadn't she, that Binbonnet was a patriot, a chauvinist? Much like Pierre, he had kept in touch with the war, as it were, by joining organizations. I had even thought of Pierre when she had told me this. He and Pierre knew each other that way.

But how Pierre should have been right there, when I needed him so desperately—and with his gun! And Lavisse arranged for!

And the entire question of Binbonnet and his identity. Gerard was then the alarmist I had first thought him to be, then decided he wasn't? An alarmist, at least, about Binbonnet? Surely Gerard had not deliberately deceived me? I thought of that possibility, but discarded it. Gerard had been too startled, too sick, to have been insincere. He had been mistaken—but why? The trouble with me was, I listened too readily. Listened too readily when Gerard said somebody wasn't who he was. Listened too readily when a stranger on a train told me to beware of people who said they came from Touraine. But probably that man under the yellow quilt would have told me he came from Touraine, had he ever spoken to me; so the stranger in the train had been only half wrong. Who was the man under the yellow quilt, by the way? Just who? And was that where the iodine had been going? What of the concierge? And why had Binbonnet lied about the phone and about Gerard?

These questions and more—as well as the gloomy details of crises and mobilization—slowed down my reading of the papers. Thoughts—frequent thoughts—of the yellow mound in the next room, too. Pierre had done his work neatly, but there was that yellow mound. And the brandy bottle. And two spots on the carpet. From time to time I read a little. From time to time I thought and wondered a little. From time to time I was conscious of a sound that before this evening had never struck my attention: the sound of room bells ringing for Pierre. Pierre was working. Working hard and well, I was sure.

And from time to time, too, I did something else—I dozed a little. I won't say that I ever slept, during those hours preceding Pierre's return—or during the hours following it, as it turned out. But I'll have to admit that there were some periods when I wasn't fully awake. I kept the light on all the time, of course.

A little before twelve there was a knock on the door and Pierre came in with Lavisse.

I had never seen Lavisse before. A stocky youngster, with a round, naïve face and large eyes which even while he was greeting me seemed to be trying to pierce through the doors into the next room. He wore a rough kind of uniform and was carrying a pail. "I have told Lavisse, Monsieur, that this person was an enemy of France," Pierre said, gravely, and, taking the hint, I immediately began to improvise a short speech on the Franco-American theme. Lavisse listened intently, his eyes now and then sliding toward the door. He and Pierre both thanked me when I finished. Then Pierre opened the doors and they went in, shutting the door behind them.

But I had to watch them, I found. Every detail of that room of mine was so horridly clear in my mind—the yellow quilt, the hand, the bottle, the two carpet stains—that I wanted to see, myself, that it was put to rights. I slid out of bed into a chair, and then hitched myself on it across the carpet to the door, and opened it and the one beyond it. Pierre already had his long-tailed coat off, and the shirt-sleeves of both men were rolled up. As I opened the door, they were staring at a great dark-red stain in the middle of the yellow quilt, which Pierre had pulled off the recumbent figure and was holding. He looked at me reproachfully. "Most indiscreet, Monsieur," he said again. "I cannot destroy the quilt—the hotel is most particular about its property. I shall have to invent a story for the cleaner."

I apologized. It hadn't occurred to me that a quilt might in certain circumstances be more valuable than what it covered.

I sat in the doorway and watched. Pierre gave quiet orders. They stretched out the quilt, rolled the body onto it, and lifted the whole thing to a distant corner of the room. They picked up the hat from where it had fallen and put it on the head, pulling it way down over the ears and eyes. Now there was practically no space between the hat and the handkerchief. Lavisse picked up the brandy bottle, washed it out in the bathroom and threw it into the wastebasket. Then he brought in a pail of water and both men set to work, each with a scrubbing brush. Fumes of Javel water filled the room. Lavisse suggested opening a window, but Pierre vetoed the idea: it was best to run no risk of being seen.

Was there no risk, I wondered, that anything had been *heard?* To me the explosion seemed so loud, in retrospect, that I wondered that people hadn't rushed from all directions. I asked Pierre what he thought. He suspended his scrubbing for a moment and assumed a judicious air. The hotel was not only massively built, he said, but well-carpeted. Carpets are great sound-absorbers. The windows were closed and the curtains drawn. The room on one side was empty; he himself had been in the other, and beyond that were the service elevator, pantry, and other service rooms, all of which had been empty. All in all, he thought it unlikely that anyone had heard. "You see, Monsieur, it was carefully planned to take place not before five o'clock, when I alone should be on duty."

Planned for five! How so? And what had been planned for five? The murder of me, or the murder that had taken place? But I didn't ask—yet. Already Pierre was back at his scrubbing.

They scrubbed at the two spots until I thought they'd wear the carpet itself away. A good half-hour. And then they spent another half-hour going around the room searching for possible other spots. But they didn't find any. As I have said, Pierre had done a neat job.

Finally Pierre said they were done. The room stank of Javel water. For the time being, the spots were bigger than they had been. Lavisse had kept going back and forth to the bathroom getting fresh pails of water. Once he had had to leave, hastily putting on his jacket, to answer the bell of his elevator. Now he washed out the pail and the brushes, and stood almost as though at attention, waiting for further orders.

"The wheel-chair from the hall," Pierre said.

The chair was brought in. There was room for it, now! The body was lifted into it, placed in a kind of slumping sitting position. It looked to me as though it would slip out before they got very far. The man's gray shoes were of suede, I noticed. I hoped they had rubber soles, so that they'd keep him in position and not let him slide onto the floor in the corridor in front of some late-returning guest.

"And now, Monsieur," Pierre said, looking a little uncertainly at me, "it is necessary that we remove the handkerchief, lest we meet someone in the corridor."

I started at once to hitch my chair back into my new room. "Thank you for the warning," I said. "I've never seen the man's face and I don't want to take my first look now."

He sprang over to me and pushed me in my chair over to my bed, so that I could swing from one to the other. They could do the rest of their work without me.

"But I was under the impression that Monsieur *had* seen the man's face," Pierre was saying.

"Never his face, Pierre. Just his brown clothes, three times."

He nodded and put his hand to his forehead. "Forgive me, Monsieur. This thing has upset me, I confess. My memory for details . . . There have been so many details, Monsieur."

I could believe that.

"Now I shall be absent again for some time, Monsieur. I shall report again to Monsieur when everything is completely over with. But Monsieur will doubtless be asleep?"

"I intend to keep my light on all night, Pierre. Come in as soon as you can."

He bowed and retired, shutting the two doors. I heard the door of the other room open, then close. A few faint sounds in the corridor. I hoped those gray suede shoes were holding tight to the foot-board.

Pierre had given me no idea of how long it would take to do the final part of the job. An hour? That should be ample, I thought, if all went well. I had no worries about the inside of the hotel. With Pierre in charge that part should go perfectly, and Lavisse was himself the operator of the elevator which they would undoubtedly use. I did worry a little about the outside part of the job. I summoned up a topographical image. The river, which I had no doubt was to be the final resting place of the man in brown, was in front of the hotel.

The hotel's service door was at the back. The building was large—wide and long. They would have to walk almost two blocks on the public sidewalk to get around to the quay, and then they would have to cross a wide street and probably go halfway over the bridge. The quarter swarmed with police, for it was a quarter of embassies and ministries. Suppose they were challenged, pushing that motionless figure in the chair? It was a macabre thought, that journey to the river. And then the journey back, with the empty chair.

I became definitely anxious when the first hour had passed.

And I waited a whole second hour. There was nothing more to read in those newspapers, and though I lay back with closed eyes spells of dozing did not come, this time, to help me with my waiting. My mind was filled chiefly with the things I had to ask Pierre. And I began to think, too, of the interview I would have with Binbonnet the next day. The thought that the next room was all cleaned up—and empty—was definitely better than before. And yet I was jumpy. I found myself jerking when the radiator knocked, for example.

Another half-hour.

Two and a half hours in all.

Then Pierre returned.

Tired, exhausted-looking in his absurd black-and-white clothes. Not disheveled. Every hair in place, as always. But a general air of having worked hard.

"It is done, Monsieur."

"Thank God. You were not seen, not challenged?"

"Oh, no, Monsieur. I took the precaution of warning everyone to be out of the way, telling them that for their own sakes it would be discreet to see nothing. Such a warning is quite often given to the staff of a hotel, Monsieur—though usually, of course, for other reasons than this."

"I see. But I meant outside, Pierre. You were not challenged outside?"

"Challenged outside, Monsieur?"

"Yes—by the police."

He looked as though he did not understand.

"There were no police at all on the streets, Pierre?"

"On the streets, Monsieur?"

The man was drunk, stupid, with fatigue. It was cruel of me to question him now. "Yes, Pierre. On the streets, between the hotel and the river."

"Oh!" A light dawned. "The streets would have been much too dangerous, Monsieur. We didn't dare leave the building. Monsieur's radiator has been knocking, perhaps? There have been one or two complaints from other guests."

It took me a moment to think that out. Was it credible? Was *that* what he meant?

"I believe I told Monsieur that Lavisse is in charge of the furnaces at night, as well as the service elevator, which descends directly to the furnace-room?"

I closed my eyes. "You did, Pierre."

"The destruction has been complete, Monsieur. Our furnaces are among the largest and most powerful in Paris."

Cremation!

But so much had happened in the last two days. Cremation took its place among the other facts. I kept my eyes closed, however. My stomach felt better that way.

Suddenly, a thought.

"Pierre!"

"Monsieur?"

"Pierre, the furnaces of the hotel are really large enough to take . . . all at once?"

"Oh, no, Monsieur. Not all at once, Monsieur. That would be inefficient, dangerous. Lavisse helped me. . . ."

I retched and gagged. Pierre rushed for a towel. Between us, we did a job as neat as the one Pierre and Lavisse had done in the other room.

I apologized for this final labor I had caused him. He assured me it was nothing. I lay back again.

Pierre arranged a few things around the room.

Now he was bidding me good-night. He would be on duty in the morning, he said. It would be he who would bring me my breakfast.

I said weakly that I was glad of it.

But I found that I couldn't possibly let him go now without asking him at least one of those great questions.

"Pierre—how did you know about me? How did you know enough to be *there . . . here?* You know Binbonnet so very well?"

He smiled, and the smile and the answer told me that I should have asked the question long before. I had been tactless, rather than considerate, in my delay. Clearly Pierre had been waiting for my question, hoping for it through all the horror, *despite* all the horror. He enjoyed answering it so very much.

"I knew Monsieur Binbonnet very well even before my sister became engaged to him, Monsieur."

He paused to let his words sink in and to savor, evidently, the expression on my face.

"It was fortunate that Monsieur came to the Clarence. I have been watching over Monsieur since his second or third day at the hotel, when Monsieur Binbonnet informed me who Monsieur was. The delay in the arrival of my revolver permit has caused Monsieur Binbonnet and me much worry, Monsieur; but such a delay is only to be expected when one's sister is in a minor position and . . . respectable, besides."

I recalled, amid my astonishment, Mademoiselle Denise's bitterness about her superior's insistence upon favors in return for favors. I recalled my surprise that a waiter should speak to me about a gun.

"It was the delay in the arrival of my permit which made Monsieur Binbonnet decide to flee to Tours. He knew that that person would pursue him. Thus Monsieur would have been assured of at least one more day of safety had he remained in Paris. Fortunately the permit arrived, and I was able to purchase the gun, this—I mean yesterday—afternoon, just before your letter to Monsieur Binbonnet let that person know that you would most probably be in your room. When I telephoned Monsieur Binbonnet to inform him that I finally had the gun, he indicated that I was to be here almost immediately, at five o'clock. There was thankfulness in his voice, Monsieur."

"But since Monsieur Binbonnet was so closely watched over, how could he speak so freely over that secret telephone?"

"Monsieur will not imagine that when I telephoned I said in so many words that I had acquired the gun. I said what it had been arranged that I say: 'The coast will be clear at five today.' For Monsieur

Binbonnet had persuaded that person that having me, a friend, in the hotel, was an advantage; that if some moment seemed particularly auspicious I might telephone to say so, and would hand them my pass-key when they arrived. I did hand them my passkey. But I had unlocked the doors of this room first."

"And arranged for the services of Lavisse."

"And arranged for the services of Lavisse, Monsieur."

"There was no telling, though, I suppose, Pierre—no telling exactly—just which of two people it would be, or for that matter, whether it would be one or two people, that you and Lavisse might be having to dispose of after the . . . the battle? I mean—the man in brown might have fired at me before you fired at him?"

"Oh, I had little fear of that, Monsieur. Not only am I a good shot, but—there was something else, and that was what made me think that Monsieur had seen that person's face. He was of a melodramatic nature, that individual. He had told Monsieur Binbonnet exactly how the thing was to be done. Just before shooting at Monsieur he was going to tear his handkerchief from his face, and astonish Monsieur with the revelation of who he was. I cannot understand how that might have astonished Monsieur if Monsieur had not seen his face before. It was therefore when I saw his hand go up toward the handkerchief that I fired."

"He was going to tear off his handkerchief?"

"Yes, Monsieur."

"And astonish me with the sight of his face?"

"Yes, Monsieur."

At this point, my friends who read detective stories have indeed reason to be scornful of me. Either I had been through too much, or else my brain is as defective in such matters as those friends think. I could not imagine who that man in brown might have been.

Pierre told me a little more. About the long-considered application for the gun permit, which Binbonnet had urged him to seek the moment the blackmailer had made his appearance. That was Binbonnet's scheme, of course—the scheme that had made it possible for him to write both Gerard and Mademoiselle Denise that "everything should be all right in a month"! About his sister's tenacity in finally securing the permit without granting the favors long demanded in return. (How her chief must hate her!) About Binbonnet's excited, surreptitious telephone call almost two weeks before, to tell Pierre who I was and what danger I was in.

I decided I was a pretty poor asker of questions. I had asked Mademoiselle Denise a good many—but if I had only asked her one more: how she had met her fiancé! On the other hand, if she had only looked at the address I had scribbled on my card, instead of just putting it into her bag!

Pierre had been able to tell me nothing, during the past two weeks, because Binbonnet had been so frantically afraid that the blackmailer would in some way learn of it and either send in the old photographs and documents to the police or else put into execution another threat he had made: merely to call the attention of Binbonnet's former customers, and possibly the police, to the fact that he was going about in disguise.

"In disguise?" That, of course, was how Gerard had been put off the track! "What parts of Binbonnet are disguise?" I demanded of Pierre.

"The beard of course, Monsieur, but also a total change in allure, and then especially . . ."

But I didn't let him finish. "Why on earth should he disguise himself?"

"He was forced to, Monsieur, by the man in brown. Forced to change his appearance overnight, not only as a means of keeping him away from his former associates but also so that his persecutor could threaten to reveal at any time the fact of the disguise, with embarrassing and even dangerous consequences for Binbonnet. If the police are informed, Monsieur, that one is going about in disguise, and investigate, and find it to be true, and then, perhaps, receive some old photographs of a fatal fight and a document that is evidence of misdoing . . ."

I nodded. A clever way of getting a hold over a man.

There were other things that Pierre couldn't, or at least didn't, tell me. There was the mystery of Binbonnet's lying, for example. But I should be seeing Binbonnet myself, and could get the rest from him.

It was the almost incredible perfection of Pierre's manners, I think, in having waited until I asked a direct question to tell me about these things, which he had so longed throughout the horror to tell me about, that impressed me most of all, as I reflected on it. That and the intensity of his look of fatigue. I wondered if I looked the same.

We said good-night. I kept my windows locked and the light on all night. For hours I didn't even doze; my mind kept whirling like a merry-go-round. I suppose a bromide would have helped me, but my bromides were in the other room. And empty though it now was, it was a room I didn't care to enter.

# CHAPTER 18

Through chinks in the curtains I saw the sky become light. Sometime after that I dropped off, and it was nine when I awoke. I was hungry—for good reason—and felt decidedly washed-out besides. I rang, and Pierre appeared with my breakfast. It might have been any other morning. He still looked fatigued, but in no other way did he differ either in manner or appearance from what he had been my very first morning in the hotel.

"Monsieur slept well?"

"Very well, thank you, Pierre, considering everything."

His complete lack of response to that last phrase gave me my first indication of what his etiquette was to be.

He pulled back my curtains and opened the window. Sun and air! Then he opened the communicating doors and disappeared into the next room. I heard him pulling back those curtains and opening those windows. After a moment he returned. "I have taken the liberty of opening the windows in Monsieur's other room. There was a slight odor of Javel water. The air will also hasten the drying of one or two damp spots on Monsieur's carpet."

I nodded. "But I think I shall keep *this* room, Pierre, now that I'm here."

"May I suggest that Monsieur retain both rooms for the present? Until the odor of Javel water . . ."

The telephone rang—the telephone in the room where I was breakfasting. It was the desk. "We are correct in thinking that you would like your former bedroom to be arranged as a sitting room, Monsieur Weavair? That was your intention, we suppose, in taking

the second room for a bedroom? We can have the first room transformed immediately, Monsieur."

I thought fast. Pierre was right. I had to keep that other room
for the present, until the odor and the spots were gone. And yet, the
odor and the spots would be perceived by whoever came to change
the furniture. A good solution occurred to me; and as it came, I
smiled. "Leave that other room as it is for the present. I expect a
friend tonight. He will sleep there. The bed doesn't need changing;
it hasn't been slept in. And today I should prefer that Pierre rather
than the chambermaid put that room in order; there are things of
mine to be moved from there to here. May I take this occasion to
express my appreciation of the hotel's service? Pierre especially is of
the greatest assistance to me, but indeed the whole staff . . . etc. I am
grateful to you for phoning, etc."

Flowery thanks were expressed. The chambermaid would be told
to stay out. Another exchange of compliments. We hung up.

"You may bring my things from that room to this, Pierre. And
then prepare it for Monsieur Gerard. I think he will be sleeping there
tonight."

"But, Monsieur—the odor of Javel water is very tenacious, and
I fear that even by this evening . . . The spots, too—moisture evaporates slowly from so thick a carpet. One more day, at least, is necessary. . . ."

"Necessary indeed, for anyone except Monsieur Gerard. But
since it will be Monsieur Gerard—"

Pierre looked at me. It was completely distasteful to him, I could
see, to have to talk even this much about things, this morning. "Back
to normalcy" was the order of the day. That he made clear. That was
perhaps one of the reasons why he had been so willing and eager
to talk the night before. Last night had been the time to talk. This
morning and the future were not. And—wasn't he right? He had told
me all he knew. Now he was a floor-waiter and I the occupant of one
of his rooms. Much better that way.

"I want Monsieur Gerard to spend tonight in that room, Pierre."

"Very well, Monsieur." He accepted it—perhaps because otherwise he would have had to talk about it. As I breakfasted he moved

from room to room, transferring my clothes and other effects. He was still there when I put in a call to Monsieur Gerard in Brest.

I enjoyed the conversation.

The hotel operator rang. "Ready with Brest, Monsieur Weavair."

"Hello?"

"Monsieur Weavair! It is really you? I have been so worried, Monsieur, so distracted. Where were you, Monsieur? And where are you now? You are in good health, Monsieur? Is there anything new?"

Anything new! The coward's question. The man who wouldn't defy his blackmailer and effect his own cure at the same time—for fear of what people like those ponderous Leblancs and Dutuits would say. The man who had fled from Paris when I hadn't returned from my "errands"!

"Yes, good news, Monsieur Gerard," was all I chose to say. "I will tell you what it is when I see you."

"You are coming to Brest, Monsieur Weavair?"

"No—but will you be good enough to come to Paris, Monsieur Gerard? Will you take that two o'clock train this afternoon, if you please?"

His hesitation made me smile. "To Paris, Monsieur? You want me to come to Paris, Monsieur Weavair?"

"I do indeed, Monsieur Gerard. Please take the two o'clock train."

"The news is really good, Monsieur?"

"Very good."

"Then—I will come, since you ask it."

"I have already reserved a room for you here at the Clarence, Monsieur Gerard," I said, smiling into the instrument.

"You are very kind, Monsieur."

"Not at all, Monsieur Gerard. Au revoir, Monsieur. Till this evening."

"Until this evening, Monsieur Weavair."

Then I had Pierre help me get shaved and dressed. On to Binbonnet's!

Before I quite realized what was happening, Pierre had brought the wheel-chair in from the hall and I was getting into it. Suddenly I did realize. "Pierre! Let me get out of this chair at once, please!"

He seemed a bit disappointed that I couldn't bury the past as completely as he would have liked us both to. He seemed to understand, however. He helped me out of the chair and accompanied me as I walked to the elevator. It did seem a long walk, as did also the walk through the lobby to the taxi. One or two of the clerks and the concierge greeted me and congratulated me on my rapid recovery from the shock of the automobile accident. I thanked them and smiled a bit grimly. After last night, the accident they referred to seemed like ancient history.

"I no longer need that wheel-chair," I told the doorman, as I got into the cab. "You can send up for it."

He promised to do so.

It would have been more comfortable for me, of course, had Binbonnet come to the hotel for our talk; but that was something I couldn't bring myself to ask him to do. For a long time, I was sure, he would be happier away from the Clarence. And on the other hand, it would have been most satisfactory for me could we have had our talk in his office; that would have best made me feel that things were back to normal and that I was merely discussing business with my broker in routine fashion. But Monsieur Binbonnet's two flights of stairs prevented that. The compromise, which I had projected before, of having him come down and see me in my taxi, seemed the best thing under the circumstances; that was why I had not phoned, since he had promised to be in anyway. Accordingly, when we had arrived at 404 Rue Saint-Martin I sent the driver upstairs to tell him that I was waiting. There was no sign of the concierge. The tape-and-braid shop looked as dreary and noncommittal as ever. It filled me with pleasure to be able to come here without fear.

Among the things that had kept going through my mind during the night hours I'd lain awake was a whole series of conjectures as to what Achille Binbonnet was going to look like in the morning. The false beard would be gone, of course; impossible to imagine even that much—Monsieur Binbonnet without his beard! And then the total change in allure that Pierre had mentioned; what would Binbonnet's restored natural allure be? And there was something else, was there not, something that Pierre had indicated was the greatest change of all . . . ? Would I recognize my broker when I saw him undisguised?

Well, when Monsieur Binbonnet appeared in the doorway I did feel a shock. Not the kind of shock I had expected, though; not a shock resulting from a great change in his appearance. On the contrary, I was shocked because he looked so fundamentally the same. The same slicked, greasy hair; the same striped suit and gaudy handkerchief and stickpin; the same sad expression; what was the removal of a beard, compared with all these things? For indeed, though Monsieur Binbonnet appeared this morning beardless, he was in my eyes much as he had been when bearded. I had asked the taxi-driver to wait, on his return, at a distance, and when Binbonnet, after hesitating a moment in his doorway, saw me in the cab and came quickly over and joined me, I asked him without hesitation, almost without greeting, to explain.

"So they were false, your whiskers!" I abruptly began.

"False indeed, but do not think I wore them willingly, Monsieur. I . . ."

"One moment, please. What I do not understand is this: Since you were in disguise, and disguised so well as to deceive even Monsieur Gerard, why were you so astonished last evening when I indicated that I too had doubted your identity, and demanded proofs that you were yourself?"

"But, Monsieur . . . ! With you I had taken particular pains to establish my identity, in a manner impossible with Monsieur Gerard or indeed with anyone else. You had never seen me before, but you knew my hand from my letters to Pearce Brothers, and that note I sent you with my present of wine and brandy—"

"Note? There was no note with the wine and the brandy, Monsieur Binbonnet."

"Oh, but there was, Monsieur Weavair! You didn't receive *that?*" He seemed greatly disturbed.

Almost unconsciously my hand slid into my coat pocket. There it was, Monsieur Binbonnet's card that had come with his double present and that I had slipped into my pocket at the time. Still there, undisturbed. But a note? I took the card out.

"But there it is, Monsieur Weavair! On the back of my card. You did not read it?"

I shook my head. I pulled the florid card out of the envelope and turned it over—as I had not thought to turn it over before. There was writing. Very pale, penciled writing—so pale as not to be very striking. And yet, there it was. I had been carrying it around with me since before going to Brest. "Do not drink the brandy. Destroy this card. The wine is a personal offering from your sincere well-wisher, who hopes that before long . . ."

I made out the faint words with difficulty and read them aloud.

"I was interrupted at that point," Monsieur Binbonnet explained. "And since even while delivering the package I was watched, I had no opportunity of finishing it."

I nodded. That the brandy had been poisoned I had gathered when more brandy had been offered me later. That the wine had not been poisoned I had also learned. And now I was learning *why*. But I could have learned why so long ago!

"I am deeply sorry," Binbonnet was saying, "that you did not read those words. I did the best I could, Monsieur. The writing is faint, but that was deliberate, necessary, lest the thing be glimpsed. I assure you I ran a risk in doing even that much. The worries you must have had, Monsieur! The danger . . . ! Some lucky chance kept you from the brandy?"

I nodded again.

"Thank God, Monsieur Weavair."

The writing was faint, very faint. And when Pierre had brought in the package, I remembered, I had been struck by the floridity of the card's engraving: even if I hadn't been thinking of packing, and leaving for Brest, would it have occurred to me to examine the reverse side of a card whose engraved side was so striking?

I thought of the cold sleeping compartment on the train to Brest; the swerve, the crash of the flask on the floor. I was thinking of my long belief that Binbonnet was not Binbonnet, but some quite different, mysterious personage who was working against me. That I should never have believed had I read that note!

"Let me thank you now for your warning, Monsieur Binbonnet."

"Ah, Monsieur, it was the least . . ."

"But another thing, then: why did you lie to me about your telephone, Monsieur Binbonnet?"

"Monsieur, Mademoiselle Richard has told you why this person was able to force me to do what he wished. You may think it cowardly and foolish of me not to have gone to the police, even in the disguise which he forced me to wear, or to a lawyer and told him my story. . . . But Monsieur Weavair, I had behaved so culpably in the past, I shrank from the difficulty of explaining my past actions—and I assure you that the thought of possibly having to stand trial for murder, of undergoing the publicity, of permanently losing my livelihood, which depends upon my reputation for integrity: I could not face it, Monsieur.

"There is no need to excuse yourself, Monsieur Binbonnet." If there was any self-excusing to be done, it was I who should begin it, I felt. That note! In my pocket for ten days!

"He watched me, Monsieur, like a hawk. He made me give up my old telephone number and take a new one under another name, to make it as difficult as possible for friends and clients to communicate with me. He wanted me entirely at his own disposal. Iodine is not the only commodity that he dealt in, Monsieur; I shall be getting back other clients besides Pearce Brothers, now, I hope. I lied to you about the telephone because he ordered me to; and while you and I were conversing, that evening, he was in the next room with his dog, as you know. But I had been able to get in touch with Pierre, and had told him to call at ten o'clock—so that you would hear the phone, Monsieur, and know that something was amiss. I was made to suffer for that, Monsieur, I can assure you. I was told it was too clumsy an error to go unpunished, and my cat . . ."

To my astonishment, there were sudden tears in the man's eyes.

"Your cat, Monsieur Binbonnet?"

"That brute of a dog, Monsieur Weavair. He was deliberately incited. That morning, after you left. I was forced to stand aside, and watch . . ."

"Give me your hand, Monsieur Binbonnet."

I gave him my sympathy by pressure. I know how people can feel about cats.

And then, after a pause: "Those things you told me about Gerard, Monsieur Binbonnet . . ." I no longer felt even like using the word "lie" to him.

"I gave such a false picture for two reasons, Monsieur. Because I knew that the person who was listening in the next room would want me to try to dissuade you from going to Brest, and because I wanted to be sure that if you did go you would see that there was something amiss. That there was something hidden, seemingly inexplicable, working against you. And at his orders I tried to get you to let him drive you to Brest, and when that failed I obeyed him by sending you the brandy. I persuaded him that the addition of a harmless bottle of wine would make the thing more subtle, and then one moment when I wasn't watched I scribbled as much of a note as I could on my card and slipped it in. He accompanied me when I delivered it at the hotel that night, so that I was unable to tell Pierre about the brandy.

"Then you went to Brest and returned. I lied to you again later: it was I who telephoned you, the afternoon following your return. I had heard by telegram that you had left Brest by train and that he was following by car. He had not yet returned; I thought it was my one opportunity of talking to you myself, enlarging on the warning I had written on my card. But you did not answer. You were back in Paris that afternoon, were you not, Monsieur Weavair? You were out?"

Again my feeling of shame. I had not wanted to talk to Binbonnet that day. I had simply not answered. And later I had suspected his call of being a trial, to see whether I was in and might conveniently be murdered! These things I couldn't confess. "Yes. I was out that afternoon," I lied.

"That was bad luck. I didn't dare leave my name, of course, and the next day when you asked if I had called, I had to deny it—for by that time he was at my elbow again, ordering me to fix a rendezvous with you—one that he would have kept with you also, Monsieur. I wondered that he had not attacked you in Brest, but he told me simply that Paris was more 'convenient.' Then you went to Holland. And then we had our encounter in the . . . café. I could say nothing to you there, of course. Oh, Monsieur Weavair—will you forgive my manner with you, during our two conversations, and on the telephone? My impertinence, my rudeness? It was necessary, Monsieur; it was part of my strategy, to pretend to that person to be cooperative—I *had* to insult you. It was like the tone of my letters—I had to do it, Monsieur. After the meeting in the café . . .”

“Pardon me, Monsieur Binbonnet, but your presence in that café . . . You seemed to be deep in papers, immersed in business. You go often to such places as that, Monsieur, for business conferences? Forgive me for asking, but to me, an American, it seems . . .”

“Ah, he took me to more shameful places than that, Monsieur! It was his pleasure to make me follow him everywhere, and I assure you that some of the places he enjoyed . . . After our meeting there, Monsieur, it was decided that . . . that . . .”

He seemed embarrassed at this point, and I helped him out. “That I must finally and unquestionably be liquidated, Monsieur Binbonnet?”

“Yes. Because you were continuing to be far too active and interfering for that person’s taste. I was in despair. I was able to telephone to Pierre at the hotel, and to my great joy he told me that in twenty-four hours the scheme that he and I had been planning could be realized. I had to secure your safety for those twenty-four hours. I escaped from the house and took a train to Tours—I could see my old mother for a few hours by going there. I left behind, on my desk, a railway time-table open at the Tours schedules; it was found by that spying concierge, as I meant it to be found by her or by that person, and I was pursued and brought back. The next day Pierre telephoned with the news I was waiting for. It was a fortunate coincidence, for we had just received your letter, indicating that you were back in Paris. Pierre said that five o’clock would be a good time—not before five, because someone else would be on duty. He loaned us his keys. I was very worried, Monsieur. I didn’t know where Pierre was planning to station himself, just how he was planning to act. I *felt* that he was behind, but . . .”

“Well, fortunately he was, Monsieur Binbonnet.”

“Ah, Monsieur Weavair, fortunately indeed. Was he not magnificent, Monsieur? Was he not admirable? He is a true Frenchman,

Monsieur; how Pierre hates his country's enemies! Pierre has longed for years for something like this! Everything was—arranged, after I left, Monsieur?" he inquired, particularly faintly.

I assured him it was.

"Thank God."

"You and Pierre had been planning this a long time, I understand, Monsieur Binbonnet?"

He looked at me for a moment, as though taking stock of what he had already told me, wondering whether he hadn't perhaps told me enough. Then he decided to go through with it.

"As soon as I found myself in bondage," he started, "I decided several things. The first was to say farewell to my fiancée until the thing was over—lest she in some way become involved or suffer. And in saying farewell to her I gave her a message for Pierre—that he was to provide himself with a gun, legally, and let me know when he had it. Except for one note which I sent her when I knew she was leaving for her vacation, I did not communicate with Mademoiselle Denise during the three months ending last night.

"Another thing I did immediately was to tell this person that I had a friend at the Clarence who could help us. I meant, of course, help me, but I persuaded him that Pierre would be useful as an ally in watching persons from out of town who were forced to come to Paris to do business with us. He agreed, and all persons were ordered to stay at the Clarence, though until you arrived there was little necessity to have any of them observed. Pierre was thus able to communicate with me, and I with him. About a month ago he referred to the gun permit for the first time, in the veiled language we had agreed upon. I smuggled out notes to my fiancée and to Monsieur Gerard, letting them know that there was hope. Then I wasn't in communication with Pierre again until I telephoned him—in excitement, I confess, Monsieur—to tell him who you were and that you must be 'watched.' It was on that same call that I asked him to telephone me at the office at ten that night. My last two conversations with him you know about.

"I am not a murderer by nature, Monsieur. When I first suggested that Pierre seek that permit I scarcely dreamed that a gun would be used so . . . so . . . *directly*. The thing has not been easy for me,

Monsieur. Even a person of that kind is a human being. It was not only the intolerable personal position I was in, Monsieur, with all the fantastic humiliation and my business falling away to nothing: there was also the terrible realization that in obeying that man I was harming my country, aiding its enemies. . . ."

"I do not think of you as a murderer, Monsieur Binbonnet." It was true. I did not. As to Pierre—well . . .

"And the other thing I did soon after my bondage began, Monsieur Weavair, was, as you know, to change my appearance, at that person's orders. It was to keep me from my old friends and acquaintances and customers, and also to serve as a reason to denounce me—publicly, as it were— if I did not cooperate. There was one thing that made my disguise easy: during the first month following the appearance of that person I lost almost fifty pounds from sorrow and worry. I had to get new clothes; that gave him the idea of changing my type entirely, as well as making me wear that beard. When I return to my normal appearance, Monsieur, and discard these clothes and accoutrements, as I have already discarded the beard, I shall still be different from my real self, until I regain some of those fifty pounds. It was that great change in my size and figure, I think, as much as the other changes, that prevented Monsieur Gerard from recognizing me. Last night, when I saw Mademoiselle Denise for the first time in several months, she did not recognize me either, even though I had already removed the beard. My own fiancée did not recognize me! I have delayed discarding these unpleasant clothes, this flashy costume, until after I should have seen you, Monsieur Weavair. There has already been sufficient confusion in our relations; I wanted to run no risk of your not recognizing me this morning."

So the beard was, as it had seemed to me it must be, the least of it. Even if I had asked Mademoiselle Denise to see a photo of her fiancé, I wondered, would I have learned from it that the false Binbonnet was the true? Perhaps not, since the changes were so great; this comforted me a little for not having asked to see it. And I regretted being deprived of one of my most cherished pictures: that of a bearded, Triton-like Binbonnet splashing up and down in the sea, doggedly searching for iodine seaweed. A beardless Triton after all: too bad!

But there was still something I must learn.

"Who was 'that person,' Monsieur Binbonnet? The man in brown, I mean. Pierre seems to have some idea that I had seen his face before, but I told him I had seen only his clothes through the door of your office and in the 'café,' and his silhouette on the road to Tours."

"Yes, Monsieur. You have seen his face. And he was angry that he should have allowed you to see his face under conditions that would make you remember it. Otherwise, he could have acted more freely with you here, and not have had to keep concealed; for if you saw his face, having seen it before, he knew that you would be antagonistic, hostile to him."

"But where had I seen him, Monsieur Binbonnet?"

And Binbonnet told me what I should have guessed the night before. But then, that incident on the *Normandie* had left my memory completely. Those gray shoes . . . That kick . . . How it came back!

"That brute? And he was following me even *then?*"

"He had gone to America, Monsieur, to see where American firms were getting their best supplies of iodine and other products; he visited Pearce Brothers to try to find out if they were getting any better iodine than Gerard's. Because if they were, he wanted that, too. He learned that you were sailing to investigate something in France, suspected what it was, and came back with you. He didn't attempt anything against you on the boat, Monsieur; considering your condition he didn't think there was any reason to. It was only when to his surprise you climbed these two flights of stairs—Oh, how it hurt me, Monsieur, that I should have to make you climb my stairs!—and then when you insisted on taking that long trip to Brest, that he decided he would have to put you out of the way."

"I see. An accomplished man, wasn't he? Businessman, gangster, linguist. . . ."

"Oh, *most* accomplished, Monsieur. Most clever at finding grounds for persecution. Most criminal and dangerous. Most highly considered in his own country, Monsieur. Oh, Monsieur—*ces Allemands!* That is what makes them such terrible foes. But do you know, Monsieur, the achievement that gave him the greatest pleasure and satisfaction?"

I didn't know.

"Having got you to come to the Clarence, Monsieur, simply by leaving a folder in your cabin. He said it proved something about Americans—that their faith in publicity statements . . ."

"*Ces Allemands*," indeed? Well, his luring me to the Clarence had been fatal—for him. And since that was so, I could not resent any slurs too deeply.

And I learned about the tape-and-braid shop. The terms that Monsieur Gerard and other producers had been forced to accept had been barter terms, of course, and the tape-and-braid shop had been enlarged to hold iodine and other stocks as well as the goods that were given in exchange. With his blackmail, the man in brown could probably have got the produce for nothing, but his superiors wanted all records to appear straight. The tape-and-braid sign was a blind. Had I investigated closely, I should have found a bell with the command "Ring" inscribed above it, and had I rung, I should have been accosted, after a few minutes, by—the concierge. She, I learned, was merely a disagreeable old crone who had been well paid by the man in brown and was therefore naturally devoted to his interests. She had spied outrageously upon Binbonnet, entering his apartment at will. But now, he assured me with a certain emphasis, her days of glory were over. It might not be possible to oust her—for in France a concierge has a death-grip on her post—but unless she behaved . . . The little man looked threatening. Even during "that person's" absence in America, he revealed, he had not dared make a mis-step, lest it be reported by that wrathful guardian and result in the disclosure of the wretched secret.

At present, in addition to cameras, mirrors, optical instruments and tools of all kinds, the tape-and-braid shop contained a goodly store of iodine, Binbonnet told me. That, plus what he had had Mademoiselle Denise buy in Brittany, would fill Pearce Brothers' wants for some time.

"You are a faithful broker, Monsieur Binbonnet."

"I have a feeling of loyalty to Pearce Brothers, Monsieur Weavair."

"Then I assume that from now on, if Gerard is willing, all will be as before?"

"I fully expect so, Monsieur."

We had a brief iodine talk, and in the course of it I learned what I had already suspected—that the man in brown and his country had wanted the iodine for munitions purposes. A question of poison gas, Binbonnet told me, though he didn't know the particulars. Something about adding iodine to the chlorine in mustard gas, to increase specific gravity so that the gas would stay on the ground. Iodine is heavier than chlorine. And in order not to decrease the toxicity of the gas the iodine had to be concentrated and pure. There is little iodine in the man in brown's country, and what there is isn't very good. So he had come to France.

As to Pearce Brothers' own iodine needs, I felt there was little need to talk with Monsieur Binbonnet. I expected that the broker's gratitude to me for letting him leave the scene, the day before, would bear fruit to Pearce Brothers for years to come.

"Monsieur Gerard is coming tonight," I ended. "I will see if he is willing. If so, I shall allow you and him to get together; my presence won't be necessary. I'm leaving for New York almost at once."

"You have not had a pleasant visit to France, Monsieur."

I admitted that I had not.

"Monsieur, would you shake hands with my fiancée? You were so courteous with her, Monsieur, she talks constantly of you. . . ."

I smiled within myself. I had turned my back on her in the train, finding her so insufferable. She had thought that courteous?

"Of course, Monsieur Binbonnet. She is here?"

"She is free Saturdays, Monsieur. This morning she came to help me begin to get my correspondence and records in order. It is almost like beginning again, Monsieur. Would you give me permission, Monsieur, to send up the driver of your taxi with a message?"

"Of course, Monsieur Binbonnet."

It was not directly to Mademoiselle Denise, however, that the driver was sent with his message. He returned with the concierge, and she was told to go up the two flights and ask the young lady to descend. It was quite pleasing to see the old woman obey. Not with a smile, of course. With just enough of her old manner to keep one from feeling the slightest pity for her wrinkles and gray hairs.

With Mademoiselle Denise my few words were almost a continuation of our conversations of two days before. After congratulating her on the restoration of her fiancé, I teased her for having failed to recognize him the previous evening. "His mother recognized him in Tours, Mademoiselle. It seems to me that a fiancée . . ."

"But his mother did not recognize him, Monsieur! She told me that at first she did not recognize him at all, and she kept crying about his being so changed in appearance, as well as unhappy. And if she didn't recognize him, Monsieur . . ."

Despite her fiancé's presence I became irritated with her immediately. "If she didn't recognize him, Mademoiselle, and told you that she hadn't recognized him, why on earth didn't you tell me? It would have given me a clue at once, a most valuable clue!"

"But, Monsieur, how could I dream . . . ?"

"And if you had only told me about your brother, and the permit you were getting for him, and his friendship with Monsieur Binbonnet . . ."

She simpered. "I try to be discreet, Monsieur."

Binbonnet beamed. His eyes were not sad now. This glorious girl . . . Try as I might, and appreciate him as I might, I could only look on Binbonnet with the eyes of Gerard.

We said farewell. I told them I was probably leaving Paris in a day or two—something I hadn't thought of doing until that moment. I was rather sorry not to see Binbonnet once as he really looked. I asked Mademoiselle Denise if she had a picture of him. She had, of course, in a locket, and she blushingly showed it to me. Hair *en brosse*, clean-shaven face that was pudgy and fat. Unrecognizable. Unornamented tie, too. A conservative bourgeois; nothing of the dandy about the normal Binbonnet. A sober broker.

They both began to act a trifle silly and giggly.

"If you wished to wait, Monsieur Weavair," Monsieur Binbonnet self-consciously suggested, "I could become myself in half an hour. Apart from the fifty pounds, of course. I plan to do it this afternoon, in any case."

But I said I'd imagine the improvement. I wished them happiness. There were fervent handshakes.

Final farewells.

I drove off.

A strange setting, somehow, for the final carrying out of Instruction No. 1!

# CHAPTER 19

I stayed out for lunch. I had it in a lavish and expensive restaurant, and tired as I was I enjoyed the perfume of the food and wine and women, and the handsome clothes and the movement about me. There were many grave faces and quiet voices, for international matters were even more frightening than they had been the previous day; but I tasted to the full of the pleasure of having my private matters devoid of frightfulness and drama—the pleasure, as it were, of sitting at peace in the sunshine under a blue sky, the pleasure of security. To the coming interview with Gerard I looked forward with a kind of malicious eagerness. I intended to welcome him to the Hotel Clarence in a way that he'd remember.

He wouldn't be arriving until about nine, and between now and then I had nothing to do; no reason to hurry back to the Clarence. And no desire to, either. It was a good hotel, the Clarence; but somehow, now that I knew how I'd got there in the first place, my fondness for it was diminishing. And my feelings about Pierre, too, seemed to be undergoing a kind of change. For the first time, now, I was in possession of all the facts in the case; my conversation with Binbonnet was allowing me to get a more general view of the mess into which I had so innocently wandered. Violence. Violence everywhere. Violence in international politics, violence in this lesser international matter, this matter of iodine. That man in brown—I reflected that I didn't know his name, and probably never would—he was a crook, an agent, and from crooks and agents one expects violence and crime. But Pierre was a room-waiter, a beautifully trained servant—and beyond that an intuitively kind human being; it was even more frightening, somehow, to think of his violence than of the other man's. Pierre's complete competence in the matter was becoming more impressive, more horridly impressive, to me every hour. And Lavisse—that youngster! The man in brown would not be missed by anyone whom one could care about; Pierre had saved my life by taking his; I could think even with pleasure that he was no longer on the scene; and yet—well, I found myself hating, with all my power, the fact that that man had been killed. Without me there would perhaps have been murder anyway; I could not think that that gun would have remained unused. But that didn't alter the fact that of this thing that had happened I was an integral part. And once before I had been concerned in the death of other people, and neither that time nor this did I seem able to stand it very well.

As I sat there, drinking my coffee and smoking in that lavish, fashionable place, my feeling of contentment, of peace, of security, suddenly turned to dust and ashes. I was miserable. I felt as I had felt during the years gone by. And yet, familiar and miserable as the feeling was, I knew, before it had gone on very long, that this time it was momentary. Generally similar circumstances had brought on this similar feeling; but even as I suffered it my mind began to forget the similarities of the circumstances for the differences. For there were differences! The man in brown was not, to put it bluntly, a wife and daughter combined. That was what I kept thinking. And if, eventually, after many years, one could feel normal and happy even after the events involving one's wife and daughter, then—! By the time my coffee and cigarette were finished I was feeling better again.

Such was my brief period of mourning for the man in brown—the only mourning, perhaps, that he received.

But I still felt no longing to return to the Clarence for the afternoon. I could think of better places to go.

It had occurred to me, while talking with Binbonnet that morning, that unless Gerard raised some unforeseen obstacle in our conversation this evening, I might just as well return to New York. The cause of Pearce Brothers' trouble no longer existed; my continued presence in France was unnecessary. Under the new circumstances I wouldn't hesitate to disobey Al and Jim's order to stay until two successive monthly shipments had been received in New York. This prospect of a prompt return to New York became more attractive the more I thought of it. This was Saturday. There would be a boat on Wednesday, I knew; in three days I could say good-by to the Clarence, to Pierre, to the whole thing.

I went to the Clarence, where I cashed a check, and from there to the steamship company. I was filled with happiness when I put the ticket in my pocket. Then I went to a movie, and then sat at a boulevard café for half an hour, and then took a taxi back to the hotel. Even there, however, I stayed away from my room as long as possible. For a while I sat in the lounge, watching people come and go, and then I dined in the dining-room. The dinner was good—but the thought of Wednesday was better. I went upstairs a little after eight.

It was almost incredible, but Pierre was still there. Once again I couldn't help exclaiming about it: "But you have been on duty steadily since five o'clock yesterday; you can't go on working like this indefinitely."

"Today is the last day, Monsieur." Yesterday and today, for example, he explained, his duties had begun at five in the afternoon; during his hours of freedom, such as this morning, when he had brought me my breakfast and packed, he had remained on duty simply for me. Besides, he reminded me, today, even throughout my hours of absence, there had been reason for him to be on hand: to see that my old room was not entered. But after tonight, there would be no further necessity for him to keep anything but his regular schedule.

It was his saying that, I think, more than anything else, which made me realize with final completeness that the state of emergency was over—that things were back to normal. I made a little speech to him then and there, telling him I should be leaving in a few days, telling him as best I could what those extra hours of service had meant to me—quite apart, I specified, from the supreme service he had rendered yesterday. As I spoke I did my best to keep from my mind the feelings that had become so strong at lunch—my feelings of revulsion and dismay at his violence. I kept my thoughts not only on the perfection and indefatigability of his service, but also on the kindness, the gentleness, that he possessed, and on the imagination which enabled him to help me in so many ways.

I could see that he was moved. And I took out of my wallet quite a lot of money, and gave it to him; God knows he had earned any sum at all. He took it, and thankfully. He said with candor that some of his colleagues were laughing at him for working so hard for me, teasing him for scenting big money. He had allowed them to think that, for the hotel would otherwise find his long hours curious; but he had wanted me to know that wasn't why he had done it.

We shook hands. I asked him to wait a moment, and I took out some more money and put it in an envelope and asked him to give it to Lavisse. That was more specifically blood money than what I'd given to Pierre; it was a transaction I was glad to put behind me.

"The windows are closed now, in the next room?" I asked.

"I closed them at dusk, Monsieur. I regret that the odor of Javel water and the spots have not yet entirely disappeared. If Monsieur would prefer that Monsieur Gerard sleep elsewhere . . ."

"No, indeed. But when he arrives, please bring him directly here, not there."

"Very good, Monsieur." He went out.

I read newspapers for half an hour or so.


Then there was a knock.

I called "*Entrez.*"

"Good evening, Monsieur Gerard."

"Good evening, Monsieur Weavair." He was in his jittery state, I could immediately see.

There was a moment's silence as the bellboy put down his bag and left.

Then came voluble words, questions.

Oh! The pleasure I was going to have in not answering them at once! I had no intention of having with Monsieur Gerard as long a conversation as I had had with Monsieur Binbonnet; there was nothing that I had to learn from him; our business could be disposed of briefly. But there were a few things that I did want to say.

"Your health is quite restored, Monsieur Gerard?" I inquired with malicious intent. "I gather you recovered quite rapidly from your attack of the other night? Because, although the doctor suggested that you stay in bed awhile, you seem to have left Paris quite suddenly the other day. I looked forward, on my return, to telling you of the adventure that had befallen me, but . . ."

"What did befall you, Monsieur Weavair?" He was all eagerness, all curiosity. Not the slightest sign of shame.

"You yourself told me, Monsieur Gerard, that I was in danger; and after I left you I discovered that you were indeed right. Our friend in brown struck straight at me, but I escaped, and returned here late that evening, only to find that you had left. I confess I was somewhat disappointed, not to find you here to tell you about it."

"But tell me now, Monsieur Weavair! I am intensely eager to learn, Monsieur. What did happen? What is the good news, Monsieur?"

Was he shameless? So intent on getting information as to be completely without self-consciousness about his desertion?

"You knew I was in danger the other afternoon, did you not, Monsieur Gerard, when you left Paris so suddenly?" I was determined to have my revenge.

At last he realized that I was driving at something, though he appeared not to know what. "I was extremely loath to leave, Monsieur. Partially for my own sake, for I assure you I did not feel like traveling. But also for your sake, Monsieur Weavair; I felt that I was deserting you when you were in the midst of danger. After all, it was I who had taken you to the Rue de Provence, where we had the encounter which made everything so dangerous for you. But . . ."

"But what, Monsieur Gerard?" It was with difficulty that I kept a sneer from my voice; even now could he not recognize his cowardice for what it was?

"But when the waiter explained the situation to me, and made me realize quite clearly how much more useful I should be in Brest . . ."

What was this?

"Pierre spoke to you, Monsieur Gerard?"

"He didn't tell you he did, Monsieur Weavair?" The man was astonished. "He hasn't told you of the conversation he had with me?"

I shook my head.

"Then . . . then . . ." Suddenly the realization dawned upon him. "Then what must you have thought of me from then to now, Monsieur Weavair?"

I felt blushes burning my cheeks. Hurriedly I protested. "Oh, Monsieur Gerard! I knew, of course, that something had come up. . . . But what did Pierre tell you? What did he say?" All the curiosity was mine, now.

"That there would soon be trouble. That he had the situation in hand, working in close contact with Binbonnet. But that, although the end of our persecution was assured, there might be an accident— by some unlucky unforeseen chance something might just happen to Binbonnet or to you, Monsieur. That I should get out of the hotel as quickly as possible, for in case anything *did* happen to you or Binbonnet, then I at least would be able to continue producing iodine for Pearce Brothers. Whereas if I too was in the hotel, then I too was in danger. He pointed out that to everyone concerned my life was worth much more than my presence in the hotel, Monsieur. And since I knew that the matter of iodine was the thing that counted with you, Monsieur, the thing that had brought you on this long journey, the thing for which you were suffering all these discomforts and dangers—I had to agree that he was right, and I left. But I was sure he would explain all this to you, Monsieur. He impressed me as a most intelligent man, that waiter. And devoted to you and your interests, Monsieur. But he should have told you this, Monsieur Weavair. What can you have been thinking of me—the brief, curt note that I left for you, with no explanations—when you were surrounded by dangers which I myself had pointed out to you, helped to get you into? . . ."

I made no reply for a time. What could I say?

Then first I exculpated Pierre. "Pierre kept this from me, Monsieur Gerard, because he knew the greatness of the service he was doing me, and anything resembling self-praise is foreign to him."

I had thought I knew the great extent of Pierre's services; now to find that they were even greater, that without a word to me he had acted to preserve the man on whom my whole iodine mission depended—!

I plunged into a recital.

"When I left you, Monsieur Gerard, I went straight to 404 Rue Saint-Martin."

And I told him the whole story, from beginning to end. Everything that Mademoiselle Denise had told me, everything that Pierre had told me, everything that Binbonnet had told me. Everything except the cause of Binbonnet's blackmail, and except the precise manner in which Binbonnet and Pierre had set about to bring the situation to an end. I did not mention their getting the gun. And I told him everything that had happened to me—on the road to Tours and in the hotel. I told him that there had been a shot, which had ended the matter once and for all. But I didn't tell him who had fired it, or even where it had been fired. And I assured him that all evidence had been destroyed.

He listened intently, asking a question here and there. And I trusted the degree of his interest and the length of the story to put out of his mind the remarks which I wished I hadn't made.

He was particularly interested in the matter of Binbonnet's appearance.

"By the time you see him," I could only reply, "he says he will be recognizable by you once more. His allure, his clothes, will be what they were—though of course the fifty pounds . . .

"And I trust you will be seeing him soon," I continued, thinking it well to do our business up at once. "I took the liberty, in fact, of saying that since you would be in Paris you would probably call on him tomorrow morning, even though it is Sunday. He is most eager to see you. I imagine, Monsieur Gerard, that now that things are back to normal our iodine business will go on from where it left off? I don't know how large a stock you have on hand . . ."

He smiled, curling his lips. "My only stock is a stock of cameras and other mechanical toys, Monsieur. If you could see my warehouses . . . Those people are the curse of France, of Europe, of the whole world, with their lack of cash and their incessant urgings to barter, barter, barter. Often one can categorically refuse to listen to them—but this one got what he wanted, at least from me."

I told him of the stock in the tape-and-braid shop and in Brittany.

"Then of course things will be as before, Monsieur Weavair."

He said it almost casually. The matter seemed simple to him. Of course it was his business, whereas to me it was the climax of an expedition which was not in my line at all.

But he repeated it, and I knew he meant it. "Of course things will be as before, Monsieur Weavair. I will see Binbonnet in the morning."

That finished our business.

He seemed almost sunk in a reverie, now that the tale was told. "You saw that foreigner killed, Monsieur Weavair?" he demanded two or three times.

"I saw it with my own eyes, Monsieur Gerard."

That seemed to make all the difference in the world to him. It had been done. I had seen it.

And then he asked me for two of the very details which I had purposely omitted. "Who fired the shot, Monsieur?"

I had no right to tell him that.

"Why should I confess to being a murderer myself, Monsieur Gerard? Or why should I pin that name on someone else?" I was firm about it, and he agreed that I should not tell. But that he should ask the other question surprised me, and that he should insist upon an answer surprised me more.

"What was the ground for Binbonnet's blackmail, Monsieur Weavair?"

A cool question indeed, from one who had refused to cooperate with me in the matter of his own blackmail! The question made me indignant.

"I have no idea, Monsieur Gerard."

"Oh—but come; what was it?"

"But I don't know."

"I see."

He gave me an odd look, a smile. He was coming out of his daze, now. I knew he was temperamental. In a moment he might well be in high spirits.

"You say you are returning to New York in a few days, Monsieur Weavair?"

"I am."

"You have gathered just now, perhaps, that I am a person of great curiosity?"

"I have."

"I confess that my curiosity is agog as to what dangerous secret could possibly be contained in the life of that wretched little broker. For he is a little man. A courageous and efficient man, but a very *little* man. That wine he chose! What dangerous secret could *he* have?"

"I don't know, Monsieur Gerard."

"You do, of course, Monsieur Weavair. And if I may be so frank, Monsieur, I suspect you too of being a person of strong curiosity. I remember that on one occasion you asked me the nature of my secret, asked me over and over again. You begged me to tell you, claiming that by learning it you could 'make things all right.' Once you even said that 'the thing could be cured.' Do I remember correctly?"

There was a slightly sinking feeling in my stomach as I admitted that he did. How wrong I had been about his cowardice in leaving Paris! About his secret too, was it possible that I could be so . . . ?

"It occurred to me, Monsieur Weavair, that you might still wish to know my secret, and since you are going to America I have thought that I might after all reveal it to you. But I should have to demand something in return. If I reveal my secret, will you reveal Binbonnet's?"

"I have told you that I do not know Binbonnet's, Monsieur Gerard."

"I know. But will you reveal it if I reveal mine?"

Now I knew I'd been wrong, of course. There would be no bandying like this, if what I had thought was right. My American lay knowledge of psychiatry! Was it to such errors as this that it led? The narrowness of my escape came over me. I had almost told Gerard what I had thought was wrong! I felt my forehead grow moist.

What could Gerard's secret be, then? Something of quite a different sort. Not a thing, evidently, of which he was ashamed in itself; for here he was cheerfully deciding to tell me after all. And yet something which must under no circumstances be known to his friends. What could it be?

I couldn't think.

"You told me you knew my secret, Monsieur Weavair. Even when I assured you that was impossible, you insisted that you knew it—and then you talked mysteriously about a 'cure.' I don't know what you suspected me of, Monsieur Weavair, but I know that if you actually knew my secret, as you told me you did, you couldn't have promised to 'cure' me. What did—or do—you suspect me of, Monsieur Weavair?"

My forehead grew moister.

And now I discovered that the nature of Gerard's secret was the last thing I wanted to know. I had come too near burning my fingers on it, disgracing myself completely; whatever it was, I wanted to hear no more about it.

"I do not know Monsieur Binbonnet's secret," I said firmly. "And I most decidedly will not tell you what I thought yours was, since I discover I was mistaken. And I do not want you to enlighten me now."

"You will not tell me Monsieur Binbonnet's secret, Monsieur Weavair?"

"No."

"Then—since I like you, Monsieur Weavair, I must tell you mine with no hope of reward."

I looked at him in alarm.

He was smiling.

And, smiling, he told me.

And as he told, I found myself not only sweating but blushing—blushing ridiculously, like a sixteen-year-old. How completely this explained everything! How dense of me not to have guessed it! And at the same time, how relentlessly it brought out the Puritan in me, all the New England blood that had ever flowed in me or my ancestors—brought it all to my face!

For Monsieur Gerard was not only a manufacturer of iodine. He was the proprietor of another business house, one which also made large profits. Monsieur Gerard was, and had been for many years, the owner of a luxurious brothel in Brest. The discreet-looking house he had pointed out as we drove by.

"You met my friends, the Leblancs and the Dutuits, Monsieur Weavair. Can you imagine *them* continuing to see socially a man who is known to be the proprietor of such an establishment? That is not to say that Leblanc and Dutuit do not patronize such places themselves—on the contrary. And it's not to say, either, that Leblanc or Dutuit wouldn't open such a place, or have an interest in one, if profits were sure and the thing could be kept quiet. Perhaps they do have financial interests in such places for all I know—it wouldn't surprise me. But to associate with a known proprietor of one would be unthinkable. It is quite rightly considered a low kind of business, Monsieur, and brings stigma and social ostracism with it. That is why I must be so careful. I cannot expose my wife and child to the contempt of society. But I know also the *hypocrisy* of society, Monsieur Weavair; and if I can provide additionally for my wife and child by doing this—and if I can keep it quiet—I see no reason not to do so. Unlike old Leblanc and Dutuit, I do not patronize such places myself. I love my wife and am faithful to her. My interest in such places is purely commercial."

I nodded. My blushes were subsiding, thank God! How completely, how very satisfactorily, this explained everything. The happy home and yet the interest I had thought to be a mania. The tour of the place in Paris, the interest in the things to be seen, the architecture, the decorations, the newest gadgets, the *dernier cri*—interest in keeping his own place up to date.

Now I was sufficiently restored, I thought, to query, "Does your wife know about this?"

A look of alarm. "No indeed."

I nodded. Previously I had asked merely whether she knew he was being blackmailed. Had I asked this newer question then, my mistake would have been revealed to me.

"How did the man in brown find this out?"

A shrug. "How do such things leak? Everything pertaining to that business has always been done through a notary in Paris. Somebody in his office . . . I shall now investigate."

"He was not going to interfere in this project?"

"Not if I continued to serve him well in the other. With me, his interests were confined to iodine, though I gather that with Binbonnet that was not so. In iodine I was being ruined, but on this I could live."

"And now, with iodine restored, you are still going to continue the other?"

"Why not, Monsieur?"

Unanswerable, it seemed to me. I found myself wishing Monsieur Gerard the best of luck in both his businesses and expressing the hope that the time he devoted to the second would never result in any deterioration of his iodine.

He assured me it would not. "One devotes no time," he informed me. "With a good manageress, the place runs itself."

I nodded my comprehension.

Other bits of enlightenment followed; he was back on his hobby horse.

I scarcely listened.

I was reflecting.

It showed how nervous and upset I had been, that I had been able to think of Gerard as a coward. I had once seen him badly frightened—but that had been for my sake, not his own. And although he had never known when he might be spied upon, pounced upon, he had four times telephoned me from Brest, trying to warn me. Cowardice had not been even his reason for consenting to be blackmailed. That, I saw now, had been a pure matter of business. Unlike Binbonnet, Gerard had money, another business; fighting the blackmailer might have harmed that other business, it wasn't worth the risk. Had he been desperate, like Binbonnet, who knows how he might have fought? Yes—this matter of iodine was purely a financial, business affair, even in its most macabre aspects.

And I reflected about something else: just how much difference would it have made, to Gerard and to the other, lesser producers, had the man in brown offered to pay in cash, like anyone else? Wouldn't it have made all the difference in the world? The man in brown was from one of those countries whose threatening behavior toward France these very days was execrated by every Frenchman one met; the iodine which he had been getting from Gerard was supplying one of France's enemies; but if he had offered cash, would anyone have declined to sell?

When I had been in the home of the Gerards, I remembered, little Louisette had sung the *Marseillaise*, and had told me that her father had her sing it every day; a kind of whistling to keep his national spirits up, I had supposed, in view of the growing tenseness of the international scene. But now I saw that it was a more personal matter than that: Gerard, a Frenchman, knew that he was not only helping to supply one of the enemies of France, but also that he was being ruined in the process. Enough to make anyone feel bitter! But if instead of being ruined he had been growing rich, making huge profits: would it then have mattered to him where his iodine was going, whether to a bad neighbor or a good one? Would he then have had his daughter sing the *Marseillaise?*

Such were my pointless reflections as Monsieur Gerard talked on and on about his favorite subject. I even heard him ask me if I should care to accompany him, now, to an address. . . . But when I pleaded fatigue, he quickly desisted, and even took the hint and rose, saying he would go to his room.

"This was my room the last time, I believe," he said. "You have moved into it? Where am I tonight?"

My heart sank. My projected joke! With what élan I had intended to play it! After making Gerard thoroughly uncomfortable about his cowardice, I had planned to startle him. Planned to call his attention to the Eau de Javel and to the spots, gradually reveal to him their causes, make his night in that room a nightmare. But now I had been so stupid, so unjust. No longer had I any wish to distress Monsieur Gerard. And distressed he would be. He was no Pierre. He was a businessman, a hard-boiled one, willing to make his money where he could; and he relished the news of that man's death; but at the realization of my danger he had been sick—I couldn't forget that again. And if the significance of the Eau de Javel and the spots was brought to his attention he would be sick once more.

"Your room tonight was to have been the next room—the one I had before," I said. "But now I think . . ."

"A very pleasant room indeed—even nicer than this one, as I recall. I shall be most comfortable there. Through this door, I think."

"Monsieur Gerard . . ."

But he had opened the two doors, and reached in and switched on the light, and now he was taking his bag. I quickly reached for my crutches and stood up and went after him, as far as the door.

"Monsieur Gerard . . ."

There was a whiff of Javel water; all I could see in the room was two great dark spots on the red carpet. But Gerard appeared to notice nothing. He had put his bag on a chair, and now was coming toward me. "Do not come any further, I beg of you," he kindly said. "You are fatigued; you must rest. I shall be most comfortable. Thank you for reserving the room for me."

What could I say? To speak now would be to reveal to him the things I had decided he shouldn't know. If he slept with open windows I hoped that by morning the odor, at least, would have been dissipated.

"Good-night, Monsieur Gerard."

"Good-night, Monsieur Weavair. And—Monsieur—if you will forgive me, I will bolt the door on my side. I am an early riser, and in Paris like to breakfast outside, at a café. If, when I am out, before you awake, the chambermaid should come and see the door unbolted, she might enter your room and disturb you. Good-night, Monsieur Weavair."

"Until tomorrow, Monsieur Gerard."

I was shutting the door when he smiled at me. "You are sure you will not tell me Monsieur Binbonnet's secret, Monsieur?"

"Quite sure, Monsieur."

"Will you not at least tell me what you thought mine was, Monsieur Weavair?"

"That I most definitely will not, Monsieur Gerard."

"I wonder what you could have thought it to be, Monsieur?"

That, I felt pretty sure, was something he would never guess.

We said good-night again; the doors were closed; I heard him slip his bolt and I slipped mine. I undressed quickly and turned out the light. Now things were really ended. Not only was the iodine business put back on its feet, but the two rooms were once more separated by their bolted doors. The other room had a new tenant—a living, happy tenant; its career as a hotel room was being normally resumed. It wasn't long before I heard, through the wall and doors, loud snores. Gerard was sleeping as deeply tonight as he had slept the last time with a sedative.

It took me a little longer to get to sleep. It was comforting to think of connections with that other room being severed, and of someone sleeping a natural sleep in it. But one other thing kept going around in my mind. Suppose I had cockily said to Monsieur Gerard that I knew he was impotent and that he might as well admit it? Suppose I had said, "Monsieur Gerard—there is hope for you. Consult a psychiatrist and your manhood will be restored." Suppose I had!

It was intolerable, that thought. "Suppose I had! Suppose I had!"

It kept me from sleeping—made me too uncomfortable.

But after long tossing and turning it occurred to me that although the thought doubtless couldn't be banished entirely, it could, after all, be justifiably modified. "Thank God I didn't," I did my best to alter it to. "Thank God I didn't!"

Put that way, it assured me that despite all my other mistakes during this iodine affair—and they had been legion—I had not, at least, made the mistake of telling Monsieur Gerard what I thought his secret to be. And yet—"suppose I had." What would he have done? Just laughed at me, doubtless, and thought me the imbecile I was.

Unconscious of any of this, Monsieur Gerard continued to snore.

"Thank God I didn't! Thank God I didn't!"

I fell asleep.

# CHAPTER 20

And when I awoke on Sunday morning, I knew instantly that I'd be leaving the Clarence not in a

few days but in a few hours. Why should I stay? Why should I continue to live, even for three days, so near those spots on the carpet of the next room? Why should I have any further contact with Gerard or Binbonnet? They could repair their collaboration between them. There were other good hotels in Paris. I'd wait for my boat in one of them; in this one I could bear to remain no longer, thankful though I was that I had come to it in the first place. Immediately after ringing for breakfast I phoned downstairs and said merely that I was leaving. No reason to tell where I was going. Mail could be forwarded to the boat or the bank.

How good it was going to be, from now on, not to have to risk running into Lavisse in the corridor! And how good it was going to be, not to see any more of that person concerning whom I had such a strange mixture of feelings—Pierre. Was it, though? Was it, I found myself wondering the moment after I had hung up? Was it, after all, going to be good, seeing no more of Pierre? I wasn't so sure about that.

My mind went back to my arrival at the Clarence just two weeks before, and Pierre's quiet moving of my crutches and braces to my bedside the next morning, and the conversation I had had with him the evening after that. "Monsieur is like me," he had said. All he had meant, of course, was that we had both escaped from the war unscathed; and his words had seemed true at the time. Now, however, I knew that in the sense in which he had meant them they were profoundly untrue. And yet in another sense they were even truer than he had known. I had escaped from the war unscathed, but Pierre had not. He had not been wounded physically, but within him he bore festering results of the fury and conflict of those years. His entire life took its color from the chauvinism which the war had generated. The things he had seen had inspired him with a lust for revenge. For him, it seemed to me, the death of the man in brown was but a successful incident in his chosen career. His aim in life, I felt, was to destroy many men in brown. No; Pierre was far from unscathed by the war.

And yet, in a sense profounder than the one he had intended, it was true that Pierre and I were alike. We had both been handicapped, warped, worsened, by the violence of our reactions to things that had happened to us. Pierre's life was a search for revenge against a human enemy. I, attacked by something mysterious, unhuman, had for the past ten years grown in upon myself, deviated from normal life as sharply as had Pierre. That was how we were alike.

Of the two I was the more fortunate. The thing that had damaged me was not human, not identifiable. For me there was no question of revenge, with all the remorse it can bring. It had taken me a long time, but now finally I had found a cure without it. A mental cure, I mean, of course; people like me aren't cured physically. During the first part of this stay in France I had with wonder watched myself returning toward normality. During the days just passed, things had been happening too rapidly to allow me to think of myself—but with that very thoughtlessness, I now realized, had come my final full return to mental health. The activity, the fatigue, the strain and the terror of the last few days had completed the process that my initial undertaking of the iodine mission had begun; they had made a man of me again. I knew that. I felt it. During the past fortnight I had re-acquired my long-lost taste for doing things. I even had plans. Once installed in my new hotel, I intended to spend my few remaining days in Paris paying calls on some old friends. My old friends the picture dealers. Why shouldn't I have a gallery again?

But Pierre—was he going on and on, seeking the defeat and annihilation of the nation, the people, whom he hated? Why, after all, should that be his goal? Millions of men had fought in the war, and

most of those millions had neither the intelligence nor the imagination nor humanity of Pierre. Why should he, out of all those millions, be as he was? Why was Pierre so close to insane on that subject—as I, for a time, had been close to insane on the subject of wives
and children? I suddenly saw that I did not know why; I knew only
vaguely that it was "the war"—and yet in Pierre's life, just as in mine,
so violent an effect must have had a specific, violent cause. What was
it? *What*, in the war, had done this to Pierre?

And, sitting there waiting for my breakfast, I found that I wanted to know just what had done it—because I found that I no longer
wanted to feel about Pierre as I did. In the restaurant, the day before, a feeling of revulsion had swept over me at the thought of him;
and later, when I had thanked him for his services, I had had to
struggle to keep that feeling from getting the better of me. I did not
want to have to feel that way about Pierre! If only I could learn that
to him there had happened, during the war, something so disrupting
that the violence of his reaction would be made acceptable! If only
I did not have to struggle against liking Pierre! Because I did like
him. For me he was a man in a million; following these past few days
I knew that I should never forget him; if only there had not been
this revulsion, and if he had been willing to accompany me . . . But
that, of course, was impossible. Now I'd not be seeing him again.
This morning he would not be on duty; his colleague would serve me
breakfast very correctly; and then, immediately, I'd be leaving the
Clarence.

I heard the breakfast table come wheeling down the hall. The
waiter knocked, the key turned in the lock. . . .

"*Pierre!*"

"Bonjour, Monsieur. Monsieur slept well?"

"But, Pierre! Just last night you said you'd go back to your regular schedule . . . now that there was no further need to . . ."

"Ah, but, Monsieur—in a hotel one's regular schedule changes;
at times one works by night, at times by day. Today it is my regular
daytime schedule that I am resuming, Monsieur."

"I see." How glad, how very glad, I was to see him! "But, Pierre
. . ."

"Monsieur?"

"Pierre, tell me . . ."

And then and there, as Pierre interrupted his arranging of my breakfast to stand at attention, clearly surprised by the fervor of my voice, all my questions poured out. "Just why do you feel this way about the man in brown and the country he comes from? Are you going to spend your life hunting and destroying people of that kind, Pierre? Why should you? All ex-servicemen don't feel as you do: what was it? Something particular and special, I'm sure—just what was it that happened during the war and made you feel as you do?"

"Ah, Monsieur—if it had been during the war!"

Pierre was standing in a formal pose, but those words of his were as fervent as mine, and they surprised me as much as mine had him. Then it was not, after all, the war?

"If it had been during the war, Monsieur, when fighting was fierce but fair, then perhaps . . . It was indeed something particular and special, as Monsieur suggests, but the very fact that it was not *during* the war that it occurred . . . Ah, Monsieur, these things I have not spoken of in twenty years! I have thought about them, brooded over them, but now . . ."

"Now speak of them, Pierre; tell them to me, because . . . because . . ."

I couldn't finish that sentence. I couldn't say to Pierre, "Tell them to me because I want to be rid of my feeling of revulsion against you"; and as I hesitated I wished for once that Pierre were not polite, so that he might find it possible to interrupt me in the midst of that sentence and save me from having to finish it. "Tell them to me because . . . because I want you to, Pierre," I finally ended, in a lame kind of a rush.

"Since Monsieur wishes to hear . . ."

"I do indeed wish to hear. It was not something in the war, then, that made you need revenge, Pierre?"

"During the war I was like everyone else, Monsieur; death was everywhere around me, and even the death of my own father at the front was but an incident of the war—a terrible incident, but one that could not be unexpected, for which one could not be unprepared. It was afterwards—afterwards, when I returned with my wife to her village, Monsieur, that . . ."

I was not as polite as Pierre. "Your wife, Pierre?" I interrupted.

"I was married when I was eighteen, Monsieur, during a leave in Paris, where my wife was living with her parents, refugees from their village in the devastated part of France."

His wife!

"It was but shortly before the Armistice that we were married, Monsieur, and shortly after it that we set out—my wife and I, her parents, and my mother and my sister who was then only five or six. My wife's village had been taken and retaken many times by both armies; it had been bombarded almost out of existence. But her parents' house was the least damaged in the place, we found. We were overjoyed. The women ran ahead towards it, Monsieur—my father-in-law and I were behind: he carrying heavy bags, and I with my sister in my arms, carrying her over the debris. I was watching when my wife reached out and turned the door-knob of the house, and I saw . . . Ah, Monsieur! I have not spoken of these things in twenty years!"

So he had told me before; and now I could see why he had not spoken of them: I could see the effort it was costing him to tell me of them now! Two days before I had been impressed to see Pierre slump in an armchair: how impressive was it now to see him turn his back upon me, walk away, stare out the window! Behavior of that kind from Pierre on duty was eloquent. But he had to tell me these things, whatever they were: I was determined that he should tell. No longer only for my sake, but for his own as well: because now I felt, suddenly, that in a sense the speaking about the past—rather than the mere exterminating of it with the man in brown—might be, for Pierre, the end of his disability. "You saw what, Pierre?"

"The stones and mortar and dust and . . . and everything fly into the air, Monsieur."

He was speaking in a strange, monotonous voice, and towards the window.

"And heard the explosion and the screams. And then there was nothing but silence, and a thick pall of dust settling over the ruins. . . ."

"I see, Pierre."

What else was there to say, to such a story as that?

I knew the sort of thing that Pierre was talking about. The enemy, withdrawing after the Armistice, had done many such things, I knew: they had loaded with dynamite many a door and window and stair, poisoned many a well. "Booby-traps," so-called. Pierre, holding his sister in his arms, had seen a booby-trap work. And, in the trap, his mother, his wife, her mother . . .

He turned around to me, left the window.

"I returned to Paris with my father-in-law and my sister, Monsieur. The old man did not live long. And I, from that day on . . ."

I nodded. "From that day on—or, rather, from that day until now—you were plagued."

"A people who could do *that*, Monsieur! *After an Armistice*—after a long war had ended . . ." For a moment his voice was louder, more passionate and agonized than it had been, and then it died away.

How clear it was! The grief, the hatred, the longing for revenge, the patriotic societies—and finally, the opportunity: the man in brown and his end. Poor Pierre! One individual of the grade of that man in brown was scarcely enough to balance *his* account! And my feelings of revulsion: where were they now? What had become of them?

"Still, there will be no more men in brown, Pierre, will there?"

"No more, I hope, Monsieur, for me. And yet Monsieur will agree that since there had to be someone . . ."

I had to agree. And I had to be glad to know that Pierre's revenge had brought with it its own end without bringing remorse.

"Pierre."

"Monsieur?"

"I had a wife, too, Pierre, and a daughter as well."

"Yes, Monsieur?"

Sitting there in bed, I told Pierre my story. I thought that he should know it. And when I had finished, he found little more to say to me than the "I see" which I had found for him.

But it was not comments on my story that I wanted from Pierre. What I wanted from him was something else. "Pierre—here I am about to leave for home and I find it impossible to imagine getting along without you. I need you: you know that, I'm sure. You could perhaps not manage to accompany me next Wednesday, but . . ."

For once Pierre didn't wait for the end of my sentence. He interrupted it, saying what I wanted him to say. "I shall be glad to follow Monsieur as soon as I can."

Why shouldn't I confess to the way my eyes smarted at that moment?

This arrangement with Pierre—which we discussed in satisfying detail then and there—didn't prevent me from leaving the Clarence that morning. There were, after all, those spots and that odor of Javel water in the next room, and I had no desire for further iodine conversations with Gerard. Pierre did my packing. I knocked on Gerard's door, but there was no answer; he was gone to breakfast and thence to Binbonnet's, and would doubtless think it strange, when he returned, to find that I had departed so hastily. I wrote a note and left it for him, saying that my nerves demanded relaxation before the trial of the ocean passage. It was a proper, convincing little letter to which he could take no exception. We would meet again, I hoped, etc. Pearce Brothers would be pleased if he restored deliveries to normal as soon as possible; and to Madame Gerard and Louisette I asked him to give my regards.

Then, after making my farewells downstairs and enjoyably concealing the fact that the best member of the staff would soon be following me, I left the Clarence. Half an hour later I was comfortably installed in another good hotel, highly recommended by Pierre, in another quarter of Paris.

It was good, my round of visits the next day to the picture dealers in the Rue de la Boétie and the Avenue Matignon. The heartiness of the men's welcome. Their immediate realization, after saying they hadn't seen me for a long time, of why that was so. The additional handshakes they thereupon gave me. Their instant comprehension of the gesture I made following their inquiries for Lucille, and the sympathy they expressed. Gestures are understood in France; that makes some things easier there.

I bought some pictures. I didn't have time to ponder and consider as I should have liked to, and therefore I took only pictures that made an immediate appeal. Not a bad idea, up to a certain point, I have decided. Nine people out of ten who buy pictures buy those that they like on sight, no matter how long they stare at them before buying; and if a dealer who knows the picture-buying public buys in that same way, then he stands a pretty good chance of selling. Of course one must consider prices, and that morning I made myself take only appealing pictures which were bargains. Astonishing how many such one can find in Paris, if one is adamant in refusing to consider anything else! It was that morning that I picked up the little Matisse portrait now in the Museum of Modern Art. All the critics have talked about its quality, but only the museum and I know the surprising modesty of its price.

On Tuesday morning I bought some more pictures, this time in the little galleries of the Left Bank—Rue de Seine and Boulevard Montparnasse. I paid for all pictures then and there and had them quickly crated and called for by the French Line. And on Wednesday morning I took the train to Le Havre and went aboard, cabling Al and Jim that I was coming and that everything was turning out all right.

During the voyage, the ship's paper carried the news that the European crisis had been settled, that the danger of war had been averted and that statesmen were shaking hands all round. I was relieved, of course, like everybody else—and yet . . . I had become too well acquainted with the methods of the man in brown to believe very much in the durability of any peace while such people as he were working as he worked for the people they were working for.

War would come eventually, and—speaking for Pearce Brothers—I only hoped that when it did it would not interfere too greatly with deliveries of iodine.

The funny thing was, in New York I discovered that the joke was on me.

Both Al and Jim were on the dock, and when they learned that I'd brought pictures back with me they exchanged a look that was clearly full of significance and shook hands gaily with each other.

I demanded that they explain. They did so, and I discovered to my surprise that I had been sent to Europe almost entirely for therapeutic reasons. My long-continued seclusion and gloom had depressed and worried my brothers-in-law and their wives, and they had determined to try to get me out of it. There had seemed to them little chance that the iodine situation could be remedied, but it seemed a good errand to send me on, and the little difficulty about my Pearce Brothers stock had been easy to fake. A few months in Paris, they had hoped, would do wonders. That explained the alarmist manner in which they had made me the proposition. When they had received the cable announcing my early return they were disappointed; and now it turned out that barely three weeks in *la ville lumière* had accomplished what they had hoped for from the longer period.

Their gaiety lessened a trifle when I told them with a certain grimness of some of the things that had befallen me during my supposed junket. I didn't tone down any of the danger-spots. Why shouldn't they consider me a hero? It was the only revenge I could think of for their duplicity. And a hero I apparently succeeded in making them consider me, for a few days later I was the guest of honor at a Pearce Brothers testimonial luncheon, one of the dullest affairs I have ever attended in my life.

It was pleasant to get back to my little Murray Hill apartment, and it's pleasant to live there now, served by Pierre as I am. He arrived about three weeks after I did, and I hope he'll never leave. He remains so very French, however, that I sometimes have my fears; I know that he misses Paris now and then, for all his devotion to me. It has been pleasant, too, to make the acquaintance of my nieces and nephews. One of the nieces looks extraordinarily like a little girl I used to know, but even so I find that I can enjoy her company immensely.

Best of all has been getting the gallery started. It's on Fifty-seventh Street, the Weaver Gallery, along with all the others, and I can usually be found there, talking about the pictures with somebody that's come in, or occasionally making a sale in the back room. Drop in, by all means!

**COACHWHIP PUBLICATIONS**
CoachwhipBooks.com

**COACHWHIP PUBLICATIONS**

COACHWHIPBOOKS.COM

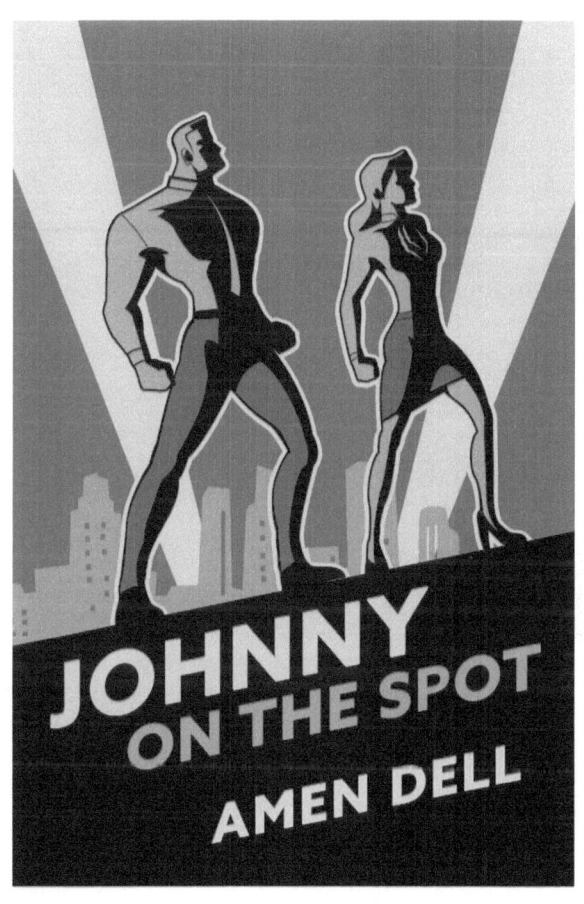

**COACHWHIP PUBLICATIONS**
CoachwhipBooks.com

THE SERGEANT HARTY MYSTERIES

# JOEL Y. DANE

## MURDER CUM LAUDE

**1**

## THE CABANA MURDERS

# COACHWHIP PUBLICATIONS
## CoachwhipBooks.com

### THE SERGEANT HARTY MYSTERIES
# JOEL Y. DANE

## GRASP AT STRAWS
### 2
### THE CHRISTMAS TREE MURDERS

**COACHWHIP PUBLICATIONS**

CoachwhipBooks.com

# COACHWHIP PUBLICATIONS
## CoachwhipBooks.com

BLOOD ON HER SHOE

MEDORA FIELD

**COACHWHIP PUBLICATIONS**

CoachwhipBooks.com

THE

RUMBLE

MURDERS

Henry Ware Eliot, Jr.